Craig gritted his teeth against the cry that begged to be torn from him,

feeling far worse pain than from any wound he'd yet sustained. He'd thought Susan was completely behind him. In the past.

Heart pounding, throat constricted, Craig forced himself to concentrate on his dangerous predicament, on the enemy just down the path. Still, he couldn't dislodge the sudden memory of Susan's parted lips, those searching eyes that tore at his soul.

Grief and loneliness cut through him like a knife. He lay silent on the hard ground, overwhelmed by loss. Because he'd never stopped loving Lt. Susan Evans. For four years he'd carried her memory in his heart.

Suddenly Craig wondered if his time was up. Susan's face had never before appeared to him like this on a mission. Was the vision a premonition?

Was he about to die?

Dear Reader,

Welcome to Silhouette **Special Edition** . . . welcome to
romance. We've got lots of excitement in store for you
this April—and, no fooling, it's all about love!

Annette Broadrick, the author of over thirty-five
novels for Silhouette Books, is making her debut
in the Special Edition line with a book in our
THAT SPECIAL WOMAN! promotion. *Mystery Wife*
is a tantalizing, compelling tale about a woman who
wakes up with a new lease on life—and a handsome,
charismatic husband she doesn't remember marrying. . . .

And that's not all! *Shadows and Light,* the first book in
the MEN OF COURAGE series by Lindsay McKenna,
is due out this month. It takes a special breed of men to
defy death and fight for right! Salute their bravery
while sharing their lives and loves!

Loving and Giving by Gina Ferris, the new addition to
Gina's enormously popular FAMILY FOUND series, is
due out this month, as well as work by other favorite
authors Nikki Benjamin, Natalie Bishop and
Ruth Wind. April is a month not to be missed!

Sincerely,

Tara Gavin
Senior Editor

Please address questions and book requests to:
Reader Service
U.S.: P.O. Box 1325, Buffalo, NY 14269
Canadian: P.O. Box 1050, Niagara Falls, Ont. L2E 7G7

LINDSAY McKENNA

SHADOWS AND LIGHT

Silhouette®

SPECIAL EDITION®

Published by Silhouette Books
America's Publisher of Contemporary Romance

To Vinton (John) Cramer and his wife, Vera—my uncle
and aunt. Holder of a Bonneville Salt Flats speed
record that still stands to this day! Bravo. And to Vera,
who has always quietly supported my uncle and his wild
adventures.

 SILHOUETTE BOOKS

ISBN 0-373-09878-2

SHADOWS AND LIGHT

Copyright © 1994 by Lindsay McKenna

Printed in U.S.A.

Books by Lindsay McKenna

*Kincaid Trilogy
†Love and Glory Series
°Women of Glory Series
‡Moments of Glory Series
+Morgan's Mercenaries
**Men of Courage

LINDSAY McKENNA

spent three years serving her country as a meteorologist in the U.S. Navy, so much of her knowledge about the military people and practices featured in her novels comes from direct experience. In addition, she spends a great deal of time researching each book, whether it be at the Pentagon or at military bases, extensively interviewing key personnel.

Lindsay is also a pilot. She and her husband, both avid rock hounds and hikers, live in Arizona.

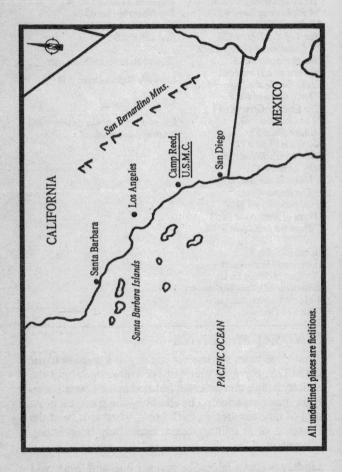

Chapter One

Captain Craig Taggart was damned if his team was going to be discovered. They were the Blue Team, the good guys—the Americans—in this war game. And somewhere, hidden in among the golden brown, loaf-like hills of Camp Reed, were the bad guys, the Red Team.

Recon training was brutal, and Craig knew that these mock war games honed his men's skills, giving them a taste of combat. Right now they lay in a rocky ravine that was peppered with cactus. Brush hid them as they waited and watched. The enemy was near; Craig could sense their presence.

The stifling heat of the huge marine base's desert setting rose up in waves as sweat trickled off his body. His face was darkened with smudges of brown, green and black to prevent his white skin from alerting enemy eyes. Flattened against the hard ground, Craig narrowed his eyes, his breath catching deep inside him.

His recon team had been out for three days, successfully meeting the challenges of their assignment. They were due to be picked up in the next half hour by a marine helicopter and flown back to the area where the scores for the war game would be totaled. Craig knew he and his men were winning. All they had to do now was wait for the helo and remain undetected.

He squinted speculatively. Several of the enemy were making their way down an old path in a ravine on the next hill, and they were headed straight toward the rocky depression where Craig and his men lay. Craig dared not move his head. But he had full confidence that the other four men wouldn't move a muscle, either. Craig knew they would wait for him to fire the first shot. Recons weren't in the business of ambush and attack. No, they were like silent ghosts moving in enemy territory, collecting data and information for their Intelligence unit. Because they carried little in the way of ammunition and had no way of being picked up if they were discovered, recons were the last to want to engage the enemy in a firefight.

Well, it looked like there might be a firefight this time. Craig's mind raced as he watched the ten members of the enemy team—all wearing fatigues similar to those of the Blue Team except the black arm bands to denote their enemy status and the M-16's slung over their shoulders—walk toward them, still oblivious to their presence. He couldn't be sure if the enemy squad would move on, make camp nearby—or discover his recons. His nostrils flared as the sluggish air brought the distinct smell of human sweat with it. At least the wind was in their favor. It was entirely possible that the enemy's point man, a young marine no more than nineteen, would smell the Blue Team's own sweaty bodies if conditions were reversed.

What should he do? Craig glanced down at his watch, attached to his wrist with a black plastic band to avoid telltale reflection in the bright sunlight. Fifteen more minutes and the helo would arrive. His first concern—his only concern—was for his men. They were good men, and he wouldn't let them needlessly "die" in this mock battle. Grimly, Craig pressed his lips together, filled with the desire to see his men safely out of this unexpected, last-minute situation.

The enemy party was still picking its way along with no obvious goal. What were they looking for? A new campsite? Craig's mind ticked off the possibilities. It was a lightly armed group—perhaps a squad sent ahead of a larger, more deadly company. They were only some three hundred yards away now, and within moments, Craig would have to make life-and-death decisions. What if they were an advance party? How far behind was the company that could easily destroy his team with their overwhelming fire superiority?

Blinking away the sweat running into his eyes, the stinging moisture momentarily blurring his vision, Craig slowly released the breath he'd been holding. His M-16 lay ready under his hands. The enemy squad hesitated, looking upward into the taller bushes, and then pointed to the surrounding foliage. That was it! They were laying trip wires for land mines!

Andy Hayes, Craig's radioman, lay directly to his right, his blond hair coated with mud so as not to attract attention. His twenty-year-old face was drawn with tension; his blue eyes squinted against the sweat. Craig indicated with a hand signal for Andy to warn the helo via radio that the enemy was present. Whenever a marine helicopter came in to pick up a recon team, another helicopter came along as gunfire support, and forewarned was forearmed. Andy dipped his head once and fingered the button on the radio he held protectively against his body. The young man was going to be married in mere days, Craig remembered suddenly. Well, the honeymoon would be a well-earned rest.

Craig quickly sized up the general area. The helicopter was supposed to hover a few feet above the crest of the hill just a hundred yards away. But the brush covering the hill—some of it twenty feet high—would require precision flying of the most dangerous kind to navigate, Craig realized. Thank God, Major Bruce Campbell, one of the best helicopter pilots at the base, had this mission; there was no one better in a tricky flying situation. The Blue Team's escape route to the helo lay directly above them. It would be a hundred-yard sprint up and over the top of the hill to reach the extraction point.

When the enemy squad heard the approaching aircraft, of course, they'd become alert. And once Craig gave the order to move, there was every possibility the enemy would spot them and a firefight would break out. They were outnumbered two to one, but Craig was used to even worse odds for their five-man recon team. If he could avoid a confrontation, he wanted to do it at all costs.

Tasting the salt leaking into the corners of his mouth, Craig slowly turned his head to his left, where the remaining three team members lay spaced a good hundred feet apart. Sergeant Larry Shelton, a redheaded marine from the hills of Tennessee, was flattened against the earth, practically invisible. Craig couldn't see Barker and Miles at all. When he gave the command, however, the other men would be contacted with a hand signal. Recons rarely spoke; everything was done with an advanced hand-signal alphabet.

The enemy squad was completely engrossed in placing wire across an old path and planting the mine. For a moment, Craig relaxed. The second hand on his watch was moving swiftly. In ten minutes, the helo would be over the landing zone to extract his team. Within five minutes, the enemy would hear the heavy whapping of the blades of the approaching aircraft. It was too much to hope they would turn back after planting the mine. As a practice, recons never followed paths made by the enemy—deadly offerings filled with punji sticks hidden beneath foliage and trip wires that could blow off a man's leg or arm.

As Craig lay waiting, Susan Evans's face suddenly loomed before him. He blinked, shocked by her appearance, and just as quickly, her image faded. *Susan.* Bittersweet memories welled up through Craig, catching him completely off guard. Where had she come from?

Craig wrestled with the unexpected memory. His heart was pounding in his chest, and as her serious, lovely face lingered in his mind, his throat constricted. Tears! With a muffled sound, he crushed his face against his hands. What the hell was going on? Her face shimmered once more behind his tightly shut eyelids. How could he ever forget her dark brown hair, which took on a reddish cast in the sunlight? Or her somber blue eyes, so innocent and wide as she looked up at him?

Opening his mouth with a silent cry, Craig felt a far worse pain than any injury he'd yet sustained in his work as a recon. He'd thought Susan was completely behind him. In the past. Lifting his head, he forced himself to concentrate on their dangerous predicament. Still, he couldn't dislodge the sudden memory of Susan's square features, classic nose, parted lips—and her searching eyes, which tore at his soul. He'd been such a fool. Why hadn't he had more gumption? Been quicker to ask her out than his best friend, Steve, who had ended up marrying her?

The grief, the loneliness, cut through Craig like a knife. He lay on the hard ground, overwhelmed by his loss—because he'd never stopped loving Ensign Susan Evans. She had been his one-and-only sweetheart, and for the last four years, Craig had carried her memory in his heart. Suddenly he wondered if his time was up. Susan's face had never appeared to him before in a situation like this. Was he going to die? Was the vision a premonition? Bitterness coated his mouth as he keyed his hearing between the sky, barely visible above them, and the banter of the enemy down the valley.

In the four years since he'd seen her, Craig admitted to himself, swallowing hard, he'd never forgotten Susan. They had met when he was a fourth-year cadet at Annapolis, when he had decided to become a marine officer instead of a navy officer. Steve Placer, his roommate and best friend, had fallen on some ice at the academy that winter, and Craig had helped him limp over to the hospital dispensary on the Annapolis grounds. Susan had been working as a nurse there and had helped the doctor wrap Steve's badly sprained ankle.

Craig released a shaky breath as he forced himself to pay attention to the enemy. Still, his heart swung around to the past—to that first time he'd met Susan.

She'd been shy around them, and Craig had been struck by her serious nature, her care and commitment to nursing. There was a vulnerability about Susan that beckoned to Craig. Although she had been thoroughly professional as Steve sat on the gurney and she wrapped his ankle in an Ace bandage, Craig had seen her cheeks flame red with the awareness that the two young men were studying her like starving wolves.

Steve, the extrovert, had managed to tease a small smile out of her, and Craig recalled sharply that as the corners of her wanton mouth had hesitantly curved upward, he'd felt a sheet of heat tunnel through him, one that had left him speechless in its wake. So Craig had stood stupidly by as Steve boldly hunted Susan, stalked her with his practiced charm and expertly maneuvered her into agreeing to go out with him at a later date when he didn't have to be on crutches.

With a violent shake of his head, Craig tried to clear away the welling memories. He lay there feeling his heart throbbing in his chest—more than a symbolic reminder of the past that walked with him into the present. Angry at himself because he was an introvert, shy rather than bold like Steve, Craig had not pursued Susan. Instead, he'd become her friend and confidant. Once he'd plucked a springtime daffodil from one of the flower gardens at the academy—a decided risk in itself—and given it to her. The night before, she'd experienced the death of a plebe who had gotten into an accident, and he'd wanted to cheer her up somehow.

The sadness in Susan's face had lifted, Craig remembered, and her face had glowed with joy as he'd given her the flower. He'd never forget how her slender fingers had wrapped around the stem. When she closed her eyes and raised the yellow daffodil to inhale its heady fragrance, Craig had breathed with her.

What the hell was happening? Craig angrily smashed the remnants of memories and ruthlessly suppressed his aching feelings of loss. He'd lost touch with her after the fateful night that she hadn't met him at the restaurant for dinner. Susan had stood him up without explanation. The next morning Craig had shipped out for his first assignment after graduating from the academy, shattered. Through the grapevine shortly afterward, he'd heard that Steve had married Susan, and Craig's anger over his inability to keep the woman of his dreams because he was too cautious ate away at him.

But it had been better to walk out of their lives—to never contact them again—because Craig had known he couldn't control his wild emotions toward Susan. He'd never forget her one innocent kiss, her shyness, which matched his own. He'd never forget the incredible butterfly lightness of her fingertips as she'd touched his shaven cheek after he'd kissed her with all the fire and love he possessed in the depths of his soul.

It's over, he told himself furiously. *Over and done. Stop thinking of her!* Was he going mad? Why would Susan's face and those excruciating memories from four years ago suddenly pop up to haunt him *now?* Craig was breathing hard, opening his mouth so that the sound couldn't be detected. Andy gave him a quizzical look, but he ignored the question in the young marine's eyes. Pressing his brow against his hands, Craig closed his eyes momentarily. He was going to die; he was sure of it now. Craig had heard other marines tell him that just before a severe injury—a life-threatening situation—they had seen their lives run in review before their eyes.

A haunting ache filled him as he lifted his head. He gave the hand signal for his unit to move out, and they did so, without ever gaining the attention of the enemy squad below. They made it across the crest of the hill and waited tensely. Craig's doglike hearing caught the first *whap, whap, whap* of helicopter blades, and his hands tightened around his rifle in anticipation. With a sharp signal, he put his men on alert. There was nothing they could do now except wait. But even if the enemy heard the engine, they could never get to them in time. Right now, his team was safe. Still, Craig couldn't shake a cold shiver of unadulterated fear. What was going on?

As he slowly got to his knees, the foliage undisturbed, he bitterly accepted that he *was* going to die. It was an intense feeling, so overwhelming that he didn't question it, although it seemed illogical. And it seemed the only explanation for Susan Evans's sweet, haunting face to be hovering before him. That was the only thing Craig regretted: not marrying Susan, not being aggressive enough—as Steve had been—to step in between them. Steve had chased Susan because she was the quarry, had focused on getting her into his arms, his bed and making love to her. With his strict Idaho farm heritage, Craig had been brought up differently. He would never dream of chasing a woman just to bed her. No, love had to be the motive, not the thrill of the chase.

As Craig slowly eased upward, using the foliage as a barrier between himself and the unsuspecting enemy, he continued to regret not having told Susan that he loved her, wanted to marry her, wanted her to carry his children. She had been mesmerized by Steve's purposeful attack, swept off her feet by his tactics to win her. And

Craig had stood by, unable to compete with Steve's razzle-dazzle approach.

Well, Craig thought as the single-rotor helicopter headed rapidly toward him, it was too late. Looking back on that last year at Annapolis, he knew he could have switched tactics—been far more aggressive and turned into a hunter—but that wasn't his way. His parents had taught him that honesty, truth and real feelings were what really counted. Well, he'd followed that guidance with Susan, winning her trust as a friend. But she'd been caught up in Steve's well-planned magic, and it had been too late. Too late....

"Susan, isn't this great?" Dr. Karen David stood just outside the emergency-room entrance to the Camp Reed Naval Hospital. A pleased smile came to her triangular-shaped face.

Susan Evans smiled over at her surgeon friend. "I think I'd rather be back in the air-conditioned comfort of the Oak Knoll Hospital, Karen. How you could trade San Francisco's beauty for this desert is beyond me."

Karen mustered a winsome smile. "Look around you." She waved her arm in the air. "There's more action here. I was getting bored at Oak Knoll. That was regular surgery. I'm a trained trauma surgeon and I wanted to be busy doing that. Reed's a major training base, and unfortunately, there are a lot more accidents and trauma situations here as a result." She gave Susan a mischievous look. "Besides, we're good at what we do. Why, these fine marines are going to be saved by the best trauma pair they've ever laid eyes on."

"Specifically," Susan said with a laugh, "you. You're the surgeon."

Karen gave her a happy look. "Yes, but you're my right-hand surgical nurse, Susan. Without you, I'd fumble a lot."

That was probably true, Susan conceded as she stood outside the swinging door that led into the trauma unit adjacent to the emergency-room area. They were both trauma trained, and Susan conceded that they hadn't really had reason to put their badly needed skills to work—until now. Karen was a brilliant surgeon who got caught up in the intensity of saving a person's life. Susan was calm, cool and collected in comparison, slapping each instrument firmly into Karen's gloved hand to make sure that rhythm between doctor and surgical nurse never got interrupted. One wrong motion could mean a life lost. Yes, they *were* a good team, and that was the main reason Susan had followed Karen out into the field.

Smoothing her nurse's uniform, Susan looked down at her sensible white shoes. The summer heat here was scorching compared to San Francisco's temperate weather, and she wished she'd put her collar-length hair up on her head. The back of her neck felt sweaty.

She watched Karen's face become wreathed in smiles and followed her friend out toward the helicopter-landing area. The asphalt was painted with a huge white circle around a red cross, where the medevacs would unload injured marines whisked out of the surrounding training areas for immediate care. She turned on her heel to study the swinging doors of the ER area and hesitated. Was this what she really wanted? Frowning, Susan turned away and followed Karen as she eagerly explored her new world.

Karen always wanted to be in the middle of the action, Susan knew. And although she didn't feel the same—out of loyalty and after a lot of nagging from Karen—she'd ended up coming along. Susan didn't get high on the intense emergency-room atmosphere that Karen loved. Her friend often referred to herself as a "trauma junky," addicted to the challenge of the life-and-death scenarios. Susan, on the other hand, was too sensitive to the pain the injured were feeling, the cries, the nauseating smells. Shoving her hands in the pockets of her skirt, she shook her head. Surgery performed under the bright lights of a stainless-steel operating room that reeked of antiseptic was far different from the crazy mayhem they'd soon be caught up in.

"This is wonderful!" Karen said as she stood in the center of the landing apron's red cross.

The unrelenting Southern California sun bore down on them out of the light blue sky. With a slight smile, Susan murmured, "You do like to be in the thick of things."

With a chuckle, Karen patted her shoulder. "Come on! This place will grow on you. Just look at it as a fantastic challenge." Karen held up her long, thin hands with their competent, large-knuckled fingers. "These hands will get to save more lives by me being out here, Susan. Isn't that worth coming for? They need trauma-ready surgeons like me in the field."

"You're right," Susan admitted, smiling in spite of herself. She applauded Karen's confidence. She wished more women would glory in their own unique assets as Karen did. She stared at her friend's hands. No one was better or faster in an operating room. With another small smile, she said, "Come on, 'Doc,' let's go check out the heart of this place, and then ICU."

With a laugh, Karen allowed her hands to drop back to her sides. She touched her blond, pixie-style hair. "Am I crazy?"

"No," Susan said, matching her longer stride to Karen's short, eager one, "just excited about the possibilities. We *will* save more lives by being here," she conceded.

Karen's smile slipped, and she became more serious. "Look," she whispered, "you did the right thing by coming here. It will take your mind off the past—off the loss of Steve."

Pain pulled at Susan, and her step slowed as they drew up to the double swinging doors of ER. Karen had been her best friend at Oak Knoll Naval Hospital. She had been with her when Steve had died. If not for Karen's care, she'd have gone crazy. Here at the marine base she would be reminded daily that life was fragile and good—and saving lives was something worth burying her heart and soul in.

"Yes," she admitted in a low tone, "it's probably a good thing we're both here."

Karen gave her an understanding look and rested her arm around Susan's shoulders for a moment. "Come on, let's check out our new turf. We're going on duty in an hour, and we need to be ready. Those choppers are sure to come in sooner or later."

With a forced laugh, Susan agreed and followed her surgeon friend through the modern trauma unit, filled with gurneys and a myriad of equipment used to save lives. Outside the unit was Recovery, a twenty-bed area where marines who were coming out of anesthesia would stay until they were fully conscious. Although Susan was a surgery nurse and most of her time would be spent in the trauma unit, she would also pull duty in ICU and Recovery, as well as other wards.

The ward area was divided between enlisted and officer areas. Susan would stand duty in both wards. Each unit held twenty beds, and navy corpsmen—enlisted men and women—would be assigned to help the medical staff take care of their healing charges. As Susan walked with Karen through the various wards, her heart was moved. Many of the beds held marines and navy personnel, staying here to recover from serious injuries before being sent back into the field.

Their faces were so young, so innocent, Susan thought, as she and Karen moved quietly down the aisles of each ward. Some of them sat up in their beds, playing cards to pass the time and keep boredom at bay. Others were swathed in white bandages, asleep or under a pain medication's domain. It was the look of some in their eyes that haunted Susan. Some held terror— unspeakable knowledge that they couldn't give words to. Other eyes, though, held curiosity, even friendly interest, accompanied by a shy smile.

Trying to prepare herself emotionally for what lay ahead on her first day of duty, Susan headed back to ER with Karen. They were opposites, Susan had realized years ago. Karen was a hard charger who grabbed hold of life, held onto it and moved with a vitality few could match. Susan, on the other hand, was more silent, introverted—moving like a shadow through life. She had learned early to be seen and not heard—to help, work, be responsible and never complain or try to throw off the burdens given to her.

Their tour completed, Susan and Karen retired to the female hospital personnel's quarters to change into fresh white uniforms, settle their clothes in assigned lockers and have a cup of coffee before their first duty. Susan was the first through the doors of ER when a black navy corpsman ran toward them, out of breath.

"Hey!" the corpsman called. "A training helo with ten marines just crashed fifteen miles from here! We got dead and injured on their way in. Two medevacs are bringing 'em right now! Get ready!"

Susan knew that only two doctors and four nurses were assigned to the ER unit. She gasped as the corpsman's message sank in and quickly moved to a small side room where she grabbed two green surgical gowns, handing one to Karen. They pulled them on, and Susan searched until she found the rubber gloves. Karen and the other doctor were scrubbing at the nearby sink. Susan's heart started pounding in dread as she heard the heavy whapping sounds of a helicopter landing outside the trauma-unit door. Its windy wake buffeted the doors leading to the landing pad, and she could make out screams and shouts mingling with the roar of the helicopter's engine.

Karen ran over to her, her hands held up, and Susan quickly slipped on the gloves. Just as the last one snapped into place, Susan heard the doors burst open. Jerking around, she saw corpsmen pushing five gurneys into the ER. Her mouth fell open as she surveyed the marines lying on them, their clothes torn and bloody, their arms hanging lifelessly.

Choking, Susan watched in a daze as Karen and the other doctors quickly began to ascertain the extent of the five men's injuries.

"We got another load of five comin' in!" a navy corpsman shouted.

Before Susan could run across the aisle to wash her hands, Dr. Benjamin Finlay, the head surgeon, caught her by the arm. "Evans, come here." Rapidly, Finlay ordered her to give the young, blond marine an IV and prep him for surgery. With shaking hands, Susan tried to ignore the extensive injuries to the unconscious boy. The area became frantic as another helicopter off-loaded five more wounded personnel. Everywhere Susan looked, the small area was jammed with gurneys, with doctors and nurses running frantically from one patient to another, ascertaining medical statuses.

Susan tried not to allow her stricken emotions to get the better of her. Efficiently, she fitted the marine with an IV and quickly cut back his clothes to expose a gaping chest wound. Finlay came back, barking orders to several corpsmen to get the marine into surgery.

"This is your first day," Finlay said, gripping her by the arm. He pointed toward three gurneys in the corner. "Take those three cases. They're the least hurt."

"Y-yes, sir." Numbly, Susan moved toward the gurneys. One marine, a redheaded youth in his early twenties, was holding his bleeding hand. The second marine was also struggling to sit up. He had a mild scalp wound, Susan surmised as she walked over to them. Scalp wounds always bled heavily, but were rarely fatal.

"Ma'am," the red-haired marine begged, "take care of our skipper. He's really hurt. Please, take care of him first."

Susan hesitated. Both young marines, their faces grim, their eyes wide with shock, pointed to the gurney behind her, which evidently bore their commanding officer. Opening her mouth, Susan started to say something. Ordinarily, she'd be the one deciding which patient was worst. But the pleading looks in their faces stifled her chastising words.

Turning on her heel, she finished pulling on the surgical gloves. As she looked down at the marine lying on the gurney, she gave a small cry of surprise and her heart slammed into her throat, her eyes widening enormously. The officer lying on the gurney, his gray eyes narrowed with pain, his hand clutching at his bloody thigh, was Craig Taggart.

"Oh, my God," Susan whispered, frozen in place.

Chapter Two

Craig bit back a groan as the nurse in the surgical gown turned toward him. The pain from the crash injury he'd sustained moved in unrelenting waves up through his body. He held a tourniquet above the wound, his fist bloodied and wrapped around the web belt that he'd called into service from around his waist to keep the bleeding to a minimum.

As the dark-haired nurse turned toward him, Craig sucked in a breath of air. His eyes, narrowed against the pain, went wide with shock.

"Susan..." he gasped, staring up at her widening blue eyes.

Dizziness assailed Susan. She struggled to breathe, unable to move as she stared down into Craig's tense, sweaty features, his gray eyes burning with undefinable anguish. A hundred fragments struck her with the force of a land mine—fragments from the past, images of how Craig had looked four years ago and how he looked now. His face had always been lean, but the lines bracketing his mouth and crossing his brow were new and deeply etched. No longer was this the young man she'd known at Annapolis. This man, his face hewn by life experiences she couldn't imagine, stared back at her through gray, hawklike eyes. His features were dirty and muddied, sweat streaking through camouflage coloring to make him look like an alien from another planet.

"What are *you* doing here?" Craig demanded with a rasp. He couldn't control his wildly beating heart or the feeling as if his breath were being choked off in the middle of his throat. Susan was here. Susan! Sweat trickled into his eyes, and he blinked rapidly. Her lovely face, now matured and impossibly more beautiful than he could ever recall, wavered before him. He opened his mouth to say more, but nothing came out. The sounds of the emergency room assailed his senses, and the smells made him nauseous. Yet Susan stood before him, clothed in green, her hands held up and encased in surgical gloves, staring down at him as if she'd seen a ghost. Well, wasn't he? Craig asked himself harshly.

"I..." Susan's voice died in her throat. "Craig..."

Nothing was making sense. Angrily, Craig glared up at her. He tried to twist around, tried to see where they'd taken Andy and Larry, who he knew had been badly injured in the crash.

"Where are Hayes and Shelton?" he demanded, his voice harsh, unsteady.

Susan snapped out of her shock. "Who?"

"My men! Andy and Larry!"

"Calm down," she whispered, forcing herself to move toward Craig.

"Like hell I will! They're my men. They were hurt in the crash. I've got to find out how they are...."

Susan realized she had to control the situation. Craig was in shock. It showed in his eyes—his pupils were huge and black, with only a thin rim of gray surrounding them. He was trying to get up, to hold onto the tourniquet tightly enough to maneuver into a sitting position. No one cared more for his men than Craig did. She had found that out at Annapolis. If possible, his loyalty to others was even more intense and consuming than her own. Using her best imperious voice, one that few of her patients ever challenged, Susan placed her hand on Craig's shoulder and pushed him back down on the gurney.

"Don't you dare move, Craig Taggart." She glowered at him as he started to protest. She added force, her hand flat against his dirty utilities, and said calmly, "Your men are getting the best care in the world. They've already been taken into surgery. Now, you lie here and be still!"

Her hands shaking, Susan took a pair of scissors and began to cut off his pant leg around the wound. Helplessly, she felt his icy response to her order. Why was he so furious with her? She hadn't known he was here at Camp Reed! Why did they have to meet now?

"I'm all right," Craig snarled, not even trying to mask the cold fury in his voice. "Why don't you see to my other two men? They're wounded, too."

Giving him a scathing look, Susan dropped the bloody pieces of fabric to the floor, then quickly cut away Craig's shirt to expose his left arm, so that she could start an IV. "Because they're injured far less seriously than you! Now be still," she said sternly. "We're in a triage situation, and the worst get helped first."

Each trembling touch of Susan's hand against his arm sent a wave of unadulterated pain straight to Craig's heart. He shut his eyes and turned his head away. He couldn't bear to look at her, because if he did, he knew he'd sweep her into his arms and hold her. Just hold her. Tears stung the back of his tightly shut eyelids, and he was only vaguely aware of the IV needle sliding into his arm. But he was wildly aware of Susan's soft, soothing touch.

When her hand closed over his to get him to loosen the tourniquet, Craig's eyes flew open. Their gazes met and clashed. Her hand hovered over his and they stared at each other, the silence drawn tautly between them. His skin seemed on fire where she had barely touched him.

"Let me have the tourniquet," she said in a low, unsteady voice.

Drowning in the blue of her confused gaze, Craig swallowed hard, his fingers releasing, one at a time, from the web belt around his thigh. At one time he would've trusted Susan with his life. God knew, he'd wanted to spend the rest of his life with her. But that was impossible. She was married. She belonged to another man. Bitterly, he relaxed against the gurney, his head tipped back, gulping several breaths of air and wrestling with his raw anger toward her, on top of his concern for his men.

Susan tried to ignore Craig's powerful hand. His fingers were bloody, many scars crossing their expanse. He'd always had wonderful hands, she thought, as she examined the gash in his thigh more closely. When the blood didn't gush, she released the web belt completely. Inside, she was shaking like gelatin, wanting to cry—wanting to be just as furious with him as he obviously was with her. But why? Why? He'd been her best friend at Annapolis. He was the one who had dropped out of her life without so much as a goodbye.

Craig's accusing gray eyes followed her every moment. "Your injury is going to require surgery," she heard herself say tightly. "First, we'll have to prep you for the general and—"

Craig's hand shot out, gripping her by the wrist as she started to leave to get the necessary medical items. "No," he growled, "no general. Give me a local. I want to stay awake. I want to know how my men are."

His fingers branded her wrist like a burning iron. Stunned by his action, Susan stared down at his suffering features. He was obviously in intense pain, but the fury in his eyes overshadowed it—and that fury was aimed straight at her. Confused and dazed, she started to pull free of his grip.

"Let go!" she whispered coldly.

Craig glared up at her, trying to combat the huskiness of her voice as it flowed over him, calming his chaotic emotions, soothing his panic and anguish over his wounded men. Instantly, he released her wrist. "A local," he said through gritted teeth.

"Let me get a doctor," she blurted and almost ran toward the central portion of ER. Everyone was busy. Karen was working quickly over one marine and Dr. Finlay another. It was chaos as she had never experienced it before. No one could have envisioned a helicopter carrying ten marines crashing on base. She went to Finlay, because he was in charge of the section. Quickly, she explained the situation and Craig's request.

Finlay didn't even glance up as the surgery nurse handed him another clamp. "These are recons," he told her. "They're tighter than fleas on a dog. They don't have the normal enlisted man/officer relationship. They're like family to one another. Well, you'll find out soon enough. Fine. If the officer doesn't want to be knocked out, I don't care. But you'd better tell the poor bastard how much pain he's going to go through when you scrub the hell out of that wound for him. Get Dr. David to stitch him up when you're done." He glanced over at the surgery table where she was operating. "She's almost finished there. I'll tell her to get to your recon as soon as possible, Evans."

"Yes, sir."

Craig twisted his head as Susan came back into view. He tried to swallow his welling anger toward her enough to find out about his team. "Well? How are my men? Did you see them?"

Stung by his cold tone, Susan stopped herself from laying her hand briefly on his shoulder. "They're in surgery right now," she told him in a low, tight voice. Trying to put her personal feelings for Craig aside, she said, "I'll let you know the moment I hear anything about their condition. I promise."

Craig lay there absorbing Susan. Her voice had always been like good Tennessee sipping whiskey, low and husky. Now that warm, almost-golden voice flowed over him like a soothing blanket. He wanted to unleash four years of terrible anger and hurt toward her. He wanted to cry for his injured men. The powerful mix of warring emotions made his voice tight and raspy. "Give me a local and clean that wound out."

Susan wondered where Craig had accumulated medical knowledge about this kind of procedure but said nothing. Under the watchful eye of his two teammates, Susan forced herself to remain professional even though she was terribly hurt by the way Craig was treating her. He'd never been like this back at Annapolis. In fact, she'd never seen him angry. What had happened to change him so much? And why aim his anger at her? The other two men had gotten off their gurneys and remained at the foot of Craig's, watching her silently. The anxiety in their gazes touched Susan as nothing else could. She gave Craig the local anesthetic and began to clean around the long, gaping wound.

"The last I saw you," she said, trying to break the palpable tension between them as she moved the gauze laden with antiseptic across his hard, taut thigh, "you were about to join the recon marines." Susan risked a look at Craig. "I don't know much about recons," she confessed. She had to talk to allay her nervousness in Craig's powerful, chilling presence. She could see the anger and anguish in his pale gray eyes, the tight set of his mouth against the pain.

"Recons go behind enemy lines," he said tightly, relieved to have his mind on anything other than Susan's firm, professional touch. How many torrid dreams had he had of her touching him? Craig groaned to himself and realized he was in shock from the crash, from worrying about his team members—and from suddenly seeing Susan again. He remembered sharply his vision of her moments before the helicopter arrived.

"I thought I was going to die," he said, placing his arm across his eyes. Susan was too beautiful, too appealing for his wildly unstable emotional state right now, and Craig didn't dare keep looking at her. Maybe if he didn't see her he could get through this excruciating ordeal without lashing into her.

"Oh?" She threw the gauze into a wastebasket. She gently tested the flesh around the wound. Craig winced, his mouth tightening, but he didn't groan. It would take another ten minutes before the local took effect enough so that she could begin the cleansing procedure on the wound itself.

"Yeah." Craig grunted, his arm still across his shut eyes, "I was waiting for that helo to come and extricate me and my team, when all of a sudden, your face appeared before me." He gave another laugh. "You! I about came unglued. I thought it was a sign I was going to die. And then, ten minutes after the helo picked up a second recon team, the blades started disintegrating around us. I saw my whole damn life pass in front of my eyes."

"You aren't going to die." Susan tried to think, but could only feel. Shaken and frayed, she asked the two younger marines to please go back to their gurneys. She couldn't stand having them watch her every move. They hesitated, looking to their skipper for confirmation, and Craig waved them away with his hand. They gave her a preferential nod and left.

"No, I'm not going to die—this time," Craig admitted, his voice low and off-key. "But I thought I was...."

Gathering the necessary items, Susan placed the steel bowl next to Craig's leg. It struck her, as she waited those few minutes, how lean and fit he had become. In Annapolis, he had been a boxing champion, but now his body was hard. Hard, tight and fit. She scrambled about for a safe topic—something to keep Craig's mind off what she had to do, which would surely cause him pain. "Tell me about recons. What do you do? Why did Dr. Finlay say you're like family?"

Craig took a deep breath, trying to steady his wildly fluctuating emotions and battle the receding pain at the same time. Why the hell wouldn't she stop talking? Stop

engaging him in polite conversation? Susan acted as if
she'd done nothing wrong! Acted as if she had no con-
science about tearing up his life four years ago and
sending him hurtling down a path that had done nothing but create more emotional pain for him. "We work
in teams of five," he muttered unwillingly. "Each
member is a specialist. I'm the paramedic on our team.
Each team consists of an officer and four enlisted men.
We're dropped deep behind enemy lines to gather tac-
tical information for our Intelligence unit." Craig's
mouth curved downward. "The last thing we want to do
is engage the enemy. Even though we have a radio, we're
often so far behind lines that a helicopter can't make it
to where they'd have to pick us up. So we're like ghosts.
We live and forage off the land, move quietly and
shadow troop movements. After ten days in the bush—
if we haven't been discovered—we're picked up at a
prearranged spot by a special helicopter team."

"I see." Susan tested Craig's leg again, and he didn't
flinch. Taking a deep breath, she warned him, "Since
you're a paramedic, you know what I have to do to
clean this wound out. Are you ready?"

He dragged his arm away from his eyes and stared up
at her. "Hell, yes!" He watched her eyes widen again
with shock at his angry response. Automatically, he
sucked in a breath, knowing the procedure would hurt
like hell itself. But it couldn't hurt as much as Susan
being here. Despite all the years, Craig realized with a
sinking feeling that he still hadn't gotten her out of his
system—or heart. The knowledge only served to make
him more furious. When he saw the apology in her eyes,
he managed a tight, one-cornered smile. "Go ahead,"
he snarled. "It's just one more way to get even with
me."

Get even? Susan closed her eyes, wavering before his obvious rage. "I don't want to get even with you," she snapped. She felt tears sting her eyes, and she looked away for a moment to get herself under control. Swallowing rapidly, she forced herself to act. Where was the friend she'd once had? The friend who'd always tried to make her feel better when she had a bad night at the dispensary? Now he was lashing out at her with anger. Well, she'd had more than enough of that in the last year of her life, and it struck a chord deep within her. She wasn't about to take Craig's inexplicable fury, Susan decided as she began the cleansing process.

"How you doing?" Karen asked, hurrying over to where Susan leaned over Craig's wound.

Craig released a shaky breath when a blond woman-doctor leaned over him and smiled. "I want a different nurse," he said between clenched teeth.

Susan jerked her head up and looked at him, her mouth open. How dare he! Before she could say anything, Karen stepped in, her voice calm and good-humored.

"Look, Captain, you've got the best right here. Just settle down and take it easy." She watched Susan critically. "Looks like major surgery to me. Who made the decision to treat this injury as a local?"

Craig wiped the sweat out of his eyes with a shaky hand. "I did, Doc. I want to stay awake. I want to find out how my men are doing. They're in surgery right now."

"I told Dr. Finlay and he said it was all right, Dr. David." Susan grimaced and drew in a trembling breath as she hurried to complete the cleansing of his wound. Hearing Karen cluck like a mother hen, Susan was relieved that her friend was here to run interference between herself and Craig.

Patting the marine's shoulder, Karen said, "Now, Captain, you just lie here and relax. The worst is over. Susan, get a needle and thread ready, please."

Craig watched the two women. Dr. David was confident, relaxed and smiling, with a distinct Midwestern accent. He liked her, he decided. Still, his gaze kept straying to Susan, who stood by, supplying the doctor with whatever she asked for. It gave him an opportunity to really study Susan for the first time since their unexpected meeting. Four of the longest years of his life seemed erased as he gazed up into her huge, and eminently readable, blue eyes. She never could hide anything from him when he looked into them, he thought, stifling a smile as he forced himself to concentrate on her rather than on the brutal pain. Not that Susan would lie anyway. But as he searched her features, his gaze came to rest on Susan's set mouth. He vividly remembered that one innocent kiss they'd shared. He'd been so hungry to kiss her more deeply. Shutting his eyes, the agony shifting and becoming more intense as the doctor worked over him, Craig felt light-headed. Susan's mouth was full, the lower lip soft, the corners turned upward to reflect her innate gentleness. How gentle Susan had been four years ago as he'd watched Steve bulldoze his way into her life, he remembered angrily.

Again the basic fact came rushing back: Susan was married. Married to Craig's own former best friend. The friend who had crushed Craig's fondest desire forever. Craig grimaced, wondering for the millionth time why Susan had stood him up on that long-ago night— that night intended to decide his future once and for all.

A groan ripped through Craig. Automatically, he gripped the sides of the gurney, the steel warm to his touch, his sweaty fingers sliding downward. Haziness replaced his sharply focused awareness. The pain was increasing by the second. Somehow, as his spinning thoughts collided with his tormented heart, Craig felt Susan's hand grip his shoulder to give him solace. Miraculously, some of the agony disappeared, and he honed in on her stabilizing touch.

No, Susan had never showed up that night, leaving Craig foolishly waiting, clutching the symbol of his chance at a dream in his sweaty palm. Finally, defeated, he'd returned to begin packing to leave. Susan thought of him as a friend. That was all. Craig had gathered his gear, grabbed a military air transport flight for the West Coast and never seen or heard from either of them again. Until now.

"He's going," Karen warned grimly as Craig's pallor increased. "The fool should've been given a general. This is too much for anyone to endure."

Susan's fingers dug into Craig's shoulder as she felt him suddenly tense. His mouth opened to release a scream. Just as suddenly, he groaned and went limp beneath her hand. Quickly, Susan tipped his head back so that his tongue wouldn't shut off the air supply to his lungs.

"It's better this way," Karen muttered. She wiped her forehead with the back of her sleeve. "Prep him for surgery. He's going under whether he likes it or not."

"Gladly," Susan breathed.

"In the meantime, I'll take a look at these other two guys," Karen said, turning to Craig's teammates.

Feeling as if someone had taken a bottle brush to her insides, Susan acted quickly, although she ached to stroke his close-cropped black hair. In unconsciousness all the harshness faded from Craig's features. His lips, now parted, revealed his true vulnerability. A sudden heated memory flashed through her, of his mouth moving in reverent adoration across her own. How could she ever forget Craig's one intense, questing kiss? He'd been so shy around her, so hesitant and always a gentleman.

Steve had been the opposite, Susan admitted, completing the last of the dressing around Craig's thigh. He'd come on strong, sweeping her off her feet, savoring life and savoring her. Steve had showered her with presents. So many gifts! Almost weekly, he would buy her something—jewelry, perfume, candy, flowers. His parents were rich and affluent. Guilt, shame and sadness flowed through Susan as she made the comparison. Craig's parents were Idaho wheat farmers. He'd had little money and often sent what he did have home to help his mother, who'd been forced to run the farm by herself since his father's back injury. No, Craig hadn't been able to afford material gifts, but he'd given Susan something money could never buy: a deep friendship—one she'd thought would last forever.

Her heart, nearly breaking at the way her life had twisted and turned, Susan looked up to see a navy corpsman, a black youth in his early twenties, standing by to take Craig to surgery.

"He ready to go, ma'am?"

"Yes," Susan whispered.

"I'm Randy Peters, ma'am," he said, giving her hand a brief, firm shake.

"Susan Evans," she responded automatically, attempting a smile.

Peters grinned. "He ain't so lucky, ya know."

"What do you mean?" Susan straightened and wiped her brow. The ER had a hushed quality now as everyone worked frantically over the remaining patients.

"This dude's injured bad enough to get a whole month's rest in this place."

Susan stood digesting the corpsman's wisdom as he pulled the gurney bearing Craig Taggart down the aisle toward the operating room. Craig would remain here, at her hospital, to recover. The realization sank into her, making her feel shaky and uncertain. Dear God, what was happening? Camp Reed was supposed to be a safe haven where she could forget the tortured past and try to collect the broken pieces of her heart. Instead, she was being ripped further apart, in ways she'd never fathomed. Craig had dropped back into her life when she was feeling the most fragile, and his anger was shocking because it was aimed directly at her.

Turning away, Susan forced herself to go help Karen, who was still ministering to Craig's two least-injured men. In no time, they had been treated and released. As she joined Karen at the sink to wash her hands, Susan saw the questioning look in her friend's eyes.

"You're pale. Are you okay?" Karen asked.

"Yes . . . fine."

"This isn't like San Francisco, is it?"

Susan shook her head. "No . . . it isn't. And you love it. I can tell."

Karen lifted her head and surveyed the ER area. "God help me, Susan, but I do love this. It's where my heart is. This is where I can be at my best. I can help save lives here as never before."

"I know."

"You're acting funny, Susan." Karen flung the water from her hands and allowed Susan to help her into another pair of surgical gloves. "Did you know that captain?"

Swallowing hard, Susan whispered, "Karen, that's Craig Taggart. My friend at Annapolis? He was Steve's best friend, too."

"Ohh . . . I remember." Karen rolled her eyes. "Did you two stay in touch?"

With a shake of her head, Susan said, "No. Craig just disappeared out of my life after I got engaged to Steve. I wouldn't have thought he'd do that."

"People are funny," Karen murmured.

"Don't I know," Susan replied, thinking of how her love for Steve had slowly turned into a dark nightmare for both of them.

"Interesting," Karen said, then grinned. "Well, who knows? Maybe you'll get a second chance."

"Second chance?"

Karen's smile widened. "Seems to me, if I recall correctly, you really liked Craig."

"He was my friend," Susan protested, frowning. "Or used to be," she added.

"This is a great chance, you know," Karen tossed over her shoulder, as she turned to go find Dr. Finlay and ask for instructions.

"Chance for what?"

"To right wrongs." She turned back toward Susan.

"There's nothing to right," Susan said, feeling her heart break even more. "My past can't be undone, Karen."

Karen patted her shoulder. "Hey, don't look so down. Chin up. Things happen for a reason. Good reasons," she admonished gently. "From what little I saw, he's upset, but I'm sure it's because he cares for his men."

Hurt thrummed through Susan as she followed Karen down the aisle to help assist another doctor. She was so confused, trying to move through a morass of emotions and answer questions about Craig's unexpected behavior at the same time. He had been so much like her back at Annapolis—open and honest. In fact, it had been their mutual shyness that initially had drawn them to each other. With Craig, she had felt safe to confide her hopes, wishes and dreams. Hurt ate at Susan. What was she going to do now that Craig was here in her nursing world? There was no way she could get transferred out, and Craig was going to be stuck in the hospital for recovery whether he wanted to be or not. Trying desperately not to allow the past to suffocate her, she tried to force her attention back to her work.

The agony and anger in Craig's eyes had sent its message, loud and clear: he didn't ever want to see her again. Susan had felt his chilling dislike. But how was she going to be able to handle it, when right now she could barely hold her own life together in the wake of Steve's death?

Chapter Three

"Miss Evans, you got a bear on your hands," warned Corpsman Peters as he ambled over to her desk outside the recovery ward.

Susan lifted her head from signing in on the watch book. From 2100 to 0600, she would be head nurse of the watch—her first night of duty in Recovery. She would have responsibility for twenty men and the supervision of three navy corpsmen who were to stand the watch with her, she knew. Randy Peters's ebony features glistened in the gloom of the small, stuffy office.

"What do you mean, Randy?" She had already decided to address the people who worked for her by their first names. Although in other spectra of the navy the enlisted were called either by rating or by their last name, Susan felt that that policy created a chasm between her and her people, one she didn't want to foster. Randy was a large-boned young man with a broad, kind face. She had appreciated his friendly manner in ER and now was silently grateful that he was on her watch section.

"What bear?" she asked, straightening and closing the book. Once an hour she would have to make rounds in the ward, checking on her various marine and navy patients to make sure their conditions were stable. Thankfully, Karen was the doctor on the watch. Susan knew the routine: one doctor for three wards, with a nurse overlooking each ward. If there was a problem, it was up to Susan to notify the doctor pronto.

Randy grinned slightly. "It's the new patient, Captain Taggart. Man, he's uptight."

Susan's heart slammed against her rib cage. Craig was in her ward. She hadn't even had a chance to look over the roster of patients, which would be her first duty. She had to check each of the clipboards that hung on the ends of the beds, noting any physician directions regarding IVs, medication, shots and such.

Susan struggled to keep her professional demeanor, so Randy wouldn't see her alarm. "Oh?" she said coolly. "What seems to be the captain's problem?"

"Ah, you know how recons are. They're like family. The captain's needing a pain med, I think. He wants to know how two of his men are doing. I told him I'd go get the duty nurse and find out what I could." With a shrug, Randy asked, "You're new to all of this, Miss Evans, but don't look too upset. The captain is tight with his men. At least he cares about them."

"How long have you been here, Randy?" Susan asked as she draped a stethoscope across her neck so both ends hung down the front of her white uniform. Sooner or later she'd have to see Craig. She might as well get it over with now. But the decision didn't stop her heart from pounding in her chest, or help her feel less shaky.

"Two and a half years, ma'am. I was a corpsman out in the field with the marines until I got my foot broke," Randy said, pointing to his left shoe. "I want to go back out, but Doc Finlay says I'll never be a field corpsman again 'cause of my injury."

"That's too bad, Randy. You look like the kind of guy who enjoys the great outdoors."

"I sure do, ma'am." His eyes twinkled.

"Why don't you show me the routine," Susan said. When she saw the corpsman's brows move up in surprise, she added, "We're a team here, Randy. I'm going to rely heavily on the corpsmen assigned to my ward for some time, until I get used to the system. The patients' welfare comes first, so consider yourself my teacher. Okay?"

Randy's shoulders squared a bit more proudly, and he pushed open the swinging door to the dimly lit ward. "Why, Miss Evans, you're talking just like a recon. Are you sure Captain Taggart hasn't brainwashed you into being one?" He chuckled pleasantly.

Susan smiled and tried not to let the young corpsman's comment rattle her. What Randy didn't know was that she and Craig did, indeed, share the same passionate commitment to people. Only, in Craig's case, the overriding concern he brought to his men had been fueled by a terrible accident that had occurred in his childhood. Craig was the older of two Taggart sons. When he was fourteen, he'd been ice-skating with his younger brother, David, on the fishing pond when David had fallen through the ice. Despite Craig's brave attempts to save his brother, David had drowned. The guilt of being unable to save him had spurred Craig to become protective of those under his command, regardless of the risk or suffering to himself. Susan had seen that quality back at Annapolis, and she was sure Craig hadn't changed in that respect.

She stopped just inside the door to the ward, where two rows of ten beds faced each other. Susan was glad to see that the windows were open to allow air circulation. Otherwise, the ward would be stuffy and the antiseptic odors could become overwhelming. Red lights above the doors at either end shed precious little light through the sleeping ward. Allowing her vision to adjust, Susan swept her gaze automatically across her sleeping patients.

Randy pointed to the end of the first row of beds on the right. Near her ear, he whispered, "That's Cap'n Taggart. Maybe you want to start your bed check there? He's fit to be tied. You probably better give him a sleep med." Randy grinned. "I think if it weren't for that leg wound he's got, he'd get up and go back to ER and demand to know about his men."

Susan's heart went out to Craig. "Okay, Randy, I'll start there. In the meantime, will you check the other patients' IVs, and if any need to be changed to do it for me?"

"Yes, ma'am, I'd be happy to."

Girding herself emotionally the best she could, Susan walked slowly down the tile floor of the aisle between the beds. She gripped the clipboard to her breast more as armor against the coming attack than as the tool it was for taking notes on each patient, to be discussed later with the watch doctor. Her hands became damp with nervousness as her gaze fastened on the bed where Craig moved restlessly.

As Susan approached, she saw that he had kicked his light blue bedspread onto the floor, and his sheet was in a tangle at the end of the cot. Like all the patients, Craig wore light blue cotton pajamas.

Susan looked at him, taking in his arm thrown across his eyes, his compressed mouth, the sweat gleaming on his face, and she realized that his pajama top was unbuttoned, exposing his chest. Swallowing convulsively, she remembered placing her hand on that chest, aware of the taut muscles beneath his shirt. But that had been so long ago—a lifetime, it seemed. Still, as she slowed, the memory of Craig's masculine power seeped back into her memory. Toward the end of their Annapolis days, her relationship with Steve hadn't been going well, and she'd confided in Craig. Upset and uncertain, she had cried in Craig's arms over what to do. Two days later, Craig had showed up at her apartment, roses in hand. By that time, Susan had been sure that she was going to break up with Steve, and she'd told Craig her decision. The roses had been such a touching surprise, because she'd known just how little money Craig had. On sheer impulse, she'd leaned up to give him a thank-you kiss for his concern. Only the kiss had turned unexpectedly passionate—for both of them. Shaken by the memory, Susan thought of the thread of hope that experience had given her. She'd never forgotten Craig's latent strength, vividly recalling how his body tautened as she shyly returned his heated, hungry kiss. A sadness enveloped her now as she came around the side of his bed. They had both been so innocent.

Well, those days were behind them, Susan acknowledged, feeling tears rise in her eyes. Then, Craig had treated her as if she were some priceless, fragile object, never forgetting his manners or trying to take advantage of her. She looked down at his shadowed form, her gaze moving to his mouth, tensed against his pain, and she fought the very real desire to put her arms around him and hold him.

"Craig?" Her voice came out low and hesitant.

Instantly, Craig jerked his arm from across his eyes. His gaze narrowed. Susan! His heart slamming in his chest, he opened his mouth, then snapped it shut as fury tunneled through him. She stood uncertainly before him, her white nursing uniform flattering her slim figure. Her brown hair hung in a simple pageboy, barely grazing her collar. The shadows caressed her square features, sad eyes and parted lips. He sensed her uncertainty, and it fueled his impatience.

Wrestling with his anger, he let his voice become hard and flat. "What are you doing here?"

Stunned all over again by his fury, Susan felt her own anger flowing to the surface, but her tone was low and controlled as she said, "I'm duty nurse for the ward tonight." She tried to ignore the accusation in his husky voice, the anger bright in his eyes. Attempting a smile to break the terrible tension, but not succeeding, she added, "You're stuck with me, whether either of us likes it or not."

Craig tried to make himself immune to Susan's presence, but it was impossible. Just that small, broken smile she had tried to give him was nearly his undoing. He saw her lay her clipboard on a nearby chair. Then she picked up his sheet and smoothed it across him. The blue bedspread followed. A wild mix of emotions raged through him as he watched her study his chart at the end of the bed. Didn't she know what she was doing to him? Automatically, his gaze moved to her long, slender hands. They were beautiful, artistic hands, Craig realized with a pang of memory, and he thought of her long-ago feather-light touch on his face, on his chest.

She was nervous. Craig saw the stain of a blush on her cheeks as she moved quietly to the other side of his bed to check the IV drip rate. When she leaned over to make sure the intravenous needle was secure in his arm, he stiffened. Instantly, she jerked her fingers away from his arm. It was then that he realized she wasn't wearing a wedding ring. His eyes narrowed to slits as she popped a thermometer into his mouth.

"I want to know how my men are," he mumbled around it.

Susan nodded and picked up the clipboard. "Just let me get your temperature and then we'll talk," she said, trying for a tone of brisk authority. It was agony to look into his sweaty, strained features, those gray eyes reminding her so vividly of a hawk. Craig missed nothing; he was attuned to every nuance. Susan swallowed hard and worked to focus on his medical record, realizing that the doctor had prescribed sleeping pills as well as pain pills. Craig had refused the sleeping pill, she saw from the previous nurse's notation. And he was well past the time when he should have been given a pain pill. She frowned. The earlier nurse had forgotten to give it to him.

Rankled, Susan said nothing as she left his bedside to return to the office's small pharmacy, which contained certain widely used drugs. She unlocked the cabinet and removed the appropriate medication, then locked up and walked back into the ward. By the time she arrived at Craig's bed, the three minutes were up and she took the thermometer out of his mouth.

"What is it?" Craig demanded irritably.

Susan recorded the temperature and shook the thermometer down with several flicks of her wrist. "One hundred point two."

"Infection," he growled. Then he shot her a glance. "I'm taking enough antibiotics to kill a horse. By morning, I'll be normal."

Susan grimly held out her hand. "Here's your pain med."

Craig looked at her opened hand. "At least you make your rounds."

He picked up two of the four tablets and popped them into his mouth, then took a large gulp of water and set the glass back on the bedside table.

"What's that supposed to mean?" Susan challenged.

Glaring, Craig held her insolent stare. "It means that the other duty nurse *didn't* make her last round. Not everyone is as capable as you, Lieutenant Evans."

Stunned, Susan tried to gather her composure. "Don't you want the sleeping pills?"

He continued to glare at her. "Why the hell would I? I just got out of Recovery. I'm drugged enough as it is."

Susan slipped the pills into the pocket of her uniform. "I'm sorry the other nurse forgot to give you the pain med."

It hurt just to speak with Susan, Craig thought. It hurt to feel her this close to him. His emotions were frayed, and the pain had made him snappish. "Look," he said in a harsh whisper, "just do me one favor and then leave me the hell alone. Find out how my men, Hayes and Shelton, are doing, will you? It's the only thing I'll ever ask of you, Susan." He was breathing hard, each breath fiery and filled with anguish.

Susan found she couldn't protect herself from Craig's anger. It was obvious that he was angry with *her*. Tucking her lower lip between her teeth to stop from snarling back at him, she held her tongue. Craig was suffering badly. The past, she realized, wasn't buried between them as she'd thought. No, it was alive and haunting both of them. "I'll find out," she promised quietly, and left his side.

Craig lay back, shutting his eyes and trying to control his chaotic breathing. He'd seen how his anger had struck Susan, as surely as if he'd hit her. Hurting physically and emotionally, he castigated himself. Sometime later, he felt Susan's presence again and barely opened his eyes to see her quietly making her rounds through the ward. Most of the men were drugged into sleep. A few, like him, had refused the pills and were either awake or sleeping fitfully. Craig's mouth lifted in a tortured grimace.

He tried to ignore Susan's serene presence, but it was impossible. He hungered to see her, to watch her, to absorb her soft, smiling face into his deeply suffering heart. She ministered to those men who were awake, reaching out like a mother to touch their hair or place her hand on their shoulders. Susan knew the value of touch; she always had. Craig remembered the way she would touch his arm or shoulder when they'd shared their many deep, involved conversations. But tonight, she was loath to touch him and he knew it. Restless and angry, he bunched the spread up in his fists, then released it. How were his men? When would Susan know? Would she really tell him—or would she continue to avoid him?

Corpsman Peters entered the ward some time later. Craig watched him go over to Susan and speak to her in a low voice. He saw Susan's face go still, and his heart plummeted. Intuitively, Craig knew the exchange had to do with his men. He knotted the covers between his fists and waited.

Her mouth dry, Susan thanked Randy and forced herself to complete her final patient check before going to Craig. He was sitting up in bed, leaning against the pillow, every muscle in his body taut. Making herself meet his fiery gray gaze, which seemed to cut into her, Susan scrambled for the right words. But as she got closer to Craig's bed, she realized he was holding himself rigid in preparation for the bad news.

Susan drew the green metal chair up to the side of Craig's bed and sat, laying the clipboard across her thighs. "Craig—"

"Just give it to me, Susan," he snapped. "Don't try to be tactful, okay?"

Wincing at his angry attack, Susan nodded. "Hayes died just a little while ago," she said softly. "They couldn't stabilize him." She saw Craig's eyes go dark. Then tears rose in them. An answering lump formed in her throat. "Shelton's in ICU, in critical and unstable condition." With a shrug, she whispered, "I'll call down there at the end of my watch and try to find out more."

Craig remained silent, absorbing the loss of Hayes. "He was supposed to get married," he rasped after a moment.

"What?"

"Andy Hayes, my radioman—he was engaged...." Craig shut his eyes and tipped his head back, a terrible, wrenching sigh ripping out of him. "It was his final mission before the wedding."

Painful, too-fresh memories staggered Susan. Steve's death had been such a long, awful slide downward for both of them. She'd tried to hold on to her love for him, but love had turned to suffering, then numbness. Still, Susan hurt for Hayes's fiancée—she and Hayes would never get to know married love at all. "I—I'm sorry," she whispered, reaching out, but stopping herself before she touched Craig. How she longed simply to hold him. She felt Craig's pain—and her own stored pain from this past terrible year. "I know how much you care for others," she began, her voice quavering with feeling.

Susan's soft, halting words washed over Craig, taking away some of his pain at the loss of Andy. He opened his eyes and looked at her deeply shadowed features. Stunned that she seemed no less affected by his loss than he was, he felt his defensive wall of anger slip. Savagely, he reminded himself that Susan was married. She belonged to another man. Or did she? Where was her wedding ring? But maybe she didn't wear it when she was on duty, his quick mind countered. With monumental effort, he whispered, "Thanks," in a steely tone.

Susan slowly stood and returned the chair to its original corner. There was nothing more to say. Craig made it obvious that he didn't want her around. And she didn't want to be his whipping post, either. She'd managed to survive a year of that with Steve, and it was time to draw the line. Turning, Susan walked away, leaving the ward—and leaving Craig to deal with the loss of his friend.

Out in the office, she logged the time of her ward round. Peters came through the door.

"Thanks for finding out that information for me," she told him.

"Bad news for the captain." Randy shook his head. He sat down on the chair in front of the desk. "You hate to see a man cry."

Susan's head snapped up. "Cry?"

Randy gestured toward the ward. "Yeah, he's in there crying."

"Karen, you have to do me a favor," Susan begged the next morning as she got off duty.

Karen yawned. "What?"

They walked out of the hospital area and headed to the parking lot. The surrounding brown hills glowed in the morning sunlight. The vast light blue sky stretched overhead, the darker blue Pacific Ocean to the west. Gulls wheeled and called nearby, looking for handouts.

"We've got ward duty again tonight," Susan began. "Can you make a call to the San Diego Hospital and check on a man for me?"

Karen rubbed her face tiredly. "Now, you know that's against regs."

She smiled. "Yes, I know that."

"Who's this for? Taggart?"

"Your mama didn't raise you to be dumb, did she?" Susan countered with a laugh.

Grinning in response, Karen said, "My mama was a sharp Ohio woman who could see straight through even the tiniest white lie."

"So will you do it?" Susan persisted. "His name is Sergeant Larry Shelton. He was stabilized and flown down to San Diego for extended treatment for his burns. He was on Craig's recon team."

Grimacing, Karen muttered, "I'll see what I can do, but no promises." Then she brightened. "How are you two getting along?"

"Like cats and dogs," Susan said unhappily.

"Why?"

Susan shrugged. "He's angry with me, and I don't know why."

"Does he know you're single again? A widow?"

"No..."

They reached the edge of the parking lot. Heat was already building on the black asphalt. "Why not?" Karen asked.

"Why *should* he?" Susan demanded. "For all I know, he's engaged or married himself."

"Is he wearing a ring?"

"No, but that doesn't mean anything. Randy, one of the corpsmen I work with, said the men don't wear any kind of jewelry because a glint could get them discovered during the war games."

"Good point," Karen said thoughtfully. Then she brightened and clapped Susan on the shoulder. "Well, don't look so glum. With time, Craig will thaw. This is just temporary, I'm sure."

Susan wasn't so sure. "With Steve dying and all," she admitted, "I was in bad-enough shape, Karen. Now, with Craig here, it's like I don't know which end is up. I can't protect myself from his anger. Each of his glares cuts a little more deeply into my heart."

"My mama always said time was a healer," Karen said gently. "Just ride this through, Susan. No sense in striking back at Craig."

"I'd never do that."

"I know. You're such a softy." Karen frowned. "That's part of your problem, you know."

They halted at their cars, parked next to each other. Susan opened the door to her blue compact. "What problem?"

"Yours," Karen said, unlocking the door of her sporty red Mazda. "Sometimes I wish you would fight back and get angry."

Susan managed a slight smile. "Be more like you? The doc that flies off the handle at a moment's notice?"

Grinning, Karen said, "I express my anger in a positive fashion."

"Oh, sure," Susan hooted, some of her depression lifting under Karen's good-natured needling. "You just use that sweet voice of yours to call some poor guy a bastard, and he doesn't even know what hit him. Diplomacy is really a code, and you forget—I know the code."

With a giggle, Karen said, "As long as those men don't realize my sweetness and smile are thinly veiled cuss words, I'll be okay." She wagged her finger at Susan. "You just be sure to get some sleep. You look awful."

Wasn't that the truth? Susan thought as she waved goodbye to her friend. The apartment she'd rented was in Oceanside, just outside the base's main gates. She longed to shower off the smell of the ward and simply sleep, but she knew herself too well. Since Steve's death a year ago, insomnia had been her bed partner. That and nightmares interwoven with guilt. Right now, Craig's burning gray eyes hovered in her mind and she wasn't sure which hurt more—the memory of Steve's death or Craig's anger. But she did know that tonight she'd be back on rounds in his ward—and she wasn't looking forward to it one bit.

* * *

"Man, I'm telling you," Randy warned Susan as she logged in for her second twelve-hour shift, "you better watch out for Captain Taggart. He's raising all kinds of hell in there, wanting to know about his man Shelton."

"Thanks for the warning," Susan said grimly. Throughout the day, she'd slept poorly. The sounds of her apartment were new to her, and the interstate was nearby. If it wasn't the aggravating roar of a truck that jerked her out of her light, restless sleep, it was the sound of a marine helicopter whapping overhead. And when she did finally doze off, Susan dreamed of Craig's anger.

"What you gonna do?" Randy asked. "He's snarly tonight."

"He's still grieving over the death of his teammate," Susan counseled the corpsman, "so go easy on him."

"Yes, ma'am." Randy grinned suddenly. "One thing, though."

"What?" Susan draped the stethoscope around her neck and picked up her clipboard.

"When the captain found out you were coming back on duty, he settled down a lot."

Susan stared at the corpsman. "He did?"

"Yes, ma'am. It was almost as if..."

"As if what?"

With an embarrassed shrug, Randy smiled. "Don't mind me. The captain just seemed relieved, I guess. Not that he smiled. No, ma'am. That's a recon marine in there, and those fellas are as tough as they come. No, he didn't smile. But he lost a lot of his restlessness, I guess."

"Well, I've got some news that might make him even more civilized," Susan said.

Randy's eyes went wide. "Thank the good Lord! Because that recon is like a caged and unhappy tiger in that ward. I heard from the off-going watch that he's hardly slept at all." He waved his finger in her direction. "Careful, he bites the hand that feeds him!"

With a slight smile, Susan nodded. "I think this news will help him sleep." She moved through the doors and stood for a moment on the other side to allow her eyes to adjust to the ward's soft red glow. A strong, good feeling moved through Susan as she surveyed her patients. Yes, these were *her* men, and she felt a trickle of pride. There was nothing like the feeling of being able to help another human being; it was something Susan lived for.

As she walked quietly down the aisle of the ward, her gaze fastened on Craig's bed. Again, he lay with his arm across his eyes, and to her surprise, he wasn't wearing his pajama top. She could see it wadded up on the deck where he'd evidently thrown it, along with his bedspread and sheet. His chest, covered with a carpet of dark, curling hair, glistened with sweat. Worried that he might still be running a fever, she rushed forward.

Her mouth dry, Susan watched Craig withdraw his arm from his eyes at the sound of her footsteps. His gray gaze narrowed speculatively. Dragging himself into a sitting position, he watched her.

"I had Dr. David call down to San Diego about your man, Larry Shelton," she said in a quiet tone, knowing he didn't want to waste time on social pleasantries. "He's out of unstable critical and they're listing him in fair condition." She managed a small smile. "Shelton will live."

Relief flooded through Craig, and he released a long, ragged breath of air. "Thank God," he rasped. For nearly a minute, he wrestled with his relief—and with his joy at seeing Susan again. Tonight, she looked pale, he noticed, and her eyes had darkness in them. He could see smudges beneath her eyes—telltale signs that she hadn't slept well. Looking away, he muttered tightly, "Thanks for finding out about Shelton."

Forcing herself to move, to start her rounds, Susan set the clipboard aside and came around the bed to check his IV drip. "Actually, you can thank Dr. David. She's the one who made the call."

Craig lifted his head and watched Susan's every movement. Her hands were trembling. He tried to steel himself against the touch that would come as she checked the point where the IV entered his left arm. As she leaned down, he could smell the perfume she wore. The fragrance was in direct contrast to the antiseptic smells of the ward, and, almost unwillingly, Craig inhaled deeply. Her touch was butterfly light.

"You asked her to make the call," he growled, willing his body to not respond to her touch.

Craig was so close, so powerful. Susan tried to hurry her IV check, but to her disappointment, she saw that it needed to be reinserted and bandaged. "You've been moving around too much," she said, trying to protect herself from his aura of fury. If only he wouldn't lash out at her again....

Craig looked down at the dark bruises on his left arm. He scowled, barely able to will himself not to touch Susan in return. Her fingers were cool against his heated flesh. "So what?"

His gray eyes seemed to bore into hers. Her mouth flattening, Susan said in a clipped voice, "I'm going to have to shift the IV to your other arm." She drew in a shaky breath. The IV apparatus was on wheels. As gently as she could, she removed the needle and pressed a bandage onto his arm so it wouldn't bleed. Craig lay stock-still, and she could feel his gaze following her every move.

He turned over his right arm so she could look for a vein. Each of her feathery touches only magnified his agony for her. He tried not to look at her soft lips, tried not to think of that sole kiss they'd shared. Forcing himself to think coherently, Craig said, "You look like hell. Don't they give you time off between shifts around here?"

Susan froze momentarily, pressing her lips together to hold back the anger threatening to bubble out at Craig. She sat down to insert the IV needle. "This is only my second day at Camp Reed," she said tightly. "And there are lots of new sounds to get used to at my apartment...."

Craig saw the unmistakable mixture of hurt and anger in her blue eyes when she inadvertently looked up at him. His breathing became suspended as he met and held her luminous gaze, which was shadowed with exhaustion.

"Why did you come here to Reed?" he snarled, pushing his emotions back down deep inside, where they belonged.

Susan blinked, taken aback by the harshness of his voice, the iciness in his eyes. Her hands stilled over his arm. "Why?" she repeated numbly.

"Coming here was stupid, Susan. You haven't changed at all since I knew you at Annapolis. For once in your life, why don't you stop helping others so much and learn to help yourself? You look like hell warmed over. You obviously haven't gotten any sleep. If you think you can keep this up, you're mistaken. Get a transfer back to wherever you came from," he snapped. "You aren't cut out for this kind of stress."

Anger bled through Susan's shock at his attack. Grimly, she focused on getting the IV back into his arm and taping it up properly. The silence grew between them as she finished the job and stood up. She took the clipboard from the end of his cot and studied it. His eyes never left hers.

"Well?" Craig goaded as she came back to his bedside. "Why did you come here?"

Susan saw the tears glittering in her patient's eyes. Intuitively, she realized he was grieving over Hayes's death. Sitting down, keeping her voice low, she said, "You're raw over your man's death, Craig. That's what's really bothering you. It isn't me!" She stabbed at his chest with her finger. "Don't forget, I know how guilty you've felt over David's death. Ever since he drowned, you've been scrambling to atone for some crazy guilt. Well, it wasn't your fault!" Her voice cracked. "I know you, remember? I saw for a year how much you cared for the men under your command at Annapolis. I saw how you cared for me. Why don't you just keep crying until you get your grief out for Hayes? There's nothing wrong with that!"

Craig watched her start to rise again. His hand shot out. "Hold it," he ordered, his fingers closing tightly over her wrist. "Just where do you get off accusing me of guilt? There's no such thing as an officer caring too much for the men of his command. And who do you think you are, bringing up David's death? How the hell do you know how I feel?" He saw her eyes go wide, but he was unable to stop the hurt from spilling out. "You talk about martyrs—well, you're one of the best, Susan! You bleed yourself dry helping others, but when it comes to helping yourself, you can't do it.''

"Let me go," she rattled.

Craig held her shaken gaze. "Not until I'm done," he snarled. "What's the matter? Wasn't marriage to Steve exciting enough for you? Didn't it fulfill you, Susan? Is that why you came here? The martyr in you just had to keep giving herself away to those in need. I guess Steve's needs weren't enough. What did you do, volunteer to come here? More than likely." He released her wrist.

Susan jerked her hand back against her. Stunned, her emotions reeling under his attack, she whispered angrily, "I may enjoy helping others, but at least I know who I am, what I'm doing here, which is more than what I can say for you! Who do you think *you* are, accusing me like this?" Tears burned in her eyes, but she refused to let Craig see her cry. She held up her left hand. "Just for your information, Craig Taggart, Steve is dead! I didn't come to Reed because I'm a martyr, damn you! I'm here because I know I can make a difference."

Shocked, Craig opened his mouth. Steve was dead? When? How? Oh, God...

With a small cry, Susan spun around and headed up the aisle and out of the ward, fighting back the tears, the hurt. She found Randy and asked him to finish the rounds. "If there's a problem, come and get me," she said, trying to control her shaking voice. "I just need some fresh air."

Randy looked at her strangely but nodded his agreement and said nothing.

Outside, beneath the stars, Susan walked away from the hospital. She was gasping for breath, her hands pressed to her heart. All her emotions overwhelmed her, and tears squeezed out from beneath her lashes. In that moment, she realized so much. Worst of all, she realized Craig's attack had ripped away the last of the pretense about her marriage. Steve had been so open and happy-go-lucky—a generous extrovert. He'd fallen in love with her the moment he'd seen her that evening at the dispensary. He'd been her opposite—filled with life, with dreams of greatness. And he'd wanted her at his side to watch him fulfill all of them.

Moving into the shadows, feeling more alone, more filled with guilt than she ever had in her whole life, Susan cried.

Chapter Four

Craig sat tensely, his hands knotted in his lap, trying to assimilate his shock over Steve's death. The horrified look on Susan's face struck savagely at him, making him feel small and guilty as never before. Steve had been his best friend for three years, even after they'd met Susan—up until that fateful day when Susan had tearfully told Craig she'd decided to break up with Steve.

Burying his face in his hands, Craig couldn't seem to think clearly. He could only feel the raging emotions battering him, tearing away at his anger toward Susan and leaving a surge of guilt and grief in its wake. Even though Steve had allowed their friendship to lapse as Susan became an integral part of his life, Craig had never hated his old friend. No, never. But he was dead. What had happened?

Bitterly, he raised his face and allowed his hands to fall back into his lap. From the moment Susan had stood him up at the restaurant, his life had taken a powerful turn away from his past, which had included Steve and Susan. He'd left abruptly, hurt and angry at Susan's treatment of him. Every day after that had been a reminder that he hadn't been aggressive enough in going after Susan—that he'd believed in some romantic notion about friendship and trust winning out in the end. Well, he'd ended up with nothing but a broken heart to show for it.

And each day since, Craig had hardened his heart, thrown himself into recon training and buried the past, buried the terrible pain of losing Susan—a pain she knew nothing about. She'd seen him as a friend, plain and simple. Pressing his lips into a thin line to stop from crying out, Craig knew his heartless aggression over the years since then had done nothing but take him from one unfulfilling relationship to another. Every woman he met he compared to Susan, whether he wanted to or not. And none of them stacked up. None of them could begin to compare. The intimacy that had naturally sprung between him and Susan in those long-ago, innocent days was something he'd searched for but never found with another woman.

So much had happened in those four long, tortured years. Since he'd walked away from Susan and Steve. But what had happened to Steve? After Craig had left Annapolis, he'd never heard anything more about his best friend beyond the fact that he'd married Susan. Ordinarily, "ring knockers" stayed in touch—or at least word about them got around. The "brotherhood"— graduates of Annapolis—were a small, tight group, and they followed one another's movements on the chess board of military life. He realized now that it was odd he hadn't heard more, but he'd been so filled with loss that for a time, much of the military world had floated by unnoticed.

Steve had been at the top of his class, destined for the greatness he'd always wanted. So why had he dropped out of sight? Scowling, Craig traced patterns on the bedspread with his finger. Suddenly, he thought again of the incalculable damage he had just done to Susan by behaving the way he did. He'd seen her anguish, so deep and telling that it made him feel worse than any other point in his life. But at the same time, he felt a tiny, rebellious thread of hope spring to life.

Guiltily, Craig tried to push the hope away. Steve was dead. It was wrong to feel this way. Anyway, he'd had great hope before, when Susan had been on the verge of breaking up with Steve, and where had that gotten him? He'd had great plans to court her himself—that's why he'd waited so long at the restaurant that night. But something had gone wrong. Evidently, Steve and Susan had made up. Still, that didn't give Susan the right to stand him up without any explanation—without any word at all. Why did life have to be so damned complicated?

If only he could get out of bed and follow Susan. But Craig knew the idea was folly, because he'd tear the wound open again and be laid up twice as long. He looked around and saw Peters, one of the navy corpsmen, approaching. Agitated, Craig waved him over.

"Yes, sir?" Peters asked, coming to his bed.

"Lieutenant Evans," Craig said irritably. "Where did she go? I've got to talk to her."

Uncomfortably, Peters looked toward the swinging doors at the end of the ward. "She was awful upset, sir."

Craig avoided the corpsman's gaze. "I know!" He gripped the covers in his fists. "I've got to see her. Call her back in. I must talk to her."

"Yes, sir. But first, I gotta make the rounds. There's IVs that need changing and—"

"Do it," Craig muttered, understanding. He wouldn't deny the men in the ward medical help just because he'd screwed things up with Susan. He lay back, breathing hard, the pain in his chest growing with every breath he took. Steve was dead. Susan was a widow. Oh, God, he'd just torn her apart with his own, selfish anger. Craig squeezed his eyes shut. He'd seen the hurt, the agony in her eyes and face when he'd accused her. What was wrong with him?

For the next hour, he watched the corpsman complete the ward rounds. It was nearly 0100, but he was anything but sleepy. Wasn't Susan right? Hadn't he attacked her partly because of his grief over losing Hayes? And was part of it to stop his hardened heart from feeling again? Craig's mouth worked into a grim line. He'd made such an ass of himself. He cared for Susan regardless of how she'd treated him in the past. And she was no longer married, which gave him a second chance. Or did it? The way he'd treated her since meeting her at Reed no doubt had burned every possible bridge. He couldn't blame Susan if she'd never have anything to do with him again. As he lay, drenched in his own sweat and pain, Craig stared up at the darkened ceiling of the ward.

The minutes kept dragging by, and he couldn't remain still. He had to talk to Susan! To his relief, he saw

Peters finish his round and leave. Was he going out to talk to her? Craig shut his eyes and wiped the sweat off his face. She *had* to come see him. And he had to apologize—for so very much.

"Sir?"

Craig's eyes snapped open. He had been so caught up in sorrow and guilt that he'd failed to hear Peters's approach. The lapse of attention to his surroundings was completely unlike him, and he quickly rose up on both elbows.

"Susan?" he rasped.

"I'm sorry, sir," Peters said apologetically, "but Lieutenant Evans said she doesn't want to see you."

"But I've *got* to see her!"

Peters shrugged. He opened his palms. "Sir, she's upset. She says no."

Craig glared at the doors at the end of the ward. If only he wasn't injured . . . If only. He glanced up at the corpsman. "How is she?" he asked unsteadily, his emotions beginning to unravel. Susan hadn't deserved what he'd said. What he'd accused her of.

"Well, sir . . . she's quite unsettled."

"Crying?" Craig tried to prepare himself for the answer. He saw Peters's mouth twitch.

"Yes, sir, she is. . . ."

"Please," he begged hoarsely, "just tell her to come back and talk with me. Tell her I—"

"Sir, she won't come. She's asked to be relieved of duty for the rest of the night. Dr. Finlay approved her request and a new nurse is coming on watch shortly. I'm sorry, sir." With a kind shake of his head, Peters left.

Craig groaned and lay back. What a bastard he'd become. He'd spent the last four years challenging death in so many ways, and it had changed him into someone he didn't even like. He'd never attacked Susan before. What was wrong with him? How could he possibly atone for hurting her that way? Rubbing his face savagely, Craig closed his eyes, consumed in the fire of his self-made hell.

"What do you mean, Lieutenant Evans isn't here?" Craig demanded irritably of Peters the next evening.

"Sir, she's left. She and Dr. David have gone to the dispensary at Edson Range. They're going to be giving vaccinations to the boots who are learning how to fire rifles up there."

Craig sat up on his bed, staring at the corpsman. Susan had left. He looked away, feeling helpless.

"I don't blame her," he whispered bitterly.

"Sir?"

"Nothing. Thanks, Peters. I appreciate you telling me."

"You're welcome, sir."

He glanced up at him. "Who's the doc on duty tonight?"

"Dr. Finlay, sir."

"Good. Can you find him? I need to talk to him."

"Yes, sir."

Craig lay back, unable to rest. It was a good hour before Finlay dropped by the ward. A large man clad in a hospital-issue green smock, Finlay was in his mid-forties, partly balding. A pair of bifocals rested on the end of his hawklike nose. He pulled up the chair and sat down next to Craig's bed.

"What's the problem, Captain?" he asked, scanning Craig's chart.

"I'm fine medically, Doctor. I need to talk to you privately about one of the nurses. Lieutenant Evans."

Finlay's bushy eyebrows rose. "Susan? What about her?"

"What happened to her?"

Finlay smiled and wrote his name on the bottom of Craig's chart. "She volunteered to be part of the vaccination team up on the range."

"Well, is that a permanent assignment?"

"No. Just a week."

"And then she'll come back? Here?" Craig didn't care what Finlay thought, although the doctor was smiling slightly as he appraised him in the gathering silence.

"Yes, Susan is due back in seven days, Captain."

"When do you think you'll release me from this place?" he asked, jabbing a hand toward his bandaged wound.

"In about a week." Finlay cocked his head and held his gaze. "Will that be soon enough, Captain?"

Relief removed some of Craig's agitation. "Yeah, that will be fine, Doc. Thanks."

Finlay nodded and got up. "Get some rest, Captain. Judging from the way you look, you need some uninterrupted sleep."

Craig gave him a measured look.

Finlay smiled. "Just settle down, son. Things will work out. You concentrate on getting well, and everything else you're so worried about will work out, too."

"Ready to go back to the hospital?" Karen asked as they climbed into her Mazda.

Susan shook her head. The week away from the hospital had been a buffer zone against these new and painful memories of Craig Taggart. Hot summer air whipped through the car as Karen drove along the

highway toward the main area of the base. Susan took
a deep, unsteady breath and wondered, as she had so
many times this past week, how Craig was getting
along. Seven days had passed. Seven of the worst days
of her life. But they were better than being around
Craig. Susan couldn't stand his anger, and the week had
gone faster than she'd wanted it to.

The time out in the dispensary had been revealing,
Susan acknowledged. When Steve had died, she had
immediately applied for Oak Knoll—and gotten the
transfer. She'd had little time to sift through her marriage, and her feelings. But in these past seven days, it
seemed as if every painful emotion she'd tried to suppress had emerged, like the cutting edge of a knife
against her hurting heart. Craig's shocking entry into
her life had ripped loose the last of the emotional scar
tissue that protected her backlog of grief, shame and
guilt toward Steve, as well as her love for him.

Worst of all, Susan had to face the fact that through
the difficult years with Steve, as his health had deteri-
orated, she'd thought often of Craig Taggart. She'd realized too late that Craig's quiet, sincere approach to
life, the steadiness he'd brought to her, was what she
really needed—and something Steve could never supply, no matter how hard he tried. Now, it seemed useless not to own that revelation about Craig, and the fact
that even though she hadn't seen him as marriage material at Annapolis, as she'd matured, she'd seen that
they had much more in common. But what good would
it do to admit that now? And at what cost to herself?
She was stuck at Camp Reed for the next three years.
And Craig was assigned to Camp Reed, too. Hanging
her head, Susan bit down hard on her lower lip. How
many tears had she spilled this past week in her apart-

ment at night? Tears no one would know about because she'd always made a point of crying alone or not at all.

Craig was an unknown quantity thrust suddenly—and viciously—into her life. Confused, Susan didn't know what to feel about him, about Steve, or even about herself, for that matter. The year since Steve's death had left her numb. Camp Reed was to be a quiet place where she would have the time to start trying to live her life again, to leave the shame and pain behind her. But with Craig Taggart hovering like a vulture ready to tear out what little was left of her heart, Susan felt trapped as never before. When had Craig thrown their friendship away? It had been such a wonderful thing they'd shared. Rubbing her brow, Susan closed her eyes and forced herself not to cry. At least, not right now.

Craig waited impatiently in the trauma-unit office. Around him, several nurses and doctors filled out forms and chatted. Shifting most of his weight to his good leg to relieve the pain in the injured one, he glanced at his watch, then searched the parking lot outside the double doors. When he'd called the Edson dispensary, he'd been told Susan would be returning in Dr. David's red sports car.

"You should see them any minute now," a nurse behind the desk said.

Craig nodded his thanks and moved out of the busy office. The afternoon sun bore down on him, the dry heat unrelenting. Drawing the bill of his utility cap a little lower until the rim almost touched the bridge of his nose, Craig squinted, restlessly searching the highway that led to the hospital. There! He saw a small red car pulling off the highway toward the hospital. His heart began a slow, insistent pounding.

What if Susan wasn't with Dr. David? What if she'd gotten permission to remain at the dispensary another week? Grimly, Craig watched the car draw closer. All his senses, all his emotions, focused on that one car, which he prayed carried Susan back home—to him.

His hands sweaty, Craig moved with a decided limp toward the nearby parking lot. He was damned if Susan was going to run away from him if she was in that car. If only she would forgive him. If only...

The sports car slowed and made the turn into the main parking lot. His eyes narrowed, and his breath caught. Two women were getting out of the car. Susan! His mouth flattening, Craig didn't wait. He moved forward as fast as he could to intercept Susan before she could spot him.

A sporadic but strong breeze whipped Susan's hair around her face. She shielded her eyes from the sudden gust with her hand as she walked unhappily toward the hospital, with Karen following at a more leisurely pace. The gust of wind died down and Susan lowered her hand from her eyes. She looked up and gasped.

"We need to talk," Craig said grimly, his hand snaking out and gripping her arm. "Right now."

Shocked, Susan stared up into his pale, tense face. Craig's gray eyes blazed with a disturbing light, and her lips parted to protest. She felt his fingers close more firmly around her upper arm. His voice, like a rasp across her raw emotions, only frightened her more.

When Craig saw the terror in Susan's eyes, he felt even angrier at himself. Instantly, he eased his grip. "Stop looking at me like that." And then he added in a hoarse whisper, "Please. I need to apologize to you for what I said last week. I had no right—"

Susan swayed, caught herself and begged, "Craig, just leave me alone!"

Instantly he released her. They were on a military base and it was against regulations to hold her hand or do anything to suggest fraternization. He saw Dr. David halt and give them a strange look, but she walked on without saying a word.

"I'm just asking for a few minutes," he said gratingly.

Spinning from Craig's unexpected presence, Susan was barely aware that she had nodded her head. She felt the grip of his hand on her elbow, guiding her. He limped badly on his injured leg, she noticed suddenly. She cast a glance at him and realized that he was back in uniform, wearing a dark green shirt and trousers, the latter bloused into a pair of black, highly polished combat boots. What made Craig even more warrior-like was the utility cap, the bill low on his brow. His shirtsleeves were rolled up to his elbows, and a web belt held a pistol in a black holster at his side, adding to his air of danger.

"You shouldn't be walking around this soon," she blurted.

He gave her a twisted smile. "Just deserts for the way I attacked you, wouldn't you say?" He led her to a wooden bench in the shade of several trees next to the main hospital building. He reached out and placed his hand on her shoulder. "This is good enough," he said and gestured to the bench. "Let's sit down." He noticed that Susan was dressed in her light blue summer-uniform skirt and blouse. Her hair was mussed and free, framing her pale face. Anxiously, Craig probed her dark, uncertain blue gaze as she tried to avoid looking at him. He couldn't blame her. He eased down onto the bench, keeping his injured leg straight in front of him to relieve some of his pain at using it much too soon.

Susan hesitated. The pleading look in Craig's eyes was her undoing, and she hesitantly joined him on the bench, keeping as much distance as possible between them. Pulling several strands of hair away from her eyes, she looked at him warily.

"I didn't ever expect to see you again," she offered, trying to steel herself against, she was sure, a coming attack.

Craig took off his cap and dangled it between his long, scarred fingers. His throat ached with tension. "I'm sure you didn't." He cleared his throat. "I can't say I blame you." Risking a glance at her, Craig rasped, "You said Steve was dead. I want to know what happened."

Anger warred within her. Tears stung her eyes. "As if you really care!"

Holding on to his feelings, Craig said, "I apologize, Susan. I was a real bastard to you a week ago." He motioned to her left hand, which no longer bore Steve's wedding ring. "I didn't know...." He looked away. Getting hold of his emotions, he said, "I didn't know about Steve dying. I'm sorry. Sorry as hell for what happened."

She watched as Craig hung his head, his lips pursed against a lot of pain. Clasping her hands, she bowed her head, too, unable to speak as emotions raced inside her. The wind was playful, the breeze tangy with salt from the nearby Pacific. She dragged in a ragged breath.

"So am I," she whispered bitterly. "I thought I knew you, Craig. You're not the kind of man to deliberately strike out and hurt someone." *Not like Steve, who would and did in the closing year of his illness,* Susan thought unwillingly. She touched her brow in a nervous gesture as Craig slowly lifted his head, his gray eyes dark with apology. "Your anger was over losing Hayes. I know how you blame yourself when one of your men gets hurt...."

He plucked at an imaginary thread on his olive green utilities. "More than anyone, you could always forgive someone else for their transgressions, Susan." And then he added softly, "Even me." He stared down at his booted feet.

"Especially you," she quavered, fighting back the urge to wrap her arms around him. Craig looked so forlorn, and Susan understood that kind of serrating loneliness that cut to the quick of her heart. His face mirrored his suffering, and she ached to take his pain away.

"Lately," Craig confided in a hoarse voice as he held her luminous blue eyes, "I've been a real bastard. Maybe it's the helo crash. Maybe it's the fact I've lost several good men." He pushed his fingers through his short, dark hair. "But those are excuses, Susan. I shouldn't have said the things I did. Especially since Steve is dead. I just didn't know...."

"This wasn't the first time you accused me of being a martyr," Susan said hollowly.

"No... it wasn't."

"You were always upset when I worked extra hours at the Annapolis dispensary."

Craig nodded. "You deserved a little happiness," he answered in a whisper. "I remember when you told me about your family. How your father left when he found out your mother had cancer." Craig shook his head.

"The bastard didn't have the guts to stay and protect your mother. He didn't have any loyalty to her or to you."

The pain of the past welled up through Susan. "I didn't mind taking care of my mom while she was dying, Craig. I know when I shared that with you, you were quiet for a long time afterward."

"I was upset, that was all."

She tilted her head. "Upset?"

"Yeah." Craig tried to smile, but it was impossible. His heart was opening of its own accord, and he felt an incredible flood of joy moving through him. "Here you were, a twelve-year-old girl left holding the bag. Your mother had to go on welfare because your father abandoned you. And then you had to take care of her, because you couldn't afford nursing help."

She took in a ragged breath. "They were the best of times and the worst of times, Craig. I loved my mother with all my heart and soul. I didn't see having to take care of her as a burden the way that you do."

"Not a burden." He groped for the right words. He wanted to say so much, wanted to catch up on every nuance of Susan and the four years he'd missed. "When I first met you at Annapolis, I was struck by how serious and mature you were for your age. You rarely smiled, and you didn't know what it meant to be a kid, I guess."

"I had to grow up fast to take care of my mother," Susan agreed. "And balance my schoolwork against what had to be done at home."

"And you took part-time jobs in the summer to make a little extra money."

"Yes."

"I got saddled early with family responsibilities, too, I guess," Craig conceded quietly. "Maybe we're not so different after all."

"You're far more intense than I am."

He lifted his head and drowned in her understanding gaze. How loving, how giving Susan was—even to him, after what he'd said to her. Now, perhaps, was the right time to broach his question about Steve. "Maybe I don't have any business asking you this—and you don't have to answer me...." He gripped the bill of his cap and settled it back on his head. "What happened to Steve? And when did he die? I never heard anything about it through the grapevine. As a matter of fact, I haven't heard a word about him since we left Annapolis."

Susan saw the anguish in Craig's eyes. His roughened voice blanketed her, momentarily taking away the pain of the past hellish year. She dropped her gaze and ran her finger absently around in a circle on her skirt. "Steve died a year ago—of cancer. Just like my mother."

Craig stared at her in silence. Shock bolted through him as he realized the implications. For six years, Susan had taken care of her ailing mother until, when Susan was eighteen, just before she'd graduated from high school, her mother had died. Susan had gone on to get her nursing degree. Five years after her mother had died, Steve had entered her life.

"My God," he rasped. "What kind of cancer?"

Susan looked across the parking lot, lost in the past. "A slow-growing brain tumor."

Craig wrestled with a barrage of emotions. As a trained paramedic, he knew a great deal about medicine in general. Staring hard at Susan's soft profile, the harsh reality of what she must have endured began to penetrate his mind—and then his heart. "Couldn't they operate?"

Susan refused to look at Craig. She had never spoken to anyone of Steve, their marriage or his death—except to Karen, who didn't know all the sordid details. "No, it was too deep in his brain."

The silence hung between them, taut and raw. Craig stared at her, trying to fathom the extent of her trembling answer. She was resisting telling him more and he knew it. The pain from it must be overwhelming, and Craig assumed that was why she hesitated.

"How long did this go on?"

"Four years."

"Four?" Craig's mouth snapped shut.

"Yes, the doctors discovered it during the last physical exam after graduation." She avoided Craig's narrowed gaze and looked down at her tightly knotted hands. "Steve was given a medical discharge from the navy at that point. I continued to work as a nurse at Annapolis. That's why you didn't hear anything about Steve's cancer—he'd already left the service."

Craig was stunned. Steve had had such dreams—and to have them crushed like that, so suddenly.... Craig's heart ached for his friend. More than anyone, he knew what it was like to see your fondest dreams shattered in an instant. Glancing over at Susan, he wondered what kind of hell she'd had to go through—again. The words nearly sprang out of his mouth. Suffering for Susan, feeling her pain, he whispered, "You came to Reed to put your life back in order?"

She nodded, unable to speak. Just the tenderness of Craig's voice was unraveling her closely held secret. This was the old Craig she'd known back in Annapolis—the young man who had such insight and sensitivity into others. Her closest, dearest friend. Panicking, Susan wondered if Craig could see that she still liked him— despite the years, despite their twisted, misunderstood past.

"I know it sounds stupid," Susan whispered, "but I wanted to do something positive. I'm a trauma-trained nurse. There are a lot more accidents out here at Camp Reed because it's such a huge training base."

"You're far from stupid," Craig observed, closely watching her expression, feeling the undercurrent of anguish in her voice when she spoke. Everything was so tentative between them. He felt as if he were walking on dynamite that could explode unexpectedly at any moment. Susan was so fragile. He heard it in her low tone, saw it mirrored in her vulnerable features. "I understand why you came here. At least, I think I do."

Susan managed a quick look in his direction. "You always knew me better than I knew myself, Craig." And it scared her. When his hawklike gaze settled on her, she felt as if he could see into the darkest corner of her heart and penetrate her deepest secret: the fact that she liked him, had always liked him.

"Not anymore," he admitted sadly. "Four years seems like four centuries sometimes."

Susan couldn't disagree. She stirred and got to her feet, smoothing out her uniform skirt. "I have to get going, Craig. I've got duty tomorrow morning, and frankly, I'm exhausted."

He got up slowly, favoring his injured leg. "Wait," he pleaded, holding his hand toward her, "don't go, Susan."

She turned and met his eyes. "Please," she whispered, "just let me go, Craig. I forgive you. Okay? It's in the past." Everything between them was in the past. Panic edged her voice. "I have to go."

"No!" Craig gripped her hand. He saw her lips part, as if she were going to cry.

"I can't let you go, Susan. I can't do that," he said slowly.

"Yes, you can!" Susan flared. She was surprised at herself. And she saw Craig's shock at her outburst.

He straightened and draped his hands tensely on his hips. "You've changed, Susan."

"Last week you were accusing me of being the same old Susan you met four years ago!" she managed in a strangled tone, the anger boiling up through her.

"That's another topic."

"Well, it's the same woman, Captain Taggart!" She took a step away from his powerful presence. Craig had grown and matured over the years, losing any trace of softness in his grim features. No, his face was hardened and deeply tanned, and his gray eyes appeared merciless.

"Look," he began lamely, trying to defuse the situation, "we need to talk some more, Susan. I—"

"No!" The word was like a howl erupting from her. Fear that she would admit to her feelings for him made her bolder than ever. Susan knew she had to leave. Now. "Just leave me alone, Craig!" she cried, turning and walking quickly to the hospital entrance. She didn't start to tremble until the heavy doors had closed firmly behind her.

Chapter Five

Susan walked slowly out of the hospital after putting in a twelve-hour shift in ER. Her first day back had been brutal, not at all like the orderly, less-hectic Edson dispensary. She knew Karen wouldn't be along for probably another hour. She was still in surgery with her final patient for the day. The dusk was a deep tangerine color above the horizon where the sun had set, but the odor of anesthesia, alcohol and antiseptic still clinging to her clothes, hair and nostrils, and she longed for the cleansing, hot shower waiting for her back at her apartment.

As she turned the corner to head to the parking lot, she noticed a marine in green utilities standing next to her car. Susan slowed her steps when she drew near enough to recognize the marine as Craig Taggart. Her mouth went dry, and she felt her knees going weak. What was he doing here? Why wouldn't he leave her alone as she'd asked? Susan's hands flexed into small fists, and she didn't know what to do.

Craig's face was deeply shadowed by the dusk. As she slowed to a halt a foot away from the car, the grimness of his features frightened her—until she had courage enough to look him in the eye.

Craig slowly moved forward. "I, uh... yellow roses are for apology." He held out a bouquet of a dozen roses toward her. "I didn't want to leave bad blood between us, Susan. Here, take them. They're my way of saying I'm sorry."

Touched, Susan gently took the huge, fragrant bouquet into her hands. "I... thank you."

Craig stood tensely, his hands at his sides. He watched hungrily as she lifted the flowers to her face and inhaled the scent. The soft smile that glimmered on her mouth made him long to kiss her. In that moment, all Craig wanted to do was step forward and embrace Susan and make long, slow love with her. But so many misunderstandings, assumptions and years stood in his way. His mouth dry, his heart beating hard, Craig asked hoarsely, "I'd like to invite you to the Officers Club for dinner tonight, Susan. Would you come?"

Susan looked up into his eyes and saw the anxiety in them. Her heart cried out to him. In that moment, she realized how many old wounds they both bore. And the new hardness and defensive barricades she felt around Craig frightened her.

"Craig," she began softly, "I—I'm just not strong enough emotionally right now." And she wasn't. Four years of taking care of Steve, who had tried to love and grow with her the best he could under the circumstances, had left her gutted.

He took a step back and looked away. "I guess I can't imagine what kind of hell you went through with Steve," he muttered. Craig thought of her being forced to watch the husband she loved sicken and suffer and die—especially after already going through it with her mother. Forcing himself to hold her gaze, he said, "I'll be here for you, Susan. Like before." He patted his broad shoulder and managed a sad laugh. "Remember? I told you in Annapolis that if you ever needed to be held or a shoulder to cry on, you could come to me? We were the best of friends...." His smile slipped and he stared at her. "The same goes for now, babe. I'll always be there for you—whether you want me to or not."

A reservoir of pain spilled through Susan as she stood holding the delicate roses. Did Craig realize that when he called her "babe," a little more of her heart tore open? She watched him touch the brim of his hat and turn away. He began limping slowly away between the rows of cars, heading toward his black Pontiac Firebird.

"Oh, God," she whispered brokenly, and turned, blindly moving to her car.

Craig sat alone at the Officers Club, nursing a cold beer. Darkness had fallen, and the jukebox played a mournful tune that only exacerbated his feeling of loss. Drinking wasn't something he did a great deal of, particularly as a recon marine. He needed a clear head and intense focus to keep his team alive. Running his hands up and down the sweaty glass of beer, he stared down at the foam edging the brim.

He frowned as he went over their conversations of the past two days. Susan was wary of him. But didn't she have a right to be after the way he'd ripped her apart in the ward? Craig took a deep, ragged breath. She was a widow. She was single again. Was there hope that he could court her? That this time he could avoid screwing up? Steve had swept Susan off her feet with his exuberant love for life, and she'd responded effortlessly to his sunny disposition.

Mulling over Steve's approach to Susan, Craig shook his head. To be honest, he told himself, Steve had gotten the jump on him. Steve had been more comfortable about being openly demonstrative. Plus, he'd had the money that Craig didn't—to buy her gifts and take her to expensive restaurants. And Craig simply couldn't give Susan a line. Whether he liked it or not, he'd always operated honestly with women, not with the kinds of lines that many other men employed to snare them. As far as gifts were concerned...well, he made a hell of a lot more money now than he had as a kid picking fruit every summer on the neighboring farm. But half his earnings still went home to his ailing mother.

Wearily, Craig rubbed his leg, which was aching like hell. He knew he would never be rich, as Steve's family had been. At Annapolis, he'd stood back and watched Steve's life-style seem to influence Susan. But had it? He wasn't sure. Craig bitterly recalled the diamond bracelet that Steve had bought for her. He'd shown it to Craig, a triumphant grin on his mouth, saying that if this didn't get Susan to make up her mind to marry him, nothing would.

Money. To be honest, Steve had always showered his friends with expensive gifts, simply because he'd had it to spend. Maybe for someone of Steve's affluence and background, material gifts had equaled affection—even love. Scowling, Craig drank a little more of the beer.

Susan just didn't seem the type to rank money high in her life. In fact, he remembered her telling him one evening while they were having coffee at the Annapolis hospital dispensary that she was embarrassed by the expensive gift—and really didn't know what to do with it. Ironically, Craig recalled suggesting to her that she wear it on special evenings out with Steve, and she'd seemed relieved to have the suggestion. No, things he'd assumed and taken for granted out of anger and hurt just didn't add up under calmer scrutiny. He needed some long, painful conversations with Susan to find out the truth of the situation. But right now he had to accept *her* needs. She'd made it clear that she was too raw from losing Steve to deal with Craig.

Dr. Finlay had told him that he was grounded from recon-training duties for the next six weeks. He'd have to stay at the main headquarters building pushing paper—unless he could come up with something more creative to do with this extra time on his hands. And the field was where Craig wanted to be. Looking around at several other officers sitting and drinking alone, Craig was struck by the loneliness eating at him. Ever since he'd realized that Susan was at Camp Reed, his world had been in a tailspin.

Well, he'd use this month wisely, he hoped. First of all, he'd leave Susan alone. Tonight, he'd pen her a letter and give her a month's breathing space. Maybe the time apart would do them good. He was convinced she needed time to adjust to the fact that he was back in her life. Draining the remainder of his beer, Craig set it aside and wiped his mouth with the back of his hand.

Sliding off the wooden stool, he limped out of the O Club and slowly got into his car. He headed toward his apartment in Carlsbad, thirty miles south of the base.

The oceanfront rental provided him with the soothing peace of the Pacific, and right now he needed that to heal his turbulent emotions. Driving along the freeway, Craig noticed the moon was full and luminous, showering the countryside with its radiance. The ocean, to his right, was as flat and dark as an ebony mirror. Arriving home, he made his way inside and immediately retrieved a paper and pen. The house was stuffy from being closed up all day, so he decided to take advantage of the salt air and moonlight out on the deck overlooking the ocean. He would write Susan a letter, then go to bed. Maybe tonight he would actually be able to sleep, but he wouldn't count on it. More than anything, Craig wished he could see the look on Susan's face—to gauge her reaction—when she received his letter.

Susan was just coming on duty in the recovery ward when another of the nurses, Becky, called her over to the front desk. What now? Susan wondered. The three days since she'd returned to the hospital had been stressful and busy.

"What's up?" she asked Becky.

"A letter just came for you," the other nurse said, waving a business-size envelope in the air.

"Oh?" No one ever wrote to her. Her mother was dead, she didn't know where her father was and she had no siblings, so she didn't have to worry about letters from home.

Hesitating, Susan frowned. "Are you sure it's for me?"

"Of course it's for you!" Becky smiled and dropped the envelope on the desk.

"Who's it from?" Susan asked as she tentatively picked it up. The letter had no return address.

"Who knows?" Becky smiled and shrugged. "Maybe it's from a secret admirer."

"Probably a bill." Susan groaned, then grinned. She slipped the letter into the pocket of her white skirt. With the duty change coming, she couldn't get caught standing around reading a letter. It would have to wait, whether she wanted it to or not.

"I'd rather have the secret admirer," Becky said with a laugh as she picked up a tray of medications. "I've got to start med rounds. See you later."

Over the next half hour, the nurse's station quieted down. By that time, Susan was done with her chores. She dutifully locked the glass cabinet containing the pharmacy drugs, washed her hands in the surgical sinks and dried them on nearby towels. Glancing at her watch, she noted that she had another half hour before her mandatory rounds in the ward. Sitting down on the nurse's station's creaky wooden chair, she leaned her elbows on the desk and pulled the envelope from her pocket.

Frowning, Susan slit the envelope open with her index finger to reveal a sheet of yellow, legal-size paper. She unfolded the letter. As she began to read the neatly printed text, her heart began a slow pounding.

Dear Susan:
I hope this letter finds you feeling a little better than when we last talked. The roses were my way of saying I'm sorry for causing you a lot of unnecessary pain. If I had made an effort to stay in touch with you and Steve, I guess I wouldn't have had such a knee-jerk reaction to seeing you again.

I know what it's like to lose someone you love; I lost Dave at the pond when we were only kids. I can understand that you're still grieving for Steve's loss, and I meant what I said about being there for you if you want me around. Right now, I don't think you do, and I don't blame you.

Doc Finlay has told me in no uncertain terms that I'm grounded for the next six weeks while my leg heals. I don't like being a "paper chaser" and generally find HQ boring as hell. I guess the outdoors will always call me. I hate sitting at a desk staring out a window.

I want you to know that I'm going to leave you alone as you asked. I feel in my heart that you need time to heal, and time to adjust to the fact that I'm here at the same base with you. So you won't see me waiting by your car again—unless you want to see me.

Susan, I can't separate what we shared in the past from the present. I don't want to. But that's not a decision that's solely mine to make. Steve fell in love with you at first sight. At the time, I was green and naive, and I didn't know how to get your attention like he did. Four years has matured me in some ways, but I won't be chasing you down. It's not me, and I'm not going to step back into your life unless you want me to. It has to be on your terms, Susan; not mine. All I can do is hope that with time, you might want to see me again.

> Your friend forever,
> Craig

Susan stared down at the letter. The emotions stirring in her heart as she reread the page seesawed among confusion, hope, guilt and uncertainty. What did she want? *Was* she really still grieving over Steve? Susan didn't know. At least Craig was offering her badly needed breathing room, and for that she was grateful.

She gently refolded the letter and placed it back in its envelope. Touched beyond words, she realized how desperately she wanted to be close to Craig again—to confide in him as a friend who cared for her. Closing her eyes, Susan sat back, rocking slowly in the chair, its comforting creaks filling the silence. What had happened to Craig in the past four years? She knew nothing about him, his romantic relationships, his pain or triumphs. Susan hoped he'd fared better than she had. He was too good, too loyal and dedicated to those he loved to deserve the kind of sentence she'd lived under for too long.

Craig sat unhappily at his desk in recon headquarters. Terrain maps were laid out before him—along with a lot of other work—but he just couldn't force himself to focus on it. All morning his mind had been wandering to thoughts of Susan.

"Captain Taggart?"

Craig recognized the voice of his superior, Lieutenant Colonel Wilkins, and looked up quickly. "Yes, sir?"

"Bad news," the colonel said, handing him new orders. "You're getting temporary assignment duties off the base." A slight smile leaked through the hard line of Wilkins's mouth. "Something I think might make you a little happier, if I don't miss my guess."

Frowning, Craig took the orders from his superior and rapidly read through them. It took everything he had not to smile broadly—or even laugh out loud.

Keeping his face carefully arranged, he gave the colonel a somber look. "This was unexpected, sir, but I'll do my best."

Colonel Wilkins nodded. "I thought you would. Carry on, Captain."

"Yes, sir." As Wilkins left, Craig looked through the TAD orders again. He and four corpsmen from the hospital were being assigned to a clinic south of San Diego. In the past, whenever possible, he'd volunteered to help at poor, inner-city clinics in San Diego and Los Angeles because, as a paramedic, he could help the few struggling doctors and nurses who handled those areas. In addition, he served as commander for the team of navy corpsmen who worked with him. Frequently, they went into poor neighborhoods to vaccinate babies and children.

As he sat, pondering the pleasant idea of getting out in the field and helping people, an interesting thought began to trickle into his awareness. Yes! Why not? Quickly, Craig took the idea and worked it into better shape. Then, for the first time in a long time, a real smile pulled at his mouth. With a lot of planning and some fancy talking, maybe, just maybe, his idea might work. The linchpin to the plan would be Dr. David, and as soon as Craig could clear the authorization and paperwork, he was going to drop over to see the woman-surgeon.

"Doc? You got a minute?" Craig stood just inside the trauma unit. Everything was quiet for now. Dr. David was shrugging out of her surgical gown and gloves.

"Sure, Captain. How about a cup of coffee? I'm dead on my feet."

Craig nodded and followed her to the back room, where a full coffeepot waited. Karen took two ceramic mugs and filled them with the strong, fragrant coffee. Then she gestured to one of the chairs.

"Have a seat. I haven't seen you in a long time. How's that leg of yours doing?"

Craig sat down facing the doctor. "Just about good as new. Doc Finlay says two more weeks, and I can go back out in the field."

Karen wrinkled her nose and took a sip of the coffee. "Being out here a month now, I've gotten a real good education on what you boys do out there." With a shake of her head, she muttered, "I can't decide whether you're crazy or the most dedicated marines I've ever seen."

Craig grinned tentatively, balancing the cup on his knee. "I think you'll find a fifty-fifty split over what recons do for a living, Doc."

"Well," she said crisply, "I know you didn't come here just to pass the time of day with me. What can I do for you?"

Craig took another sip of coffee and set his cup on the desk. "Doc, I'm going to be taking a week off from my normal duties to help in a special inner-city program that I helped launch a year ago when I first got to Reed. There's a Hispanic neighborhood, a barrio, down near National City, which sits right across the border from Mexico. A lot of illegal aliens and families who don't speak English make their homes there. Health conditions aren't good, so a medical team from here at the base goes in now and again to assist at a free clinic. We help their doctor and nurses with a wide range of medical demands. It can mean going into the barrio as a team and vaccinating children, or just trying to educate pregnant mothers to come to the clinic for check-ups and nutritional information. I'm a paramedic, and I've even helped deliver a couple of babies down there. We've got a number of mothers that are due any day now. I know Lieutenant Susan Evans has a background as a surgical nurse, and I could sure use the help in this field program, if you could see your way to letting her go for seven days."

"You've delivered babies, Captain?"

"Yes, ma'am, I have."

With a smile, Karen said, "I'll be darned. That must make you feel good."

He smiled a little. "Yes, it does."

"In your line of work you're trained to take lives, not save them."

It was a harsh truth, but Craig couldn't disagree. "Normally, recons like to avoid any contact with the enemy, Doc. As the paramedic on my team, I've had occasion to save one or two of my men's lives."

"Admirable." Karen nodded in approval. Then she sighed and studied the ceiling. "You're a surprising man, Captain. And I like what you're doing by trying to help the poor."

"I grew up on a wheat farm," Craig explained, "but the Johnsons' farm next to us was a huge fruit-tree acreage. They employed Hispanics, and I worked side by side with them every summer to earn extra money. They don't get much help from the government, and I know their problems."

"So you want my best surgical nurse for a week? Is that what you're telling me? To assist you with the birthing of these babies?"

"That's the idea," Craig agreed. "She could meet me at helo pad A at 0900 tomorrow morning. I'll be responsible for packing all the supplies. All she needs to do is show up with a week's worth of clothes—we wear civilian clothes when we go into the neighborhood, so we're not mistaken for police." Craig prayed that the doctor would go along with his plan. He knew Susan's love of children, and he felt this would be a great opportunity to get reacquainted with each other under less stressful circumstances. It was the perfect strategy. And the only thing standing in the way was Karen David, Susan's immediate supervisor.

"Well, let's see..." Karen frowned. "Lieutenant Evans has been working her tail off around here lately. She's been awfully tired."

"Oh?" Craig couldn't keep the concern out of his voice. He sat up, alert as never before. True to his promise, he'd not contacted Susan since sending the letter. Despite the fact that she hadn't contacted him, Craig felt he had to try one more time. If only Dr. David would give her permission...

"She hasn't been sleeping well for almost a month now...."

Craig swallowed hard. Had his letter upset her? "Look," he began quickly, "this is strictly business, but I'm sure Lieutenant Evans would get a lot more rest there. We'll be working eight hours a day, not the twelve that she does here. This could be a perfect opportunity to let her rest up, don't you think?"

Merriment twinkled in Karen's eyes as she studied the marine officer. "Now, I'm just a little ol' gal from Ohio, Captain, but I don't think my eyes deceive me, do they?"

Craig's mouth relaxed. He knew that the doctor intuitively understood there was something between him and Susan. "No, Doc, I don't think much gets past those eyes of yours."

Laughing prettily, Karen waved her hand in the air. "Captain, I declare, all you marines are alike: so easy to read. I'll order Susan to go with you, so stop looking worried."

"Er, Doc, could you maybe ask Susan if she'd like to go instead of ordering her?"

"Why, Captain, you're such a polite devil. It's not often I find a man who is so sensitive in that regard. Of course, I'll ask Susan. Now, you wipe that frown off your brow and go about your business. Susan will meet you at 0900 at the helo pad. You two have a good time."

Craig could've hugged Dr. David on the spot. Unconsciously, he'd been holding his breath. When the surgeon authorized Susan's release to him, he let it out as relief, sweet and joyous, flooded through him. He rose. "Thanks, Doc. I owe you one."

Karen laughed huskily. "Are you sure there isn't a twin of you around somewhere? Why, that nice Dr. Finlay could stand to take some lessons from you. He's such a sweet man!"

Although Craig was a Northerner, he knew that words such as *nice* and *sweet* were the kiss of death when spoken in such sugary terms. Dr. Finlay was grumpy by nature, but being the lady she was, Karen David wouldn't be caught dead saying a wicked word about the good doctor. "Yes, ma'am," Craig murmured, curbing a smile at her admission. Her secret was safe with him.

He felt as if he were walking on air. He'd have a week with Susan—something they both deserved.

* * *

"Hey," Karen called to Susan as she saw her come off ward rounds, "I need to talk to you a sec."

Susan detoured and met Karen halfway down the hall from the nurse's station. "What's going on?"

With a smile, Karen said, "How would you like a week's reprieve from this place? I've got a set of TAD orders for you to go down with a medical team from base here to a Hispanic inner-city area south of San Diego. It will mean working out of a local clinic there and generally helping them as needed."

Raising her eyebrows, Susan considered the request. "Is this an order or a volunteer situation?" she teased.

Her smile widening, Karen said, "It's your choice. It's not an order. Of course, I'll miss you at my side in surgery like the dickens, but you've been looking really tired of late. This request was dropped in my lap, and I thought you might like first dibs on it."

Exhausted would be a better word than *tired,* Susan thought. "It would probably be like working out of the Edson Range dispensary?"

"Somewhat," Karen hedged. "Captain Taggart is heading up the team, and I think you should know that before you decide."

Her heart slammed once to underscore Craig's name. Susan tried to look unaffected by this new information. "Well..."

With a sigh, Karen muttered, "The guy was practically on his knees begging me to let you come along. He was very nice about it, Susan. Why don't you go?"

"Why should I?" Sudden panic was eating at Susan, and she couldn't keep the quaver out of her voice.

"Because he was sincere about his request, that's why."

Susan stared at her friend. "I don't want to go."

"Look, things aren't settled between you two. Any idiot can see that."

"They are from my point of view."

"They aren't from Taggart's perspective," Karen warned grimly.

With a shake of her head, Susan rasped, "No. I don't want to go."

"Then you owe him—"

"I don't owe Craig anything!" Trying to keep her voice down, Susan looked up and down the hall. "Look, I appreciate what you're trying to do, Karen, but I don't want to see Craig. He's part of my past. Not my present." And not her future, as much as she might wish it could be. No, too much water had flowed under that bridge.

"We've been friends for a long time," Karen began gently, "and even though you think Captain Taggart is part of your past, I don't think he sees it that way."

"Then let me handle this in my own way!"

Karen studied her for a full minute before speaking. "Ever since he mailed you that letter, you've been hiding, Susan. Look at you—you look like hell."

"Thanks for your professional opinion."

"It's an opinion from a friend!" Karen flared. "I care about you. I saw what taking care of Steve did to you. Craig Taggart isn't such a bad guy, Susan. From where I'm standing, you're avoiding giving him your ultimatum."

Susan swallowed hard. "I—yes, that's right. I'm scared, Karen."

"Of him?"

"No... Of myself."

"You have feelings for him?"

Susan glanced at her friend. "Yes. Panic and fear, among others. Not to mention guilt. More than any other person in my life, Craig was my friend."

Taking Susan by the arm, Karen led her into the doctor's lounge, which, thankfully, was empty. She let go of Susan and stood with her back against the door to prevent interruption. "Look, what I'm going to say is for your ears only, okay? Ever since Craig gave you that letter, you've looked strained. You've got circles under your eyes. Did he tear you up in that letter or what?"

Wrapping her arms against her breasts, Susan turned away, and her voice came out with a strangled sound. "No, just the opposite," she admitted. "It was a beautiful letter...."

Making an exasperated sound, Karen walked around and confronted Susan. "Beautiful? And you're acting like you're going to die? I don't understand."

Giving her friend a sad smile, Susan whispered, "I don't, either."

"Something's going down here, and I think it needs to be resolved." Karen wagged her finger in Susan's face. "Bottom line is this: you're going with Taggart on that seven-day clinic run. And don't even try to protest. Maybe this is what you need in order to face him and work out whatever needs to be worked out."

"But—"

"No buts, Susan. It's an order."

Craig couldn't still his pounding heart as he saw a jeep driving up to the helo pad. As the vehicle drew to a halt a few yards from the helicopter, he spotted Susan and beamed a welcoming smile. Craig could see wariness in her face, but he wasn't about to allow her distrust of the situation to ruin this very special morning.

"I'm glad you could make it," he said, approaching the jeep and taking the duffel bag that the driver handed to him.

Susan gave him a nervous glance. "I know you went to Dr. David. You might as well know I didn't want to come along. She ordered me to come."

Groaning internally, Craig nodded and tried to suppress his happiness over her presence. "I asked her not to order you, if it makes any difference."

Susan's mouth opened—and she quickly shut it. One of Karen's bad habits was her confidence in knowing what was right in every situation—for herself and others. Realizing that nothing could be done at this stage, Susan sighed in resignation.

"I believe you," she whispered.

Relief flowed through Craig. "Thanks, I needed to hear that."

"Karen is one of the most opinionated people I know," Susan groused, "and she frequently takes things into her own hands."

With a slight smile meant to make her feel better, Craig murmured, "I'm glad you're here, if that helps anything."

Susan didn't know what to say in response to his obviously happy statement. Her emotions were mixed and sharp, and her heart had begun pounding for no apparent reason.

Craig grinned and handed Susan's duffel bag to the crew chief standing at the helicopter door. Unable to stop himself, he cupped her elbow and helped her on board. "I thought you'd like delivering babies," he teased.

Susan gaped at him. She stopped putting on the safety belt. "Babies?"

"Yeah. Didn't Dr. David tell you about the clinic and how we work with pregnant mothers and new infants? Oh, we'll be doing normal clinic stuff like vaccinations and all, but this particular inner-city clinic is one of the few around that tries to focus on prenatal care."

Nonplussed, Susan forced herself to buckle the seat belt. As the door to the helicopter was closed, she looked around and noted four men besides her and Craig on board—the full medical team going to the clinic, she supposed. "I love babies," she answered. "But I've never assisted in a delivery. Besides, I'm very rusty on my Spanish. I had it in college, but I haven't used it since."

"It will come back," Craig assured her. His heart was pounding erratically, and although he tried to appear calm, he felt anything but. In the month since he'd seen Susan, she seemed to have grown even prettier.

"We'll primarily be helping with nutritional information," he continued, "educating mothers-to-be and things like that. My Spanish is fluent, and I can act as an interpreter for you if necessary. Don't worry, Susan, things will work out fine."

She said nothing. Simply being next to Craig made her feel panicky. With an effort, she forced herself to sit quietly and pretend as if nothing was going on inside her. She watched as the blades of the helicopter began to slowly turn. He was so close, so vital. And the unexpected light shining in his gray eyes told her how happy he was. Her feelings skidded from momentary joy to guilt and back again.

The noise in the cabin grew as the rotors picked up speed. It would only be about a forty-minute flight to

National City, she estimated. Craig motioned for her to put on a pair of headphones and situate the mike near her lips, so they'd be able to converse.

"There's a little airstrip near the clinic," he explained as the helicopter flew down the beach coastline toward their destination. Inwardly, he was feeling jumpy, with memories of the helicopter crash still fresh in his mind, but focusing his attention on Susan eased his tension. One look into her compassionate blue eyes soothed his raw nerves. "Dr. Jesus Espinoza, the physician who runs the clinic, will meet us there with his truck. His wife, Maya, is a nurse, like you. They've run this free medical clinic for the last ten years, and it's all the barrio has."

"Maya's a beautiful name."

Craig nodded. "She's in her fifties and very committed to the health and healing of their people. I really admire her. I know she'll be glad we brought a woman down with us. Usually, it's five men."

Susan gave him a glance but said nothing.

"I come down with this team every three months," he went on, wanting to give Susan the broader picture in the hope that she would become as enthused about it as he was. "I know most of the families who frequent the clinic." He smiled proudly. "I've even delivered babies."

"You're one up on me, then."

"Don't worry. Maya will teach you the ropes of prenatal care in no time. She did me."

Susan gave him a measuring look. She saw such genuine sincerity in Craig's eyes that she couldn't help but absorb his happiness. "You really like doing this, don't you?"

He shrugged shyly. "I believe in helping the poor. I saw their hard lives on my neighbor's farm as a kid, when I picked fruit with the Hispanic migrant workers. They got to be like a second family to me. Every season, the same families would return. I kind of adopted them and vice versa. So when I got to Reed, I helped create two TAD medical teams—one for National City and the other in the heart of southern Los Angeles." He smiled a little. "The south Los Angeles clinic is more mixed ethnically, with Latinos, African Americans and Koreans. But the bottom line is the same: they need help."

Impressed, Susan nodded. "It must give the Marine Corps a good name among those people."

He leaned forward, his elbows resting on his knees. "We're becoming a peacetime military, and I think we ought to be doing some positive things for the people around our base."

Susan felt a surge of pride for Craig and his hard-working compassion. Steve had aspired to helping the poor, too, although he'd done it through hefty financial donations. "I can hardly wait to meet the people," she said—and meant it.

They landed on a flat, asphalt area that had once been a large mall, now abandoned, near the clinic. Disembarking from the helicopter, the team was met by the Espinozas. Susan liked the fifty-year-old obstetrician, Jesus, and Maya was a strikingly beautiful woman. Greetings were warm, Susan noticed, between Craig and the husband-and-wife team, with much back-slapping, joking and smiles, and she felt herself getting caught up in their enthusiasm.

Susan sat with Maya in the back seat of the couple's beat-up Blazer on the way to the clinic. Everywhere she looked, dilapidated housing, raggedy-looking, brown-skinned children and generally poor living conditions were very much in evidence. Maya looked fresh by comparison in her white nurse's uniform, and Susan felt a warmth toward the tall, thin woman with the ebony hair and eyes.

"So you know this hombre, Captain Taggart, eh?" Maya offered in stilted English.

Susan smile a little. "Yes...Craig and I go back many years."

"Ah, this is good. I have been pleading with this hombre for many months on end to get a woman to come down and help us. You know, the mothers are very shy in front of men, eh? They feel better if a woman is with them. Everything in our society is gender based. The women stay with women, and women care for the mothers and help during birthing. The men, they do their thing, but I feel it is important to keep the women's tradition."

With a small laugh, Susan said, "You sound like a feminist, Maya."

With an eloquent shrug, she said proudly, "Women are stronger of the two, eh? We bear the children. Our world continued because we care for our families." She frowned. "Here in the barrio there is much poverty, and the mothers, even though they have the support of other women, suffer greatly. They do not get proper food. The babies are born with low birth weight, and many are stillborn." She shook her head. "It is a sad thing." She brightened and patted Susan's hand. "But for seven days I thank the Mother Mary for you, a woman. We will be a good team together, eh? That hombre Taggart did a good thing by bringing you down here. We are most grateful that you have come.''

How could she possibly regret coming when Maya made her feel as if her presence meant life instead of death? The deep warmth between Craig and the couple was apparent, and Susan sat back and absorbed this side of Craig—his ready smile, his deep laughter and the effortless care he bestowed on the committed Espinozas. Once, Craig turned to deliver a comment, his gaze pinned directly on her, and she felt heat nettle her cheeks. She gave him a shy smile in return, and she saw the pleasure dance in his eyes. Perhaps this wouldn't be as bad as she'd anticipated. Although the entire team, with the exception of her, spoke fluent Spanish, no one left her out of the conversation on the way to the clinic, and Susan felt not only needed, but like a much-loved member of a cosmic family.

The clinic was a small, one-story stucco building with a red tile roof, crowded into what seemed to be the poorest section of the barrio south of National City. Susan's heart ached for the children she saw playing around the clinic's parking lot, for their potbellies and stunted growth indicated lack of nutritious food. As Dr. Espinoza parked at the rear of the building and the doors opened, Susan felt depressed. How could anyone work here and not cry daily over the paltry living conditions?

Craig waited until Susan stepped out of the Blazer, then caught her gently by the arm and held her back until the rest of the group was headed toward the rear door of the clinic. ''Well? What do you think? Is this better than ER?''

Susan looked at the squalor that surrounded them. Mutts, mangy and starved looking, roamed everywhere. The air was filled with various scents ranging from a spicy smell to the odor of rotting garbage. She cast a spurious glance up at Craig as he walked at her side. "I don't know," she answered softly, emotionally torn by the sight of these people's living conditions.

"Are you glad you came?"

"Ask me that in seven days."

Craig frowned. "For what it's worth, Susan, *I'm* glad you came."

She nodded. "You could have picked any nurse. Why me?"

"I knew you." His mouth stretched into a happy smile. "Hey, delivering babies shouldn't be done by strangers." He gestured toward the barrio. "Jesus says we've got four mothers ready to birth any time now."

"You know these mothers-to-be?"

"Over the last year I've gotten to know a lot of the Hispanic families that live in the area, yes. My medical team works out in the neighborhood for the most part, not in the clinic itself. We usually sleep and eat with various families around the area. They've more or less adopted the five of us." Craig showed her a gold crucifix that hung from a leather thong around his neck. "An old grandmother, Doña Juanita Marniquez, gave this to me as a gift six months ago when I helped her oldest daughter Maria give birth. She is in her early forties. Isn't that something? She told me to carry it for good luck, and I'm convinced it helped me walk out alive from that helo crash last month. Juanita's granddaughter, Consuela, is just about ready to give birth. She's just eighteen. I'm going to tell her about the crash and tell her to keep praying for me every Sunday. In my line of work, I can use all the help I can get."

Susan realized that Craig was truly a part of the fabric of this neighborhood. And the discovery was unexpectedly sweet and filled with promise. Prejudice had no part in her life, either. The color of people's skin, their religion or country of origin should never be held against them. Although Steve hadn't been particularly prejudicial, his affluence had isolated him in a mostly white society. Susan cast a glance up at Craig as they slowed their pace. "I'm glad I came," she said, meaning it.

Craig said nothing, but his heart responded to the luster in Susan's eyes. Yet he could see a shadow in their depths, and he wanted to find out what still haunted her. Well, they had seven days together, and he intended to make the most of it.

"The pregnant women are going to be glad to see you," Craig said as they entered through the clinic's back door.

"And if I know these older women, I think they'll also be relieved to see a woman at my side."

Susan wasn't sure *she* was relieved to be at Craig's side. Her emotions still skidded dangerously from bursts of sudden euphoria back to that numbness that had cloaked her for the past year. What did it all mean? Confused, she followed Craig into the clean, brightly lit clinic.

Chapter Six

Susan was unprepared for the warm welcome that the medical team received as they stepped into the crowded reception area of the clinic. At least thirty people, mostly older women, mothers and children, sent up a shout and started to applaud.

Craig smiled down at her. "Our welcome party is here. Come on, let me introduce you around."

His hand on her arm was steadying as the women, many dressed in bright-colored cottons, surrounded them. A short, spindly grandmother, with a bandanna on her gray hair, came forward.

"Welcome," she called to Susan in poor English. "I am Doña Juanita Marniquez."

"Gracias," Susan said self-consciously. "I'm Lieutenant Susan Evans." She reached forward to shake the old woman's arthritic hands, hands that had seen much wear and tear through the years. The air was hot and stifling in the clinic because the Espinozas couldn't afford the high electric bill for air-conditioning.

As the women milled around, many looked at Susan with open curiosity, and she traded smiles with women of all ages. Somehow, she got separated from Craig, who was instantly surrounded by at least fifteen children.

The old woman patted her hand. "That one is a good man, Señorita Evans. He carries a good heart."

Susan smiled down at Doña Marniquez, whose slightly hunched figure was in black. "He is a good man," she agreed. "Everyone seems to know him."

"That is because Captain Taggart is loved by all of us," Doña Marniquez explained. "He is a man of war, but his heart holds peace. You see the niños? The children? They know who loves them. Look at how they cling to his legs, how they embrace him. The little girls bring him flowers. They knew he was coming. That is my daughter Maria who stands at his side. The beautiful girl next to her is my granddaughter, Consuela. See how big she is? Consuela was hoping to have the baby after the captain arrived. He helped my daughter birth last year. Did you know that?"

Susan nodded, caught up in the contagious, festive atmosphere of the clinic. Several women had brought fruit drinks, which were being passed around to eager hands in white paper cups. Indeed, it was like a coming-home party, Susan thought, with Craig and his team as the guests of honor. She had never seen Craig like this—all smiles, his laughter booming across the room, hugging and kissing each shy child who came up to him. Doña Marniquez was right: Craig had a good heart. But no one knew that better than she, Susan realized, sadness overwhelming her. If only she hadn't been so young, so naive when she'd met Craig. He was a man of great warmth, great compassion, she was discovering, and her heart swelled with a sudden joy as the Mexican women and children showered him with their affection.

Finally, Craig made his way back to Susan's side, once he and the rest of the team had greeted the many callers. Craig noted how wide with surprise her eyes were at the enthusiastic welcome they were receiving. Without thinking about it, he slid his arm around her shoulders as they were being tightly surrounded by the friendly families. Too late, he realized what he'd done. Quickly removing his arm, he stole a look down at Susan. Her lips had parted, soft and provocative over his faux pas. It had been a gesture of sharing, he realized as he was forced to turn his attention to more approaching women. But had Susan seen it as that, or as him taking advantage of the situation? Probably the latter.

Toward the end of the hour, the crowd gradually began to dwindle. The Marniquez women were the last to go, but before they did, Doña Marniquez limped forward, her arthritic hand extended toward Susan.

"Here, *señorita*. This is for you and your man with the good heart in his chest."

Stunned, Susan opened her palm as Doña Marniquez handed her a thin gold chain. "Why, thank you, Doña—"

The old woman smiled toothlessly. "A gold chain symbolizes the completion of two into one. Keep it. It will bring you much luck, just as the crucifix I gave him last year saved his life in the helicopter crash."

Craig started to speak, but the old woman waved her finger in his face, saying to him in Spanish, "And you, my adopted son, you take care of this woman who is your equal. *¿Comprende?*"

With a helpless smile, Craig nodded. "I will, Grandmother."

"What was she saying?" Susan asked after they were alone. "I couldn't pick up all of it. Something about me being your equal?"

Uneasily, Craig looked down at the slender gold chain Susan held in her hands. She had lovely hands, work worn and reddened by the frequent scrubbing for surgery.

He whispered conspiratorially, "Doña Marniquez is the grande dame of the barrio. She may be old, but she rules this place, to a degree. I guess she thought we were a nice-looking couple and decided we were, ah, together."

"Oh, no!" Susan tore her attention from the chain and turned it on him. "Well, tell Doña Marniquez we aren't!"

"No way," Craig said with a grin.

"Why?"

"Because she's been trying to get me to marry one of her granddaughters for the past year. I guess she saw you come in with me and put two and two together."

"Then I'll give them back the chain."

"No, don't do that. You'd hurt their feelings."

"Oh, dear..."

"It's not the end of the world," Craig soothed, leading her down the hall to begin acquainting her with the waiting room, the meager pharmacy, the small rooms where patients were examined. Afterward, they got busy, with the rest of the team, vaccinating the waiting children for measles and smallpox. Craig had already worked to raise money from local business people to buy the necessary vaccines. Now Susan helped him hour after hour, inoculating at least 200 children by the time the clinic closed its doors at five p.m. With their work for the day done, the Espinozas, who lived behind the clinic in a small house, invited the team to dinner.

Twilight embraced the barrio as Craig walked Susan across the parking lot toward the empty clinic. "This is where we'll be staying each night," Craig explained. "The Espinozas don't have room, so they've let us use their spare room at the clinic."

"Us?" Susan halted, openmouthed.

With an innocent expression, Craig put his hands on his hips. "Yeah." When he saw her fear, he explained, "When I started up this program I didn't want to spend needless money on motel rooms and food. The Espanozas kindly offered this room with two cots, and the rest of my team stays with different families in the barrio each night. It cuts costs, Susan, and puts more vaccines and medical help where they're needed—in the homes of these families."

He opened the clinic door with the key and allowed her to walk past him. Some of the fear and wariness still showed in her face even after his explanation.

"But that—that isn't..." Her voice faltered after he'd locked the door behind them and they stood in the hall.

"It's temporary," Craig pointed out benignly.

"I—"

"And there's plenty of room. Come on, follow me. You'll sleep on one side of the room, and I'll be on the other."

Susan looked at Craig's shadowed features and saw the happiness shining in his gray eyes. Although he was struggling to remain serious because he knew this topic was serious to her, she could see the corners of his mouth edging upward. "You planned this!" she said accusingly.

"Me?" He touched his chest. "No way. Usually one of the team members and I stay here, but since your Spanish is a little shaky, I thought you'd feel more comfortable here than staying with a family where they speak no English."

He was right, she realized with an awful, sinking feeling. Perhaps she was acting gun-shy, but why? Susan tried to get a grip on her wildly fluctuating feelings about the arrangement as they halted at a door at the end of the hall. Craig moved around her and opened it. Flipping on the fluorescent light, he stepped inside.

Susan slowly entered the small, rectangular room. Two cots were pushed against opposite walls. Other than a bedside table with a lamp and a wastebasket, the room was bare. But the sparse conditions weren't what bothered her. Her heart pounding, she whispered, "I can't stay with you." And she couldn't. Oh, God, she just couldn't!

Taking off his utility cap, Craig groaned. "Susan, you'll hurt the Espinozas' feelings if you leave. These people like you. They love me like a son."

Susan moved nervously around the room. The pillows were thin and worn, but the floor was clean. A small window was open to permit some air into the room. But black, wrought-iron bars covered the window, and she felt like a prisoner.

"Why don't you go sleep with the rest of the team?" she challenged.

"Because each of the marines is staying with an individual family," he explained calmly. "That's part of the beauty of this effort to blend our people with their people. The marines eat with them and sleep in their homes. We're trying not to destroy their culture or way of life, but instead to fit into it and help them understand better health methods. Living with the people as part of the pacification program was one good thing we learned over in Vietnam. Unfortunately, the army negated the marine idea and entire villages got moved to compounds, destroying an entire way of life and culture," he added, shaking his head. He looked around and opened his hands in a supplicating gesture. "Besides, dangerous gangs roam this area at night and I wanted to put you someplace safe. Someplace where I could protect you if I had to."

"Gangs?" Susan didn't like the darkness; she never had. The idea of gangs skulking around at night made her even more uncomfortable.

"Yes," Craig said soothingly. "But that's a good reason to have me here with you." He smiled slightly. "Just think of me as kind of a big guard dog." He scratched his head, then settled the utility cap back in place. "If you don't want me here, I can post another marine to stay with you and I'll stay with one of the families."

Susan crossed her arms over her chest and glared up at him. "This is just too convenient," she accused hotly.

He held up his hands, upset at her genuine wariness of him. "You have nothing to be worried about. We'll be busy from dawn to dusk. We'll eat with the Espinozas at night, and when it gets dark, everyone goes to bed. We'll be so tired that we'll drop dead on those cots."

His husky voice washed through her, and Susan studied him in the turgid silence. "I don't sleep well at night," she warned him. "I'll probably wake you up. You won't need that."

With a sad smile, Craig shrugged. "Then that makes two insomniacs in the same room. I don't sleep too well, either, Susan."

Her arms dropped to her sides. "Why not?"

Craig turned and looked out toward the hall. "Ever since that helicopter crash, I get replays of the damn thing at night."

"Nightmares?" Susan guessed softly, hurting for him.

"Yeah, sometimes . . ." Turning, he met her caring gaze. "Sometimes I wake up screaming." He shrugged. "It's normal after a crash, don't you think?"

Susan moved over to where he stood. Craig looked so stalwart, so alone in that moment with his hand resting on the frame of the door. His profile was lean and rugged, his mouth thinned, as if he were holding back a lot more than he wanted to say. Reaching out, she tentatively touched his arm. He barely turned his head, his gray eyes nearly colorless, the pupils huge and black. She felt as if he were looking into her soul. Dropping her hand again, she tried to smile.

"I think I can handle your nightmares." And then she added in a strained voice, "I just hope you can handle mine."

Craig's eyes narrowed. He opened his mouth to ask what she had nightmares about, but just then, one of the navy corpsmen, James Duncan, approached them.

"Cap'n, Dr. Espinoza would like to see you, sir."

"I'll be there in a moment, Duncan. Thank you."

The dark-haired corpsman, not more than nineteen, nodded. "Yes, sir."

Craig turned to Susan. "Why don't you stay here, unpack and make yourself comfortable?"

Susan's heart sank, and she struggled not to show her disappointment that their sleeping arrangements couldn't be changed. "Okay," she said, crossing to her olive green duffel bag.

Craig hesitated, but decided it was best to leave. The disappointment on Susan's face struck at him. She didn't want to be in the same room with him. Trying to balance his own hurt against her needs, he left quietly. As he walked down the hall with Duncan, he tried to rationalize Susan's reactions. She'd been horrified by the prospect of being seen as his fiancée by the patients. She'd looked absolutely frightened about staying in the same room with him at night. Did she see him as some kind of ogre? A man capable of jumping her against her will? The bitter taste in his mouth didn't leave, because he had no definitive answers to his questions.

It was too soon to call his idea a failure, he rationalized as some children suddenly appeared out of the alley. They ran up to him, grabbing playfully at his hands and laughing as he crossed the parking lot. Craig's worry lifted as he drank in their upturned faces, their smiles, combined with shy but curious looks. Ruffling the silky dark hair on several heads, Craig smiled down at them.

"Okay, you caught me," he told them and stopped in the middle of the well-lit parking lot. The children, at least a dozen of them, aged two through twelve, danced and shouted around him as he dug into the deep pockets of his utilities. Craig knew most of the children by name, and he knew they'd been waiting impatiently, but respectfully, right outside the clinic doors.

As he crouched down, small hands fell eagerly on his shoulders and back as the children surrounded him.

"Let's see," he said in Spanish, "what gifts did I bring for you?" Slowly he opened his large hands to reveal gum and candy. Over the past year, Craig had taught the children not to crowd, grab or take more than their share. Pleased at the way each child waited his turn to choose one item from his hands, he grinned. They were beautiful children, and he hoped Susan would enjoy her time with them as he always did.

Susan looked out the small window toward the parking lot and saw children crowding around Craig. Her heart blossomed with unexpectedly fierce emotion as she watched his hard, expressionless mask drop away while he talked to them. His mouth lifted in a warm smile, and she pressed her hand against her aching heart. She remembered that smile from his days at Annapolis—when he'd still been her friend. His eyes had always held that dancing warmth whenever he met her. She'd not seen it since then—until now, with the children, she realized.

The children adored Craig, that was obvious by the way they reacted when he mussed their hair and talked to them. Susan realized the children weren't as excited over the candy he'd brought them as they were eager for Craig's hugs and attention. He took one girl, about seven, and lifted her to his shoulders, her tiny legs straddling his neck. She shrieked with delight and clutched at his head. Then Craig scooped up a boy of four in his arms, and the rest of the children trailed him, as if he were the Pied Piper.

Susan hung her head. Craig loved children. How could she have forgotten that about him? Unwillingly, bitter memories squeezed at her heart. Steve hadn't wanted children. Ever. As she had matured in their marriage, Susan had wanted a baby, hoping it would help Steve mature—and that she'd be left with a part of him after he died. Steve had refused, afraid that if she had a baby, her attention would be focused on the child instead of on him. Turning slowly toward the room to begin her unpacking, Susan felt more old emotions rise to the surface within her. As she opened the duffel bag, she spotted a small dresser by the door that she hadn't noticed. Claiming two of the four drawers, she put away her clothes and toiletries. Oh, how was she going to handle the coming nightfall with Craig here, in the room with her?

"Well," Craig said genially as he walked into the darkening room about an hour later, "I'd say we made great progress today."

Susan sat on her cot, her white shoes off and set to one side. She laid the paperback historical novel she'd been reading in her lap.

"Yes, it was a good day," she agreed hollowly.

Night was rapidly gaining on the barrio. Her heart began beating more strongly, and she tried to busy herself by spreading the thin blanket across the cot.

Craig sat down on his cot and placed his holster and pistol next to him on the floor. He saw Susan give him an odd look. "Nights are usually safe around here," he explained. "But I'll sleep in my gear just in case one of the gangs decides the clinic might be a good place to steal drugs. Not that I think they will. This area is considered one of the safest in the barrio."

Susan looked at her shoes. "Then . . . maybe I'd better put mine back on."

"No, don't worry." In the failing light, Craig studied her profile. She sat tensely on the cot, her hands on her long, slender thighs. Craig sensed her nervousness, and didn't quite know how to defuse the tension. His gaze zeroed in on her nose. What was different about it? Frowning, he studied her profile as she made up her bed.

"Hey," he called, and got to his feet. Walking across the room, he crouched down in front of her.

Susan lifted her chin warily as he approached. "What?" Taken off guard by Craig's unexpected move, she stiffened as she squatted less than six inches away from her, one hand on the edge of her cot to steady himself.

He smiled and lightly touched her nose. "Is it my imagination or what? Didn't this used to be straight?" He cupped her jaw and gently moved his fingers across the bridge of her nose.

Susan pulled out of his grasp, her skin tingling wildly where he'd touched her. "I—uh . . ." She looked away, casting around for some kind of explanation.

"Whoa," Craig chided, and placed his fingers beneath her chin, forcing Susan to look at him as he continued to study her nose. "What did you do? Go and break it?" He noted there was a decided bump at the top of her nose where there hadn't been before.

Susan couldn't stand Craig's tender concern. She closed her eyes, her lashes sweeping downward. Her throat constricted and she realized that it was useless to try to lie to him. "I—it's a long story, Craig."

He smiled slightly, feeling her pain, watching her lower lip tremble. "I've got all night," he whispered, releasing her. "What happened, babe?" When she opened her eyes, he saw the haunted shadow in their depths.

Susan quickly averted her eyes and a shudder went through her. Every time Craig used that endearment, the walls around her heart were ripped away, leaving her exposed. Vulnerable. Trying to make light of a subject that was too painful to talk about, Susan joked weakly, "I never really liked my nose the way it was, so it was fixed for me."

His eyes narrowing, Craig felt the volume of pain Susan was holding on to. He saw the corners of her mouth draw in with pain. "Wait a minute," he said huskily, touching her flaming red cheek. "Did Steve do that?" His mind raced with the possibility. Steve had never been prone to violence, but a brain tumor could sometimes change a person's personality, depending on its exact location. His voice deepened as he saw Susan flinch at his question.

"Look at me," he demanded hoarsely. "Did Steve do this to you?" It hurt even to ask the question, much less to think that his one-time best friend would ever lay a hand on Susan.

Craig's fingers seemed to burn into her skin where he touched her, and Susan wanted to run. But there was nowhere to go. She couldn't jerk away and race out the door. The barrio night could be dangerous. But the danger to her heart where Craig was concerned right now seemed even more frightening than what the darkness held. Fighting back tears, she whispered, "He didn't mean to do it."

A guttural sound tore from Craig's mouth. Sliding both hands along her jawline, he forced Susan to look up at him. "He hit you?" The words came out strangled, filled with utter disbelief.

Unable to stand the torment and emotions swirling between them, Susan pulled out of his grasp. She stood up, moving away from him. "Steve didn't know what he was doing," she said quietly. She saw the agony in Craig's eyes, the disbelief.

"When did that start?" he demanded tightly, coming over to her until mere inches separated them.

"Craig, I don't want to talk about it."

"I do." He studied her face critically, recalling every soft curve and line of it. "How else did he hurt you?"

Her mouth quirking, Susan could barely stand Craig's intense inspection. The need to simply fall into his arms and sob out the pain her heart held was almost overwhelming. "Look, it happened, okay? It's over! It's in the past, and I don't want to talk about it."

Gripping her hands, he rasped, "But I need to know."

"No!" She backed away, breathing hard. "Leave me alone, Craig! Just leave me alone!"

She was going to run if he didn't back off. Grimly, Craig backed away from her. Susan's breasts were rising and falling rapidly, her face contorted and pale. Just what the hell had Steve put her through? Craig turned and stalked over to his cot. The darkness was nearly complete.

"Let's go to bed," he said quietly. "I'm sorry. I won't ask you again, Susan. It's all right. Come on, just go to bed."

Standing in the darkness, Susan felt the warm tears spilling down her cheeks. She was thankful that he couldn't see them as she returned to her cot. Agony pulsed through her as she lay down on her side, facing the wall, her back to Craig. She pulled her legs up toward her chest in a self-protective, fetal position.

Somehow, she had to get to sleep. Somehow, she had to hold herself together in Craig's presence. *But why had he touched her so gently?* her mind seemed to scream in the silence. The tenderness burning in his eyes had almost destroyed her ability to withhold the truth.

"No! No!" Susan's voice rolled off the walls of the room. She sat up, shrieking the word over and over again, her hands shielding her face. Sobbing in the gloomy darkness, lit only by a dim streetlight filtering through the small window, she gasped for breath.

"Susan?"

Still caught up in the nightmare, she gave a little cry as she felt a man's hands grasp her shoulders and draw her into the safety of his arms. At first she struggled to escape.

Sleep was torn from Craig as he tightened his grip around Susan. "It's me," he rasped thickly, pressing his head against hers. "Susan, it's Craig. Take it easy. Easy..." he crooned. He felt her fingers digging deeply into his chest through his shirt. Trembling sobs escaped her lips.

He dragged her closer against him and held her tightly. She was having a nightmare, he realized belatedly. His mind was fogged with sleep. At first, he'd thought the clinic was being broken into by a gang.

"It's okay, babe," he soothed thickly, caressing her hair with his hand. Craig rocked her gently against him, much as he would a frightened child, murmuring soft words to take away the terror that still coursed through her. "It's okay," he told her, pressing a small series of kisses against her hair, its silky texture fragrant beneath his lips. As his mind cleared, he devoted more of his attention to her.

"You're soaked," he murmured, running his hand over her damp cotton gown. Frowning, he realized that Susan's nightmare was virulent, not just a bad dream. Moments passed, and gradually her gasps softened and her fingers slowly released the fabric of his shirt. He kissed her hair one last time, glad that he was here to help her.

"What happened?" he asked her in a low voice, continuing to stroke her back and shoulders.

Susan squeezed her eyes shut, her face buried against Craig's chest. His heart was comfortingly slow and even in beat, unlike her own. "I—it was Steve. I dreamed of him hitting me, breaking my nose. . . ."

Craig uttered her name and tightened his embrace. "I'm sorry," he murmured in a choked voice, "I shouldn't have brought it up, Susan." Damn his need to know.

"N-no," Susan whispered, "it's all right."

"Maybe you need to talk this out, babe," he pleaded huskily, looking down at her suffering features. "I can feel you holding in so much pain. Please use me as a sounding board. Talk to me the way you used to. Remember how we used to talk for hours? As friends? Get rid of that stuff you're carrying."

His voice was balm to her shattered emotions and Susan had no strength left to stop the torrent of words that suddenly began to come out of her. As she trembled in Craig's arms, she felt truly safe for perhaps the first time in her life.

Craig felt more than heard Susan began to speak, her voice terribly low and off-key. He bent his head, holding his ear close to her lips to hear what she was saying.

"...He would fly into these rages. I didn't know what to do. The doctors gave him drugs to try to control his changing behavior, and sometimes it worked. Other times it didn't. I never knew what Steve would be like when I came home from the hospital. Sometimes he was moody and wouldn't talk to me. Other times, he'd start screaming at me, accusing me of being late because I was with another man. I tried—oh, God, I tried—to tell him I wasn't, but he wouldn't believe me. One night, as I was sleeping, he turned over and started hitting me. I remember hearing my nose crack, and I remember the blood pouring all over my gown.''

Craig shut his eyes and took in a tortured breath. He felt Susan's trembling begin to dissolve and, intuitively, he understood that talking was helping her to heal. No matter how horrible it made him feel to hear it, she had to keep talking. ''Did you go to the doctor?'' he asked.

''I—no.'' Susan gave a little laugh, more of a hysterical sound. ''Two months earlier, Steve had broken my jaw, and I'd had to go to the emergency room for an X-ray. The doctor at the navy hospital was really upset. He wanted to commit Steve to a mental ward to protect me. But I knew if they did that to him, he'd die. I knew he couldn't stand being caged like that. I—I just couldn't do that to him. I tried so hard to make his last few months bearable. . . .''

Tears stung Craig's closed eyes. He slid his hand against Susan's face, his touch tender. ''So you didn't have your nose fixed because you were afraid the doctor would put Steve in the mental ward.'' Poignantly, he remembered her reaction to animals in a zoo; she'd been distraught and tearful at their lack of freedom. No wonder she'd been unable to do that to her husband. Grimly, he felt her nod her head once, and he continued to stroke her hair in an effort to soothe her. So she had sacrificed herself for someone else, just as she had done as a young girl growing up. First her mother, then Steve.

Hurting for her, Craig asked, "How long did this go on?"

"It seemed like forever...." Trying valiantly to stop from trembling, Susan said, "No, it wasn't forever. It was just the last year. Steve couldn't help it. I know he was always bragging and boasting, but he'd never hurt a fly, much less me. It was the tumor...."

Emotion overwhelmed Craig, and he couldn't speak. All he could do was hold Susan, hold her and absorb the pain she had borne by herself. The minutes spun together, the weak glow from the streetlight cascading over them, and gradually Craig felt Susan begin to relax, her breath evening out and her heart rate slowing.

"I wish," he told her hoarsely as he tunneled his fingers through her soft hair, "I'd known. I wish you'd called me. Written me. I could've helped some way, somehow...."

Susan sniffed, feeling Craig's powerful care and tenderness. She lay against him, too weak to move away, needing what he was giving her too much. "How could I? You just disappeared out of our lives, Craig," she said in a scratchy voice. "Wh-when I stood you up that night after graduation, you disappeared. I—I wanted to find you... to apologize, but you'd left. I didn't have much time after that to try to locate you, because Steve needed me."

Craig sat very still. His throat constricted. "Why didn't you show up at the restaurant that night, Susan?"

Susan blinked away the tears. Sitting up, she felt his arms loosen, but his hands encased hers as she faced him. His face was harsh and alive with feelings. Susan felt too gutted to hide her own feelings any longer. Craig deserved the truth, she realized, even if it was coming four years late. She felt the strength of his hands around her own and drowned in the tenderness of his gaze, giving her the strength to go on.

"I went to see Steve earlier that day, to tell him it was over. But when I got to his apartment, he met me at the door, crying. It shook me as nothing ever could, Craig." She took a deep, shuddering breath and continued. "I asked him why he was crying, and that's when he told me he'd been diagnosed with a brain tumor. He said he wanted to marry me. He pulled out an engagement ring. He said he might have less than five years to live, but he wanted them to be happy years—with me."

Craig's mouth parted and he stared at her, stunned.

With a grimace, Susan continued, "I was so torn up, Craig. I cried with him. A part of me loved him.... I felt so sorry for him. All he did was cry and hold me and beg me to marry him." She hung her head. "I'd never seen a man cry before, and it tore me up in ways I can't even begin to tell you. I—I agreed to marry him, Craig." Her voice fell into a painful whisper. "It wasn't until a long time after all that that I remembered we'd planned to have dinner that night, Craig. I felt so terrible. Steve stayed with me that night and—" she frowned, ashamed of herself "—we slept together...." Sniffing, she looked up at him. "I tried to call you the next morning at Annapolis, but the man on duty said you weren't in. I left a message for you. Because we all three were friends, I figured you'd understand and forgive me for not showing up. Steve didn't want anyone to know about his cancer. He felt so ashamed."

Taking in a shaky breath, Craig gently caressed Susan's damp cheek. What she didn't realize, even to this day, was that he'd been planning to ask her to become engaged to *him* that night at the restaurant. All these years of blaming her for standing him up had been for nothing, he realized bitterly. Susan had no idea how he'd felt about her—and he hadn't let her know. But how could he have? She was Steve's girlfriend. He was her friend.

"I left early that next morning for Camp Lejune," he said in a roughened voice. "I never got your message. I'm sorry...." And he was, in a million ways. With his thumbs, Craig removed the last of the tears from beneath her anguished eyes. "What happened next?"

"After I tried to get hold of you, Steve and I were married by a justice of the peace that same day," Susan whispered. "It all happened so fast. I was so confused. I didn't know if I'd done the right thing or not. But how could I leave him when he needed me so much?"

Bowing his head, Craig nodded. He could see that Susan would never have been able to leave under those circumstances. She'd been young and inexperienced with men in general, and Steve had been courting her strongly for nearly a year. "I understand now," he rasped.

With a slight nod, Susan sniffed. "I—I tried to love him that last year when he turned violent. I tried so hard and—" she gulped "—I feel so horribly guilty. I was angry with Steve, even though I knew he couldn't help himself. I—I'm ashamed of myself for getting beat up like I did. But I didn't know where to turn for help. His poor parents were at their wits' ends, they were so grief stricken about his illness. All the money in the world couldn't stop Steve from dying before their very eyes. I know they felt better because I was there and because I was a nurse. Steve had the best care I could give him.''

Craig wondered in anguish who'd cared for Susan during that period. Probably no one. Not even him— the friend who had run out on her when she'd needed him the most. Turning the anger on himself, Craig knew he'd been blaming the wrong person all along. *She* deserved to be angry with *him*.

''Shh,'' he whispered, touching her lips with his finger. ''You have nothing to apologize for, don't you see?''

''Yes, I do.'' She scrubbed her eyes with her hands and looked away. ''The reason I wanted to break up with Steve in the first place was I'd realized we were both too young. I wanted to go out with other people and follow the dreams I had. I felt if I married Steve, I would be cheating him and myself. But when he told me about the tumor, I just died inside. I couldn't say no.''

''We all make decisions we're sorry for later,'' Craig whispered, avoiding her tear-filled gaze. It would hurt Susan terribly if she knew how much he'd misplaced his anger toward her for the last four years of his life.

''I made a mistake in marrying Steve, but I tried to love him,'' Susan said in a strained voice. ''As I grew up, I realized our values were so different. Steve enjoyed a shallow, superficial kind of life. I was the opposite. He always put the blame on other people or external events rather than taking responsibility himself.''

''Steve was always a little boy at heart,'' Craig agreed hoarsely.

''I thought if we had a baby, it would help, but Steve was jealous that my attention would shift.''

"He liked being the center of attention." Craig wrestled with the terrible hurt in Susan's eyes. More than anything, he knew, she loved children and wanted to be a mother. How much it must have hurt her when Steve denied her the one thing that might have helped her through that time.

Craig sat there, his hand lightly cradling her cheek, absorbing her way of seeing the world. "Listen," he urged finally "you need to lie down and try to sleep. Come on." He got to his feet. If he didn't, he was going to sweep her back into his arms, kiss her until she melted like hot sunlight and love her until the pain finally left her eyes. Swallowing hard, he moved back, letting Susan settle back on her cot. He took the thin cover that she'd thrown aside and gently laid it over her. She curled up on her side, her hands beneath her cheek.

"You'll sleep now," he promised her as he knelt beside her on one knee and tucked the blanket around her shoulders.

Getting up, Craig moved back to his cot, his mind working like a steel-jawed trap. He lay down facing Susan's darkened shape. Never in his wildest dreams had he managed to hit on the truth about Susan and Steve—and himself. He stared into the darkness, thinking and feeling deeply. Susan had been naive to the world, conditioned to taking care of others. With her soft heart, Steve's tears had persuaded her to marry him, Craig had no doubt.

On the other hand, Craig felt helpless and grief stricken about Steve. As a paramedic, he understood the medical implications of such a tumor. But because Craig cared so deeply for Susan, he had trouble separating logic from boiling emotions. How many times had Steve beaten her up? Susan had become a victim in the worst sense of the word. Perhaps it was that shame that made her stay away from him—because he wanted the truth, and the truth had been too painful for her to share with him. Until now...

Sighing softly, Craig closed his eyes. Six days. He had six more days with Susan here at the clinic. Once they got back to Camp Reed, he knew their time together would be severely restricted. Not that Susan had shown that she wanted to spend time with him, he reminded himself. Still, perhaps with this quieter time here at the clinic, with their focus on pregnant mothers and babies, Susan would begin to relax and begin to trust him as she had four years ago.

Finally, as dawn stole over the horizon, a plan began to form in Craig's head. A plan he prayed would give Susan the courage to put the past to rest, so that she could begin to live and, perhaps, look at him again as a friend—and more....

Chapter Seven

Susan awoke slowly, feeling groggy. Grayish light drifted into the room from the small window. Memories of the night came back in bits and pieces, accompanied by powerful emotions. Craig had held her, had comforted her when she'd never needed it more. Her mouth gummy, she sat up on the cot and pushed the hair away from her eyes. Her gaze strayed across the room to where Craig lay, still in his uniform. He was sleeping soundly.

What she needed was a hot shower, so she got up and padded quietly to the bathroom. The hot spray washed away some of her leftover pain, but it couldn't erase the memory of Craig's hoarse words: "You have nothing to apologize for, don't you see?" Nothing? Closing her eyes, the water trickling across her hair and streaming down her face, Susan wanted to cry. The shower was a safe place to do that; she'd done it so many times when

Steve had been alive. He'd never known she'd cried—for him and for herself.

Losing track of the time spent in the shower, Susan toweled herself dry and slipped into some clothes. Craig had explained how uniforms could make them stand out rather than blend in. Also, he didn't want their uniforms confused with police uniforms, which could cause trouble with the ever-present gangs who "owned" certain turf in the barrio. Susan had to admit her soft pink pullover and comfortable jeans, pink socks and sneakers made her feel better. As she combed her hair, she didn't want to see herself in the small, round mirror, but it was impossible not to look as she parted her hair.

She tried to avoid noting the darkness in her eyes—and the shadows beneath them. Her mouth was compressed, the corners pulled in as if she were experiencing pain. Well, wasn't she? Her hand trembling, she set the brush aside and finished getting ready. By the time she left the bathroom, it was six a.m.

"You okay?"

Susan halted abruptly just inside the door to the room when Craig's voice, husky with sleep, broke the silence. Her hand tightened on the doorknob and she forced herself to look in his direction. When she did, her heart mushroomed with such fierce longing that it made her momentarily speechless. Craig's eyes were soft from sleep, his hair tousled. Whatever hardness he normally wore was gone—replaced with heartrending vulnerability.

Susan parted her lips and managed to whisper, "I feel okay, I guess."

Rising to a sitting position, Craig gave her a sleepy smile, rubbing his eyes. "You look beautiful," he said,

HERE'S HOW TO PLAY
"MATCH 3"

1 Detach this, your "MATCH 3" Game, & the page of stamps enclosed. Look for matching symbols among the stamps & stick all you find on your "MATCH 3" Game.

2 Successfully complete rows 1 through 3 & you will instantly & automatically qualify for a chance to win a Big Money Prize—up to a MILLION-$$$ in Lifetime Income ($33,333.33 each year for 30 years). (SEE RULES, BACK OF BOOK, FOR FULL PARTICULARS.)

3 Successfully complete row 4 & we will send you 4 brand-new SILHOUETTE SPECIAL EDITION® novels—for FREE! These Free Books have a cover price of $3.50 each, but they are yours to keep absolutely free. There's no catch. You're under no obligation to buy anything. We charge nothing—ZERO—for your first shipment. And you don't have to make any minimum number of purchases—not even one!

4 The fact is, thousands of Readers enjoy receiving books by mail from the Silhouette Reader Service®. They like the convenience of home delivery...they like getting the best new novels months before they're available in stores...and they love our discount prices!

5 Successfully complete row 5 &, in addition to the Free Books, we will also send you a very nice Free Surprise Gift, as extra thanks for trying our Reader Service.

6 Play the "Lucky Stars" & "Dream Car TieBreaker" Games also enclosed & you could WIN AGAIN & AGAIN because these are Bonus Prizes, all for one winner, & on top of any Cash Prize you may win!

YES! I've completed my "MATCH 3" Game. Send me any Big Money Prize to which I am entitled just as soon as winners are determined. Also send me the Free Books & Free Surprise Gift under the no-obligation-to-buy-ever terms explained above and on the back of the stamps & reply. (No purchase necessary as explained below.)

235 CIS ANSM
(U-SIL-SE-04/94)

Name

Street Address   Apt. #

City   State   Zip Code

©1991 HARLEQUIN ENTERPRISES LTD.

NO PURCHASE NECESSARY—
ALTERNATE MEANS OF ENTRY

You can of course qualify for a chance at a Big Money Prize alone by not playing rows 4 & 5 of your "MATCH 3" Game or by printing your name and address on a 3" x 5" card and sending it to: Silhouette's "Match 3"(III), P.O. Box 1867, Buffalo N.Y. 14269-1867. Limit: One entry per envelope. But why not get everything being offered! The Free Books & Surprise Gift, are after all, ALSO FREE—yours to keep & enjoy—with no obligation to buy anything, now or ever!

looking at her. "Like a dream I've dreamed for a long time."

His words were like a caress, sending tingles coursing through her. Susan swallowed convulsively, ensnared in his tender gaze. There was such longing in his eyes, in his husky tone. "I don't feel very beautiful this morning," she admitted.

He hunched over, resting his elbows on his knees. He heard the raw pain in Susan's voice and struggled to wipe away his sleepiness so he could think coherently. "Last night had been coming for a long time," he murmured.

Nervously, Susan nodded and worked to put her cot into order. "I feel so stupid and embarrassed."

Getting up, his clothes badly wrinkled, Craig moved over to where she stood. "Listen," he said as he reached out and captured her arm, "you weren't stupid for having a nightmare." He felt her stiffen, and her eyes were shadowed as she looked up at him. Never had he wanted to kiss Susan more than now. Bitterly, Craig realized it was impossible—at least, for now it was. He eased his hand across her tense shoulders, which had carried too much weight for too long. "I'm glad I was here to share it with you, babe. You loved Steve and you were loyal to him until the end. That takes a kind of courage I can only try to imagine."

Just the gentle touch of Craig's hand on her shoulder sent tears rushing into her eyes. Struggling to speak, Susan whispered, "It was young love, Craig. I'm older now, and I realize that. And yes, I wanted to be loyal to him. I'd never want someone to walk out on me under those circumstances."

With a sigh, Craig said, "That's why you wanted to break up with him back at Annapolis. I think part of you knew it was young love."

"If you saw that, why didn't I?"

He managed a sad smile. "That's not a fair question to ask. You were a lot younger then. Maybe naive is a better word to use."

Shaking her head, Susan gave an embarrassed laugh. "I still am! I think I'll always be."

Craig fought himself, fought not to take that last step and pull her into his arms, where she deserved to be. "Don't confuse naïveté with idealism," he reassured her. "You've always been an idealist, and I think the world needs more of that. Idealists give us hope. Realists tell us what isn't possible."

His hand slid off her shoulder, leaving her feeling lighter and happier than she could ever recall. Smiling softly, she met and held his dark gaze, which burned with an inner light she couldn't interpret. "And which one are you?" she teased.

With a groan, Craig said, "A hard-core realist."

She watched him walk back to his duffel bag and pull out a towel and washcloth. "Steve was one, too," she admitted.

"Most men are," Craig said as he walked toward the door to the bathroom. "It's the women of the world who keep not only themselves going, but us men, too." He sobered as his hand fell over the doorknob. "I hope that part of you never changes, Susan. I think it was your idealism, your boundless hope that got you through that last year of hell with Steve. A realist might have thrown in the towel. Might have committed him to the hospital."

"Loyalty was part of the reason I stayed with him," Susan said in a low voice, "but I also know I stayed out of guilt, because my love for him was never as strong as his was for me."

With a shrug, Craig rasped, "You did what you felt was right at the time. You're human, babe. We all make mistakes. We screw up big-time. Don't keep beating yourself up for what's done. You were loyal to the end, and you can be proud of that." He gave her a slight smile meant to make her feel better. "How about a hot cup of coffee and a little breakfast when I get out of the shower?"

She rallied beneath his warm gaze. "What did you have in mind?"

"McDonald's is a couple of blocks down from the clinic. It's 0600, and they'll be open. What do you say?"

"Sounds nice, Craig. Thank you...."

"Well? How's our star mom-to-be doing?" Craig asked in Spanish as he walked into the examination room after Maya and her husband had left. Consuela Sancho, daughter to Marie, was dressed and standing next to Susan. It was early afternoon, and the clinic was crowded and busy.

"Any day now, Craig!" Consuela answered in her native tongue with a bright smile. She patted her swollen belly. "Dr. Espinoza says it will be soon."

Craig smiled at Susan. She was looking better with every passing hour, and he was sure that last night and this morning were partly responsible for her demeanor. "Then you'd better stick close to home and that phone," he told Consuela as he ambled into the room.

"I know." She sighed and raised her eyes upward, "As soon as I go into labor, I'm to call the clinic and then 911 for an ambulance."

Grinning, he came to a halt next to Susan. "You got it, young lady."

Craig had feared that the intimacy that had sprung up so strongly between them over her nightmare would be destroyed with the coming daylight. Instead, to his surprise and gratitude, Susan hadn't closed up as she had before. She was quieter, subdued, but she no longer looked at him as if he were an ogre stalking her.

Consuela's sweet smile melted away the last of any sadness he'd seen in Susan's eyes earlier. If he'd ever had doubts about her ability to connect with people, they were resoundingly laid to rest. Consuela had gravitated to Susan like a flower to sunlight.

Susan smiled over at the pregnant woman. The morning had gone so quickly, with one patient following another in rapid succession. Word of the extra medical help in town had sent the mothers and children of the barrio flocking to the clinic for free treatment. Susan arranged the stethoscope across her neck and began to prepare the room for the next patient. Although Craig wore a red polo shirt, beige slacks and loafers, he still looked like a marine, Susan thought, smiling to herself. It was his proud bearing—the way he squared his broad shoulders and held his head—that broadcast that powerful confidence always emanating from him. As she moved around the room, she was grateful for his presence this morning. About once an hour, he'd pop in from his other duties just to check on her—although it wasn't anything that obvious. Craig knew most of the patients and always struck up a conversation in Spanish with them. And the patients always left the room smiling or laughing under his sunny influence.

Susan put fresh paper across the table and glanced over at the others. Craig was watching her intently, and her heart gave a little pulse of surprise. Just the tender gray flame in his eyes gave her courage to remain vulnerable to him. After last night, she no longer had the strength to maintain a defensive wall against his presence.

The joy Susan saw in the Marniquez family's eyes over the arrival of this baby was wonderful, in her opinion. Someday, Susan wanted a baby of her own. Trying to choke back the rising emotions, she concentrated on what she was doing.

Craig grinned as Consuela gripped him by the arm and chattered away in Spanish. "Hey, Susan."

She looked up. "Yes?"

"Consuela says that you can help her deliver the baby if the ambulance doesn't arrive in time."

Susan straightened and grimaced. "Tell her I have absolutely no experience in birthing! Anyway, I'm sure the ambulance will get there in plenty of time."

With a one-shouldered shrug, Craig said, "In Mexico the mothers are helped by midwives and never go to the hospital at all."

Susan finished smoothing the paper across the examining table and turned toward them. "Tell her I'd love to be there, but I'm not a midwife."

Translating to Consuela, Craig knew that the reason she would want Susan with her had to do with Susan herself, not her experience. Craig didn't blame the Marniquez family for wanting Susan nearby. Her warmth and compassion were something rare in the medical arena these days. His smile deepened, and he drowned in the dark blue of Susan's eyes. Did he dare believe that some of the shadowy darkness was gone? He'd like to think that their holding each other and caring for each other last night was responsible. "Consuela says you remind her of her older sister, who died a few months ago. She says she wants you at her side, an adopted sister."

Touched, Susan came over and gave the Hispanic woman a hug. "Tell her I can never replace her sister, but I'd love to be there." Then she gave an embarrassed laugh. "But the only thing I'd be good at is holding her hand through labor."

Craig translated, and Consuela giggled, while Susan squeezed that small, delicate hand. She was so petite, even in comparison to Susan. "I wouldn't want to miss this for the world."

Craig nodded and translated. He sobered slightly as he got to his feet and waited for the two women to say goodbye. Two of Consuela's aunts waited at the door. He liked the strength of the Hispanic women, who supported one another totally.

"What's next?" Susan asked, feeling strangely light and happy. She didn't want to look too closely at the reasons, but she knew that Craig holding her last night was somehow responsible for her mood.

"Consuela's grandmother, Doña Marniquez, is next. She's got a bad case of arthritis." He smiled slightly. "She's the one who gave you that necklace yesterday, remember? She's special."

Susan colored briefly. "How could I forget her?"

"I'll bring her in."

With a nod, Susan moved to the window, which, like the one in the bedroom, had bars across it. Work at the clinic was demanding but had its own kind of reward, and she found it hard to believe that gang wars were raging sporadically all around them. But the wrought-iron bars were silent testament to the violence that the people of the barrio lived with daily. Although it sometimes felt as if she'd stepped back into a "Dodge City" sort of environment, being here nonetheless left her with a good feeling rather than a bad one. As always, there were the children, who would come from all directions every time Craig appeared in the parking-lot area, calling his name, pulling at his hands, dancing around him and pleading for more candy or gum.

From a nursing point of view, Susan realized that the children all needed some medical attention. She worried that the many dogs that roamed the streets, starved and looking for food, could carry rabies. More than once she'd heard of a baby or small child being bitten by such an animal. If not for the clinic's rabies vaccine, they could die.

Late in the afternoon, Craig ambled into the examination room after another patient had left. Susan looked up and smiled in greeting. "You never said we'd get worked to death, Captain."

He grinned. "But isn't it worth it?" He gestured around the room. "Look at how many women and children we're helping."

"I know." She sat down to rest for a moment. "And I'm really glad I came. I wouldn't have missed this, Craig."

"So you've forgiven me for trapping you into coming?"

"You know I have."

"Whew, that was close." He moved over to the examination table and leaned against it, enjoying the moment of quiet with Susan. "You're looking better with every passing hour."

Touching the area beneath her eyes, she said, "You mean I don't have shadows anymore?"

His smile deepened. "No more shadows."

Basking in his warm gaze, Susan murmured, "I guess you could apply that statement to my life in a lot of ways."

"Shadows and light. Life is a bit of both." Craig looked around the room. "Take this clinic. It's a light in the darkness of this gang-torn barrio. People get shot on the street—innocent victims of an underground economy of stealing and drugs."

"Yet the Espinozas have committed their lives to their people," Susan murmured in understanding. "I worry for them. This place is more dangerous than I first realized."

"The gangs usually give this clinic a wide berth," Craig said reassuringly. "It's seen as a neutral zone, so there's never been the violence or warring that goes on in other areas."

With a shiver, Susan said, "I don't know how the decent, good people of this barrio manage to live with it, Craig."

"Patience, endurance and belief in humanity. And idealism."

She smiled up at him, catching the reference to their earlier talk.

"If Consuela has her baby this week, we're all invited to a feast afterward. Did you know that?" he asked, changing to a more cheerful subject.

"No, I didn't."

"Yeah, it will be a real shindig. I was here six months ago and helped deliver a baby for a woman in her home.

She couldn't afford a telephone, and my team just happened to be in the neighborhood giving vaccinations when she went into labor.'' Craig smiled fondly in remembrance of the unexpected event. "I never saw such a celebration for a kid.'' He shook his head, amazed. "I wish our medical system would recognize the value for some mothers of having babies at home.''

Intrigued, Susan wanted to hear more of Craig's thoughts. She found herself starved to get to know him again. "As a paramedic, you realize the value of a hospital birth,'' she countered.

"I do.'' Craig shrugged. "Call me old-fashioned, but the pioneer women had their babies in wagons, in their sod homes or alone in the wilderness. I'm glad the system is moving back toward more natural surroundings, with birthing rooms, keeping the mother and baby together, breast-feeding and going home twenty-four hours after a normal birth.''

"My heart be still. A man who supports breast-feeding.''

He flushed slightly. "Isn't that a sexist remark?''

Susan smiled tenderly. "I was teasing you. I think it's wonderful that men are becoming more interested and involved in pregnancy and the birthing of their babies. You're such an open book, Craig Taggart. Your farm-and-country heritage is showing.''

"Well,'' he responded good-naturedly, "farmers value women more than most men do, I think. I know my father never looked down on my mother. He didn't see women as the weaker sex—my mother is one of the strongest people I've known.''

"Yes, and your parents passed that positive view of women on to you.''

"I think stereotyping women—or anyone—can be a dangerous trap."

"It's refreshing to see a few men get rid of the labels," Susan agreed. "I, for one, am tired of being seen as something to be ordered around. I have a brain, I'm intelligent and I have experience that I wish would be respected and used more."

Craig lifted his hands in a sign of surrender. "I'm the first to support women being all they can be."

"Are you poking fun at me?"

He grinned. "Not really. Women need to realize that they're worthy, too. I grant that men have been sending them a lot of coded messages that they aren't as valued—or valuable—as the men of the world, but things are changing."

"One grudging, hard-earned inch at a time," Susan reminded him, delighted to discover Craig's sensitive views. She gazed around the room, feeling a contentment she'd never known before. "You really do belong here, Craig. I feel you understand these people like few ever will. You're not trying to change them or their beliefs and values. You're trying to fit in and become a part of their living experience. I find that admirable."

Susan's praise made Craig feel ten feet tall. "You're happy here, too," he offered.

"Oh?"

"I saw you with Consuela—the way you touched her, calmed her. You know the value of touch, Susan. It's healing. In our hurried world, touch is too often overlooked. Here, the people are always reaching out and touching one another. You see mothers with their babies all the time. They're never separated from one another. The mother carries that baby with her wherever she goes, no matter what she does." He held her luminous gaze and smiled slightly. "You're like that. You'll make one hell of a mother someday...."

Shaken by the gritty tone of his voice, Susan felt heat prickle her cheeks. She was blushing. Drowning in the warm gray of his eyes, she choked back sudden tears that threatened to overflow. His mouth, so strong and yet tugged into such a tender smile, made her go weak with need. She'd been without love, without care for so long that she felt as if she were becoming unhinged inside for exactly what Craig had talked about: touch. Only, it was his touch she hungered for. His love....

Caught in the web of his gaze, Susan managed to stutter, "I—I think we should go see if Maya needs help."

The heated thought that Susan could carry his child within her left Craig silent. As he searched her eyes, he saw hope in them for the first time. He ached to reach out and stroke her flushed cheek and tell her how much he cared for her, how much he wanted her. Instead, he nodded and walked toward the doorway.

Craig prayed that the magic of the clinic and these wonderful people would continue to give Susan the courage to open up to him, to reveal her past, no matter what it held. Armed with that knowledge, he would finally be able to plan a future for them. And never in all his life had he so much wanted fate to give him a second chance. He knew he'd been handed that second chance with Susan, and he was damned if he was going to blow it this time. No, no matter what herculean tasks were thrown in front of him, he wasn't going to give up on getting Susan into his arms again. He wasn't going to abandon her—as he'd done before.

Realizing that Susan was nervous again, he stepped out into the hall. "The rest of the team and I are going to a neighborhood about eight miles away, where they're setting up for evening vaccinations. So you'll be here by yourself tonight.''

Surprised, Susan looked up. "And the Espinozas?''

"Maya is teaching a prenatal course up at the local college in National City and Jesus will be with us. I thought it might be better if you got some rest this evening.''

Susan realized that she *was* tired. "I'm sure I'll get along okay here. What time do you think you'll be back?''

"No later than 2100.''

"But that's after dark. What about the gangs?''

"You'll be okay. I've contacted the police, and they'll swing by the clinic more often than usual while we're gone. We'll be all right, too,'' he said soothingly. Glancing at his watch, he muttered, "I'd better hightail it out of here. We're scheduled to leave in ten minutes. I'll see you late tonight.''

When Craig left, the room seemed to lose its vitality. Susan stood for a moment absorbing his words. Worry plagued her as she stepped out of the room and walked down the hall to Maya's office. The barrio wasn't a very safe place. She'd just found Craig again; she didn't want him hurt or killed by one of those bullets that always seemed to go astray when gang members began shooting.

Susan was at the front door of the clinic, ready to lock it up for the night when she saw a car screech to a halt out front. Twilight had fallen, and she was alone. She opened the door and stepped outside as she recognized Blanca, Consuela's younger sister.

"Señorita Susan! Señorita Susan!" Running breathlessly up to her, Blanca gripped her hand and tugged on it.

"Come! Come! Consuela! Consuela!"

Susan tried to understand the girl's high-pitched voice.

"What's wrong?"

The young woman rattled on in Spanish, and Susan wished fervently that Craig was here to translate.

"What is it, Blanca? What's happened?"

"My sister! She have the baby! Come! Come! You help!"

"Oh, no!" Susan saw the stark pleading in the girl's eyes. Consuela was in labor! Her mind spinning, she urged Blanca to come into the clinic with her, where she raced for the phone in the reception area. The line was dead! Stricken, Susan stood holding the receiver. Maya had warned her that from time to time the electrical and phone services would suddenly stop—such was the life in their barrio. It might take hours before the lines would be restored.

Reeling from the situation, Susan hurried down to one of the examination rooms and retrieved a physician's black leather bag. It would have everything necessary for delivering a baby. But could she do it? Susan wasn't at all sure. She hurried back to the entrance, with Blanca gripping her hand. Susan had no idea how close the nearest hospital was, but her thought was to get Consuela into the car and take her there—if possible.

"*¡Ándele!* Hurry!" Blanca begged. "She is close! Close to having the niño!"

Susan locked the clinic with shaking hands and ran to the awaiting car. Blanca gunned the motor, and they sped down the avenue. Gulping in air, Susan sat with the black bag on her lap. Her mind spun with options and alternatives. Craig had said he'd be back with the medical team around 2100. She looked at her watch. That was an hour away.

The Marniquez house was a single-story home scrunched between two other dilapidated houses. As they pulled up to the front, Susan couldn't help but notice the poverty they lived in. A few toys were scattered across a lawn fried brown by the hot sun, and peeling paint told her they couldn't afford much but the necessities for survival.

Breathing hard, she raced up the cracked sidewalk to the porch. There, several of the husbands waited, including Consuela's, Alfredo, who nodded toward her, gratefulness written in his face. Blanca guided her through the gloomy interior of the house to a rear bedroom. There, Susan recognized the rest of the Marniquez women hovering over Consuela, who lay moaning on the bed. The relief on Maria's face made Susan feel shaky. The grandmother, Juanita, who sat in a chair holding her granddaughter's hand, looked up and nodded deferentially to her. Susan wondered briefly where the rest of the extended family was, and realized with the phone system out, they couldn't be reached in time to attend the birth. She knew the families lived in far-flung reaches of the barrio from one another. Setting the bag on the bed, Susan looked to Maria, who knew more English than anyone else in the family.

"Maria, do you have a phone?"

"*¿Que?*"

"Umm . . ." Susan desperately looked around. She didn't remember the word for telephone, so she mimed talking on a phone.

"No." Maria shook her head sadly. *"No hay telephono."* She reached out and gripped Susan's hands. "Gracias for coming, *señorita*. Consuela has been crying for you, for help."

"Can you send Blanca and some of the men out to call 911?"

"Sí." Maria turned to her youngest daughter.

Blanca gave Susan a stricken look. "The phone lines no working all over the barrio, *señorita*. I have to drive five miles to get outside."

"Then do it! And please hurry!"

"Sí, Señorita Susan." Blanca rushed out of the room.

Susan moved toward Consuela. "When did she go into labor?" she asked Maria.

"¿Que?"

Feeling helpless, Susan gripped the hand Consuela extended to her.

"Susan!" the mother-to-be whispered, sounding relieved.

"Didn't I promise I would come?" she replied unsteadily. "It's all right," she crooned to the girl.

Consuela lay atop the bed, the covers pushed aside. Clean bowls of water, fresh towels and soap had been placed on the bedstand next to Juanita. Susan quickly noted that the blanket beneath Consuela was darkened. Her water had broken. She gripped the woman's small hands and gave her a slight smile.

"You'll be okay," she breathed, turning her attention to the older women, who were watching her intently.

"May I?" Susan held up her hand and pointed to Consuela's swollen belly.

Maria nodded. Juanita gestured sharply and said something that Susan didn't understand.

First, Susan opened the physician's bag and checked the contents. Everything she'd need was in there. Oh, why wasn't Craig here? She'd never delivered a baby, and these women were looking at her as if she knew what she was doing.

"I'll be right back! I have to wash my hands." She held them up and made scrubbing signs. The women nodded sagely. Maria got to her feet and guided her toward the bathroom. Susan turned at the doorway. "I'll be right back, Consuela, I promise."

Running down the hall, Susan shakily washed and scrubbed her hands with the bar of soap she found. She tried to pull from memory, from her few days on an obstetrics floor, what to do. All her life she'd been a surgical nurse, not connected with labor or birthing procedures. What if Consuela got into trouble? What could she do? Swallowing hard, she grabbed a towel and dried her hands on the way back to the bedroom.

Trying to look calm, Susan entered the bedroom. All three women looked at her with great hope in their eyes, and her stomach went queasy. She came and sat down at Consuela's side. The girl's face was damp with perspiration, so Susan retrieved a clean cloth and gave it to Maria so that she could wipe her daughter's brow. Juanita nodded and smiled in her direction, as if to give Susan encouragement.

"I don't know what I'm doing," she told Consuela in a low, shaky voice as she took her blood pressure. Fortunately, her patient had already divested herself of her skirt and underwear, and only a sheet covered her. Gently, Susan placed her hand on Consuela's leg and examined her. She was fully dilated. Shaking her head, Susan realized that she must have already been in labor when she'd been examined by Dr. Espinoza this morning. Biting down hard on her lower lip, Susan rummaged through the medical bag, locating a sterile pair of surgical gloves. Maybe Consuela hadn't known she was in labor, so hadn't mentioned it to the doctor. Maybe she'd thought it was just a bad case of cramps.

If only Craig were here! He had experience delivering babies. Susan felt nearly helpless as she heard Consuela groaning and breathing in choppy gasps. Her back bowed with each grinding contraction.

Susan kept her hand on her patient's leg. Trying to think coherently, she allowed her instincts to take over. The baby would need to be washed once it arrived, and the cord tied, sterilized and cut. She could do those things. The three hovered around the bed, consoling the young mother. Susan felt a calm flowing through her in response to the older women's strength. They had each had many children, and perhaps that was why their quiet presence was so stabilizing to her and Consuela. Their wise eyes, dark and shining, spoke to her, and her initial panic dissolved.

Offering the family members a trembling smile, Susan remained at Consuela's side, checking the dilation, gently rubbing Consuela's leg to soothe her and allow the miracle of birth to occur naturally. Nearly an hour later, Susan knew she was close to giving birth. The girl's eyes were wide with pain and her face slack from pushing so hard, while perspiration made her golden skin glow.

Maria spoke and Juanita nodded. Susan watched as the two women conversed with Consuela in low, coaxing tones. Then they helped the girl sit up. Susan was about to protest when she realized that these women had far more birthing experience than she. Getting out of the way, she stood and watched as they positioned

Consuela on her knees, so that gravity would help her push her baby out of the birth canal into the world.

Susan felt like an interloper to such a mystical, poignant moment. Juanita gestured for her to come over and hold her hands between Consuela's legs. Susan nodded, tears in her eyes. Juanita wanted her to catch the baby as it slid into the world. Moving forward, she knelt next to Consuela, holding out her hands to receive the child. She saw the baby's head slowly ease forward, and she gasped.

"It's coming!" she cried. "It's coming!"

The next few moments spun to a halt as Susan cradled the baby's head, then its shoulders, her trembling fingers creating a cradle for the infant to slide into. Consuela's cry sank into a groan as the baby arrived with seeming ease into Susan's waiting hands. The other women helped the new mother lie back down, soothing her, clucking over her as they took damp cloths and wiped her brow, face and arms with great tenderness and love.

Susan was on her knees, holding the newly born infant. It was a girl, she realized belatedly. A tiny, perfect little girl with sparse black hair across her small head. Then Juanita was there, her toothless mouth pulled into a smile as she quickly blotted the baby with a wet cloth and then dried her with a nearby towel. Susan looked up at the grandmother, tears streaming down her cheeks. The baby moved her small arms, but never once cried. Juanita pinched the baby's nose with the towel, and Susan realized she was cleaning away any mucus that might interfere with her breathing.

Clucking delightedly, Juanita pointed to the umbilical cord, which still pulsed with blood being pumped into the baby. Susan realized how important these last moments were to the child's health, and she cradled her protectively, feeling more powerful and good as a woman than she ever had before. Juanita held out a small blanket, and she smiled, tucking the baby girl into it.

A few minutes later, Susan tied off the cord in two places and made a cut in between. Holding out the antiseptic, she allowed the grandmother to cleanse both ends of the cord. Then Juanita tied a string around the cord near the infant's belly. Everyone was smiling—smiles of triumph, of celebration of life and birth.

For the next half hour, Susan watched in mute silence as the baby girl suckled strongly at her young mother's breast. The colostrum, a clear yellow liquid, would bubble at the baby's bow-shaped mouth, and Consuela would smile and gently wipe it away. The tears in the new mother's eyes were telling, and Susan noticed that none of the women had dry eyes. The placenta was passed, and Susan helped Juanita clean Consuela and remove the stained, bloody sheets from beneath her.

Blanca finally came bursting into the house, with an ambulance crew not far behind. She hurried into the room, giving a cry of joy when she saw the baby. When Susan left not long after, she was convinced that mother and baby were in the best of hands. She looked down at her own hands, realizing she'd caught the baby and brought her into the world. Juanita had known on some instinctive level that she had wanted to do that.

Silvia, one of the aunts, drove Susan back to the clinic. Anxious to see if Craig and the team had returned, she felt disappointment as the car pulled up in front of the clinic. No lights shone from the clinic windows.

Once inside, Susan tried the phone, hoping it would be working by now, but it wasn't. Sighing, she went back to the rear room that served as the bedroom. She'd have to wait until Craig got back to notify Dr. Espinoza and Maya about the birth.

Just as she was getting ready to take a shower, Susan heard voices out front. At the sound of Craig's quiet laughter, she realized the team had returned from their duties. Sitting down on the cot, she quickly slipped on her shoes again.

Craig appeared at the door and gave her a welcoming smile. "And here I thought you'd be in bed by now."

Rising, Susan laughed softly. "Consuela just had her baby! We need to tell Jesus and Maya. The phone lines are dead and I couldn't call an ambulance, so I had to go over and help."

Craig's brows rose in surprise. "What? Is she okay?"

With a little laugh, Susan said, "Everything's fine, Craig. Mother and baby are doing well, as far as I can tell. Blanca drove out of the barrio to make a 911 call, and the ambulance came to take them to the hospital."

"I never expected her to have the baby this soon." He realized how happy Susan appeared. "Let me go tell them right now. I'll be right back and we can talk some more."

"Go ahead. I'm due for a shower anyway."

Craig hated to leave, wanting to stay and share Susan's joy over the incident. First things first. He left without a word and hurried toward the front of the clinic. Since the phones were out, he'd have to walk over to the doctor's house. Whistling, he unlocked the door.

Susan was sitting on her cot, toweling her hair, when Craig reappeared. He looked tired, and she realized he'd put in a fourteen-hour day. A dark growth of beard accentuated the planes of his face and emphasized his inherent strength. She gave him a slight smile as he quietly closed the door to the room and turned toward her.

"Well? Were they surprised, too?"

Tiredly, Craig ran his fingers through his short hair. "Surprised isn't the word. They're driving over to see them at the hospital right now." He walked to her and crouched down in front of her, his hands resting lightly on her robed knees. "I'm really proud of you, Susan."

She held up her hands to him.

"I got to help, Craig," she said softly. "Juanita let me catch the baby as it was born. I actually got to hold the little girl. Isn't that something?"

Touched, Craig reached out, his hand settling on her shoulder. Tears were making her eyes look huge and luminous, he noted. "I think it's wonderful," he murmured.

Susan laughed. "Look at me! I'm crying. Again! All four of us women cried when the baby was born!"

His face lost its usual hardness as a slight smile curved his mouth. He saw such joy mirrored in Susan's face that he wanted to lean those extra few inches forward and kiss her, to breathe her joy into himself. "I cry every time it happens," he confessed with a choked voice.

Gazing up into his shadowed gray eyes, Susan fought back a sob. "It was so beautiful, Craig. So beautiful. I mean, I held this little warm life in my hands. Now I know why so many nurses and doctors want to go into obstetrics. It's wonderful!"

Without thinking, Craig pulled her to her feet and into his arms, burying his face in her loose, dark hair. "You're wonderful," he said, his voice muffled as he held her tightly. "I'm so glad to see you smiling again, Susan. So glad...." The words jammed in his throat. All he could do was hold her and feel his heart opening to her, to her discovery that there was an incredible magic and mystery to life. He felt her arms slip around his waist, and felt the tension drain out of her as she pressed her face against his chest.

Shutting his eyes tightly, Craig absorbed the feel of her form, her warmth. She was small in his arms, small and almost fragile. He felt the tenuous trust stretching between them and he held his breath, afraid that it would shatter as he held her. "I'm so proud of you," he whispered unsteadily. How much courage she must have to open up again and reach out to others. She'd reached out to Consuela, and now to him. "Miracles," he said thickly, "are what life is made of, did you know that?"

Sniffing, Susan raised her eyes to meet and drown in his warm gray gaze. Craig's mouth was so close, so strong and male, that she ached to reach up on tiptoe and kiss him. Just to have his mouth on hers...

"I—I feel like some kind of miracle took place," she said brokenly. "That little life in my hands...she smelled so new and so good, Craig. She didn't cry once, not even when I cut the umbilical cord. It was as if she knew she was loved and welcome." Susan blinked back her tears and gave a sad little smile.

With a long exhalation of breath, Craig forced himself to release Susan. She was far too fragile, he realized, fragile in ways he could never have fathomed. Four years of hell had left her a tangled, confused woman. But now she was being given a chance to step out of the past and into the present. Would she?

The silence grew in volume as he stared down at her clasped hands. Susan had such lovely hands. Craig vividly recalled her telling him once that she dreamed of someday taking art classes and learning to paint. With a shake of his head, his voice low with emotion, he said, "Life takes some real twists and turns, doesn't it?"

Susan agreed. She clung to the sight of Craig's shadowed profile, his mouth set in a thin line against his feelings. But what was he feeling? Afraid to ask, afraid of his judgment of her, she could only answer, "Yes. Twists and turns."

Raising his head, Craig glanced at her enigmatically. "One good thing, though," he told her, "at least we're alive. I do believe in miracles." He closed his hand over hers. "Whether you know it or not, Susan, you're a miracle walking back into my life. When I first saw you at the hospital, I came unglued. I'd tried to put you behind me, what we'd shared, what I'd dreamed of for us...and then, seeing you, I thought I'd snapped." His fingers tightened momentarily. "And when you touched me for the first time, I knew I wasn't dreaming and I wasn't crazy. You were there. And you were real."

Chapter Eight

Craig tossed restlessly in his cot. It was over an hour since they'd gone to bed and he couldn't sleep. Assuring himself that Susan slept deeply and without nightmares, he quietly got up and left the room. He needed fresh air, so he unlocked the rear door to the clinic and walked out into the empty parking lot. As he stood there looking up at the night sky, which was blotted out by millions of lights reflected upward from the sprawling city, a dog came over, wagging its tail in a friendly fashion. Craig knew the gangs were active at this time of night, and he remained on guard as he absently petted the mangy black dog.

Studying the friendly but bedraggled mutt, Craig realized that Susan was in just as rough shape in an emotional sense as this dog was physically. He shook his head. His mind wouldn't seem to shut off, nor would his heart stop feeling deeply for her. Steve had been his friend, too, though. Craig recalled all the good times the two of them had shared those first three years at Annapolis. They'd almost been inseparable—until Susan had come into their lives.

Rubbing his face tiredly, he stared up at the quarter moon high in the sky, the one celestial body visible over the barrio. Any anger he'd held against Susan was gone now. She had experienced enough anger as the unwitting victim of Steve's uncontrolled rages. He could barely stand the pain of realizing that his old friend had broken her jaw and nose.

"Hell," Craig muttered, wiping his mouth. He blamed himself for not remaining in Susan's life regardless of whether she'd married Steve. Why had he abandoned her in a fit of what he'd thought was righteous anger? If he had come back, what would have happened?

Looking up at the moon, Craig wished he had been more responsible and not so damned immature himself, stalking off like some ego-stung male. He was far from blameless in this situation. Between him and Steve, Susan had hung suspended—guilty only of being idealistic, young and naive. Craig watched the progress of a small bat flitting across the night sky. If he hadn't been so hurt about being stood up, he would have gone to see her the next morning. Instead, she had no idea that he loved her.

Rubbing his hands together slowly, lost in thought, he wondered if there was any hope of Susan loving him now. How could she after he'd abandoned her to Steve? He'd not proven he was worthy of her by going back and confronting her. If he had, he'd have found out the truth.

Innocent. Susan had been a pawn between the two of them. Bitterly, Craig realized that if he'd been a little more assertive, Susan would have married him instead. But all that was water under the bridge, his mother would tell him.

So what was left? Anything? Craig's head sank down against his chest as he explored the alternatives. Marriage to Steve had left Susan badly scarred. That was why the wariness, the fear always hung in her eyes, Craig surmised. Was she afraid of him, or just men in general?

How could he win Susan back? Or could he? What would it take?

Time, he realized. Grimly, he looked around the dark, sleeping barrio. Time was something he didn't have much of, unfortunately. He was due to be rotated into the field in another week. His life would once again revolve around ten days of training, a week's rest at base headquarters and then another ten days of training, not only at Reed, but with other arms of the military, on war-game exercises that could take place anywhere in the world. Those kinds of war games kept him and his men at peak efficiency.

Craig didn't even know how long Susan intended to remain at Camp Reed. It could be a two- or three-year stint.

"Dammit," he whispered harshly.

The dog, lying at his feet, pricked up an ear and looked at Craig.

Worse, Craig had already signed up for another four years. He was due to be sent to Paris, France as an embassy officer in less than six months. It was too late to get out of it now. He'd have thirty days' leave between rotations, but that was it. No, the next twenty-four months of his life were planned. Paris was going to be his home. Feeling frantic, he tried to figure out when he could court Susan. And what if she wasn't over Steve? Was there room in her heart to love two men in her lifetime?

He remembered more of his mother's words of wisdom: *take one day at a time.* She'd always gotten after Craig for daydreaming—for hanging too much on an unclear future. Being the commonsensical woman she was, she had warned him time and again about dreaming too big, or for too much. Rubbing his sweating hands on the thighs of his trousers, Craig knew he was dreaming bigger than he had ever dared to in his life. He dreamed of Susan loving him as much as he'd always loved her. And in that moment, he realized that he'd never stopped loving her, despite his attempts to bury the past in anger and work.

Still, Craig believed in miracles. The chances of having Susan land in his life a second time hadn't been lost on him. Standing, he leaned over and petted the mangy black dog. This time he was going to hang in there no matter what happened, no matter how many hurdles Susan threw in front of him. He wasn't going to abandon her a second time.

"Señorita Susan! Look!"

Susan was busy giving vaccination shots to a group of youngsters in one of the examination rooms the next morning when a black-haired girl of seven came running up to her. Tears were streaming down her cheeks as she held up a small brown puppy.

"Craig?" Susan called. He was giving shots to a group of energetic, restless boys in the adjacent room, and the door was open between the offices. Susan

smiled as the girl drew near and began talking breathlessly in Spanish. She twisted her head toward the
doorway as Craig entered the room to see what all the
excitement was about. All morning she had felt oddly
happy for no discernible reason. Now, as Craig came up
beside her, she had the urge to kiss his smiling mouth.
His eyes broadcast a warmth that seemed to envelop her
like invisible, comforting arms.

"What's she saying?" Susan asked as she finished
giving the last vaccination.

Craig smiled and leaned down to speak to the little
girl. "Oh, I see," he replied to her rapid-fire Spanish.
"The pup has a broken hind leg, I think."

"Oh, no!" Susan squatted down in turn. The puppy
was scruffy-looking, with huge brown eyes. It lay on its
back, tucked in the arms of the girl, seeming to trust her
completely. Susan leaned over and watched as Craig
carefully examined the dog's leg more closely. All the
while, the girl was crying and talking excitedly.

"Her name is Odessa," he told Susan. "She says her
puppy ran out into the street and a car hit it." Scowling, he studied the injured leg.

Susan knelt down, gave Odessa a reassuring smile and
touched her long, straight black hair. Gradually, her
tears stopped and she looked anxiously at them.

"What can we do, Craig?"

Quirking his mouth, he gently stroked the puppy's
head. "Her family obviously doesn't have the money to
take this dog to a vet." He sighed. "I can try and set it
for her, but I've never dealt with a dog's leg before."

Smiling gently at Craig, Susan whispered, "I'll get
your bag," and stood up.

Craig watched her move quietly out of the room. He
would never tire of seeing her swaying walk, he thought.

Her every movement carried such grace that he some-times felt like a starving man just trying to absorb every moment with her to the fullest. Shaking his head, he continued to soothe Odessa and her hurt puppy while he waited for the physician's bag.

Susan returned shortly and set the bag on the table. "Let's work up here," she said. "I'll assist you."

With surgical gloves on, they went to work to set the puppy's right hind leg with two small splints, securing them with gauze. Before they were done, Susan real-ized that several children had made a circle around them and were silently watching. A number of mothers and older women also came to the room, curious about the crowd outside the door.

"You always were for the underdog," Susan told Craig later, when they were alone again. She went to the counter and began to roll lengths of cotton strips into bandages.

He smiled absently and washed his hands with soap and water. "Oh? Why do you say that?"

"I have a feeling that little girl brought that puppy here because she knows you have a soft heart."

"Mmm, soft head would be more like it," Craig said, grinning over at her.

Susan's mouth compressed. "A happy ending for once."

He chuckled and dried his forearms and hands with a towel. "My, don't we sound like a dyed-in-the-wool pessimist all of a sudden," he teased.

Glancing up from her duties, Susan felt as if she were drowning in his dancing eyes. Her heart started to beat a little harder. "Maybe at one time I believed in happy endings, but I don't anymore and you know it."

"No," he said slowly, calculating the intensity behind her words, "I don't know that."

She gave him a dark look and resumed rolling the bandages. "Life has taught me well."

"Life has been hard on you," he agreed softly, "but I hope it hasn't stolen your dreams, babe."

Susan's hands froze momentarily. She frowned and forced herself to continue her work. *Babe*. Craig always caught her off guard with the endearment! "My dreams," she began in a strained tone, "were crushed a long time ago."

"Tell me what they were."

"They were just silly, childish dreams, Craig. Nothing special."

"I'd still like to hear about them."

"They're part of my past, too," Susan countered grimly. She reached for another strip of cotton.

"Okay. What were they?" Craig persisted. Setting the towel aside, he studied her. Susan's hair was slightly mussed, and she wore absolutely no makeup, but she was supremely beautiful to him.

With an embarrassed shrug, she muttered, "Oh, you know... Before Mama got sick, I used to go out to the meadow behind our home. I'd lie on my belly with the flowers waving back and forth all around me, and I used to imagine... imagine having a family of my own. Having lots of children. My best friend, Annie Farnsworth, had a great family. Her father laughed so much, and he hugged us all. I remember how happy her mother was just baking bread in the kitchen. She taught us how to make donkey tails from leftover pie-crust dough."

Glancing up, she frowned. "I guess I was jealous of Annie and what she had with her parents. I dreamed of a happy home, lots of children and..."

"And?" Craig prompted, holding his breath.

"Nothing," Susan said flatly.

Craig remained silent for a long moment, realizing Susan was upset. She was winding the cotton material almost angrily. "A happy home, lots of kids and a husband who loved you as much as you did him?" he posed softly.

Wincing, Susan said nothing. She just kept wrapping the rolls and tying them off with thin strips of cotton.

"Nothing wrong with that dream," Craig continued in a few moments. "Just because your dad abandoned you doesn't mean you can't someday be happy, Susan."

"Men mean disappointment to me," she whispered. "Since Steve died, I've avoided any relationships."

"I don't blame you for the way you feel," Craig said. "First your father, then Steve. I made mistakes with you, too."

Susan lifted her head. "You? No, you didn't."

Taking a deep breath, Craig knew she deserved to know the whole truth. He jammed his hands in his pockets and leaned against the examination table. "I should have come back the next morning and found out why you didn't show up at the restaurant, Susan. If I had, maybe things wouldn't have gone the way they did for you—or for me."

Confused, she stared at him. "You had every right to be angry that I stood you up."

"You were my best friend. I owed you the chance to explain."

Susan tore her gaze from his burning one. "I felt guilty, Craig. It's one of my favorite feelings. Someday, I hope it'll go away."

"With time it will," he informed her softly. Craig saw the pain in her eyes. "You're still blaming yourself, and you shouldn't, Susan."

"My martyr complex that you accused me of back at base?"

He grinned slightly. "Yeah, maybe a little of that. I just feel that all your life you've had to take care of others." He stepped over to where she stood. The cotton rolls lay in neat rows across the table. He picked up another of the strips and slowly began to roll it up. "You grew up thinking that all your worth, your value, was in helping others," he told her softly. "What you don't realize is you're allowed to have things for yourself, Susan. You were victimized by family circumstances two times in a row."

"I never saw myself as a victim." Her hands stilled and she absorbed Craig's closeness. This was what she craved, what her heart cried for—the intimacy he always established effortlessly with her.

"No, you wouldn't. You're too kind, Susan. I don't think you'd be in nursing if you didn't hold out hope for the hopeless. Coming to the barrio with me is about as hopeless as you can get, yet you know in your heart you can and do make a difference for these people." He held her luminous gaze, wanting desperately to kiss her parted lips. But Craig knew that if he moved too fast, all his grand dreams of a future with her would be shattered.

"And if you really didn't want to come out here, you wouldn't have. I know that. You do, too." He slowly rolled more bandages, a strained smile working its way across his mouth. "No, I don't believe you when you say you're a pessimist. I believe you've been hurt badly, and for now you might feel that way, but in time, the dreams will come back. The hope, too."

Susan absorbed his words—and the emotions behind them. She didn't speak for a long time, continuing simply to roll the cotton. "I always knew in my heart that you knew me better than anyone," she said finally.

"Yeah?"

She glanced at him from beneath her lashes. "Don't pat yourself on the back about it."

Chuckling, he felt another load lift from his shoulders. He was euphoric that Susan would talk this openly with him about such a painful topic. "No, believe me, I've learned my lesson in abject humility where you're concerned."

"You have a lot of humility, Craig, and I see that as something good in you, not something bad."

"In some ways, we're a lot alike," he offered quietly, holding her vulnerable gaze.

"I've been thinking lately that our similarities were the basis for our friendship," she admitted. "I was such an introvert!"

"You're shy," he amended gently. "Shy, pretty, vulnerable and giving. That's not a bad combination, in my book."

Susan shook her head. "My shyness kept me from having the gumption I needed sometimes."

"Oh?"

She shrugged. "Steve's folks were in deep denial about his disease. Steve was their only child, and they wouldn't believe me about the changes in his behavior. His father had taken him to so many doctors and got-

ten so many different guesses about how long he would
live. They wanted to believe that he would live another
ten years. When I went to them after he broke my nose
and begged them to help me, they accused me of starting a fight with him.''

Disbelief flared in Craig's eyes. "What?"

"They loved him, Craig. Don't blame them. They fell
apart when Steve died. They just loved him too much
and couldn't face the truth of the situation."

"So you were a convenient scapegoat?"

"I guess so." Susan sighed. "But I couldn't walk out
on him. What would that have made me? I know what
it feels like to be abandoned. I wasn't going to do that
to Steve. And his actions were dictated by the tumor,
not him."

Craig shrugged, needled by guilt. He'd abandoned
Susan, too. "I don't think anyone has the right answer
to a situation like that. At least, I don't."

"Well, I don't, either. Steve was like a hurt animal to
me. In some ways, he reminded me of my mother.
During her last days she was so helpless . . ." She knotted her hands. "I felt so sorry for him. I just wanted his
suffering to be over."

A fierce love for Susan's courage welled up in Craig.
He reached over, his hand closing on her fingers. Her
chin snapped up, her eyes widening. "You have a very
special kind of courage," he said huskily, his voice
laden with feeling. "I only hope that if I'm ever faced
with something as terrible as you've survived, that I
have half the courage you've shown."

Craig's grasp felt strong and tender at the same time.
Slowly, Susan turned her hand so that their fingers en-
twined. "You don't know how much better I feel since
you made me start talking about all of this."

With a grimace, he whispered, "If it hurts me this much to listen to it, I can't begin to imagine how you feel when you talk about it." He stared down at their hands. Susan's fingers were long, the nails blunt and clean. His own hand was darkly tanned with many lighter scars covering it, and dark hair sprinkled across the back. Light and dark. Sunlight and moonlight. Susan had lived through a hellish darkness, without the support even of family to help her survive it.

"Notice the color of our hands," he said slowly. "Yours is light and mine is dark."

"Yes?"

"When I first met you, Susan, I was struck by your lightness. It had nothing to do with your skin color, of course—it was that smile you always had, and the laughter dancing in your eyes. You always lifted my spirits, no matter how tough I thought things were for me at Annapolis."

The warmth of Craig's hand sent a tremor of longing through Susan. She gave a slight shrug. "And look at your hand. Look at the awful scars on it." She touched them lightly with her fingers.

"Your scars may be invisible," Craig said hoarsely, "but you carry them inside you, on your heart."

Her hand stilled over his. Closing her eyes, she whispered, "Craig, I'm not the same person you knew at Annapolis. Four years has changed me. I don't smile very much anymore. And I don't like to look in the mirror and see the darkness in my eyes. I've changed."

He turned and gently slid his hand along the clean line of her jaw. "No," he whispered, "you've matured. And I like what I see. I like who you are, Susan. You owe no apology to me or to anyone for who and what you are right now. Life has molded you, made you stronger in a lot of ways than before.'' He was wildly aware of the velvety softness of her skin beneath his fingertips. Susan's eyes, so blue and large, shimmered as he leaned down . . . down toward her parted, trembling lips.

As he ever so lightly brushed her lips with his, Susan took in a gasp of air. His fingers slid behind her neck, gently holding her captive as he tenderly offered himself. The second time he graced her lips, he felt her tension dissolve, felt her fingers—still interlocked with his own—grow boneless. This time, he molded his mouth to hers with a blinding certainty that he wanted to give back to Susan. Her mouth was soft, opening to his tentative exploration.

Susan's moist breath flowed across Craig's face as he pulled his hand free of her fingers and framed her face, tilting her head back just enough to explore her even more. In his heart he wanted to kiss away all the pain she'd ever experienced. He wanted to absorb all the sorrow that she'd held inside—to silently express that she was a woman of great emotional worth and that somehow he wanted to atone for the wrongs that he'd done to her.

Never had he drowned in a woman's kiss as he did now with Susan. Her mouth was at once yielding, giving and heated. Just the shy movement of her lips beneath his, the sweetness that was Susan alone, nearly moved Craig to tears. He molded his mouth to hers, feeling her returning fire, the raggedness of her breathing and the hesitant touch of her palms against his chest.

Slowly, ever so slowly, Craig eased back, opening his eyes and drowning in her blue gaze. Tenderly, he touched the slight pout of her lips with his fingertips.

He wanted to kiss her again, this time hungrily, giving in to his own body's driving need. But as he saw the tiny flecks of golden light in Susan's eyes, he felt humbled. Desire nearly convinced him to lean those scant inches and claim her lips again, but his heart silently counseled him that this was enough for now.

He allowed his hands to trail down her shoulders and arms to her hands as he ever so gradually pulled away. Susan's face glowed with such trusting openness that it took his breath away, and Craig stared at her in the gloom, wondering for the first time if there really was hope for them. Could the gold in Susan's eyes really be there for him? Did she want him as badly as he wanted her? Swallowing hard, he managed a small smile and pressed her hands between his.

"Just give us a chance," he heard himself plead hoarsely.

Chapter Nine

Susan awoke from a deep, healing sleep the next morning to the sweet scent of flowers. As she dragged open her eyes, she inhaled the unexpected fragrance. She had been lying on her side, her hands cradling her head. Now, blinking, she saw five small, white flowers lying next to her.

Craig. His name lingered hotly in her awakening memory as she pushed herself up into a sitting position. It was well past sunrise, and light was spilling brightly into the room. Craig was gone, his blanket neatly folded at the bottom of his cot. Memory of yesterday's tender, searching kiss made her close her eyes again and sink back into all the wonderful feeling it had evoked.

Opening her eyes, Susan wondered if she was in some fevered dream brought on by all the stress of the past. Picking up the daisies, she brought them to her nose and took in their heady scent. Only Craig would be this thoughtful, this sensitive to her needs. Just as he had been at Annapolis. She vividly recalled that night he'd brought her the daffodil at the dispensary after she'd gone through a particularly traumatic time working on a young cadet who'd been in a car accident. The nineteen-year-old boy had died right in front of her, which had shaken her terribly.

Her fingers gliding over the delicate white petals, Susan smiled fondly. Craig had known she had the duty that long-ago day, and as financially destitute as he was, he'd found a way to bring that single perfect flower to ease her pain. Now, holding the daisies lovingly, Susan felt her heart burst with such emotion toward him that she didn't know what to do.

"Ah, you're finally awake," Craig teased, slipping into the room.

Susan looked up and saw the happiness in his gray eyes. Craig was comfortably dressed in a dark blue polo shirt, jeans and white tennis shoes. His mouth, usually pulled taut, was relaxed. His mouth... Susan felt herself go shaky with need all over again.

Craig sauntered over and crouched down in front of her, smiling into Susan's still-sleepy eyes. Her hair was tousled, and he entertained the thought of taking her brush and pulling it through the dark brown strands to tame them into order. His smile deepened as he realized she was holding the daisies in her slender hands, as if they were a precious, wonderful gift.

"You like the flowers?"

"I love them." Susan stared up at him, aware of his enticing nearness. Her emotions were in chaos. "Where on earth did you find them in this concrete-and-glass jungle we're living in?"

"Now, how did you know *I* got them for you?" he teased, joy seeming to bubble up from inside him. Susan's lips still beckoned to him, and he ached to take her in his arms again. But he was afraid it would be too much, too soon. No, he must go slowly with Susan, allowing her time to adjust to the changing facets of their relationship. Craig remembered how her eyes had gone wide with shock when he'd assured her that he wasn't angry at her for the past in any way. Only then had he realized how much she'd needed to hear that from him.

"I know *you*," Susan said, clearing her throat. She laid the daisies aside. The look in Craig's eyes made her feel a yearning that cut through her with the loneliness of an eagle searching for her mate. Self-consciously, she rummaged around until she found her hairbrush on the nightstand. She had to have something to do beneath his hooded appraisal!

"I was out walking early this morning before the clinic opened and I found them growing in a vacant lot," Craig said in answer to her earlier question. The pleasure of watching Susan brush her hair flowed through him. Each of her gestures was simple and graceful, and he couldn't help but wonder what it would be like to have her hands slide across him with such smooth, certain strokes.

"It reminded me of the daffodil you gave me that time, remember? When you heard about the cadet dying in our dispensary at Annapolis?" The brush stilled in her hands as she held Craig's warm gaze. She watched his mouth curve slightly.

"Oh, yeah..." He managed a slight laugh and stood quickly, knowing that if he didn't, he was going to embrace her and kiss her breathless. Shoving his hands into his pockets, he muttered, "I didn't have much money then, did I? I figured you were a friend in need, so I risked getting caught swiping one of the daffodils from the academy garden."

Susan tilted her head and smiled deeply into his eyes. "You'll never know how much that daffodil meant to me. It was the only gift I ever got from you."

Craig frowned and nodded. Even now, Susan wasn't aware he'd waited in that restaurant with a dozen red roses and an engagement ring for her. Trying to make light of it, he said, "Yeah, I guess my stingy farm heritage was showing."

"Don't you dare try to cover up the truth, Craig Taggart! I knew how your family was struggling to make ends meet. I know you sent most of your paycheck home so your father could hire a man to help because of his back injury." Susan shook her finger at him. "Don't you dare say you're stingy! I happen to think your farm values are wonderful."

"You do?" Craig's heart sang with joy. Susan's face was flushed, and she was passionate in her defense of him.

"Yes," she muttered defiantly, "I do." She continued to brush her hair in quick, sure strokes for over a minute before she was able to speak again. Her voice dropped to a hesitant whisper, "And lately, I've realized what you gave me back at Annapolis was something money couldn't buy."

Craig stared at her, stunned by her admission. "What was that, Susan?"

"Care, unselfish concern, giving of yourself... You were always totally honest with me. I remember the day after I told you I was going to break up with Steve and I was feeling awful. Like the good friend you were, you tried to cheer me up. You suggested taking me to a movie. I wanted to go, but you didn't have the money to buy gas for your friend's car, much less the movie tickets.''

He shrugged at that painful memory. "That was right after my father's fourth back operation, and Mom needed every dime I could spare to get the mortgage paid on time every month. I didn't want them to lose the farm."

Without thinking, Susan reached out, her fingers closing over his. "I felt terrible for you when you admitted you didn't have the money."

"I was pretty bullheaded about you not paying for the gas or the movie," Craig recalled, thrilled that she was holding his hand. Gently, he placed his other hand over hers. "That wasn't right in this day and age, but I guess my pride got in the way."

Susan closed her eyes, feeling Craig's fingers stroking the back of her hand. His touch was galvanizing, sending longing singing through her. She looked at his somber features through her lashes. "We went through some crazy times together back then, didn't we?"

"Yes, we did. But I never regretted any of it, Susan. I liked being your friend," he told her quietly, holding her shimmering gaze. "I'm glad you came to Reed."

"When Karen wanted to come here, I thought, why not? She convinced me that diving back into trauma work was the best thing for me. She thought I was grieving, but I was numb emotionally. I saw Reed as a place to finally heal."

"So," Craig said slowly, stroking her hand, "you didn't have a lot of grief to work through?"

"I'm not sure, Craig. I sort of numbed out the last year with Steve. Most of the time I feel guilt."

He lifted her hand to his lips and pressed a kiss to her skin. Susan's eyes widened beautifully. "Over what?"

The tingles racing up her arm made Susan momentarily speechless. There was such naturalness between them, just as there had been years before—only then it was on a friendship level, without this romantic edge of intimacy. Craig, she realized, was a man of deep passion—a passion that dictated his feelings toward her. She tried to think coherently despite his hand around her own. "Guilt that I married him when I wasn't sure how much I loved him. I know he loved me so much."

His hand tightened. "You loved him the best you knew how. It has to be enough."

"I'm just beginning to realize that now," Susan admitted in a hushed tone.

"And get rid of the idea that you didn't love him enough. The only thing I'm angry about is that when he became abusive and emotionally unstable, his parents didn't send him somewhere that he could be cared for to keep you out of danger." His eyes blazed with anger and frustration. "I blame Steve's parents for that, not you. Not him."

Susan managed a slight smile. "You're good for my self-esteem," she joked weakly.

Craig held her shadowed blue eyes, seeing past pain that still needed to be worked out, he realized as he studied her in those quiet moments. "I think I know why we were given a second chance," he told her in a low, unsteady voice. "Let me help you piece your life back together again, Susan. We've always been good for each other."

Craig's words flowed across Susan, easing the guilt that threatened to eat her alive. "How?" she whispered.

Craig smiled and released her hand. He didn't want to, but he knew he didn't dare push her too fast. Right now, he was grateful that she trusted him. "Let me be your friend, like before, at Annapolis."

Susan stared at him in disbelief. "Yes," she managed to utter, "I'd like that." Was there really hope for her and Craig? She glanced down at his hands. He wore no wedding ring. Gathering her courage, she pointed to his ring finger.

"Aren't you in some kind of relationship?"

His mouth curved ruefully. Craig realized that most of their time had been spent exploring Susan's past, not his. He shrugged. "Not right now. I have been off and on in the past, but I've just never found the right lady, I guess."

Susan's heart took a plunging beat, and her mouth felt dry. "But you're such a good man—"

"A good catch?" he said.

Flushing, Susan nodded. "That, too." She forced herself to ask the most important question. "Why didn't you marry?"

"It just never worked out," he murmured. Then he lifted his eyes and met her confused gaze. "Maybe I had this dream about a dark-haired lady with the most beautiful blue eyes I'd ever seen. She captured my heart a long time ago, and no matter how many women I met, she never left my heart." He saw Susan's eyes go wide with shock.

Craig got to his feet. He'd said enough—perhaps too much. "I've got to get going, whether I want to or not. Dr. Espinoza and I are going over to the local junior high school to talk about AIDS prevention to the kids. I'll be back in a couple of hours at the most." If he didn't leave, Craig thought, he was going to kiss Susan again. The kiss they'd shared the night before in the darkness had arisen out of his need for her, in response to the yearning he'd seen in her eyes. That kiss had been healing—helping to close old wounds they shared from the past.

"I'm supposed to go with Maya to visit Consuela and her baby," Susan murmured, realizing she needed to be ready to leave in half an hour.

His head racing with new revelations, with more questions than he dared ask, Craig moved to the entrance of the room. "You always loved babies," he stated. And what a wonderful mother Susan would be. He lifted his hand. "I'll see you in a while."

Susan remained frozen in place on her cot, still working through Craig's surprising admission. He'd never married because he had dreamed of her. Holding the daisies, she didn't know whether to be frightened or happy. Life had always forced her to buckle beneath it and carry loads for others. She lifted her head and stared at the entrance where Craig had been standing moments before. What was he saying to her? That he loved her? That he'd always loved her and therefore wouldn't marry another woman?

Confused, Susan realized that only time and more honest, open talks with him would clear away the confusion. He wanted to be her friend, he'd said. Not her lover. Then why had he pressed that achingly beautiful kiss to her lips last night? He'd leaned over, claimed her lips, and for the first time in her life, Susan felt whole. He'd kissed her with a reverence that brought tears to her eyes even now as she remembered the act.

"Time," Susan warned herself, getting up. "We have to have the time." But would their hectic, pressured lives give them that precious commodity? As she shook out her blanket and folded it, Susan didn't have answers, just more questions. All too soon, their stint at the clinic would come to an end. They had come so far so soon by being here, removed from the demands that both had to respond to back at Camp Reed. Swallowing hard, she realized she couldn't hurry her heart. She was old enough, mature enough, to know that as she worked through her terrible guilt from the past, it would leave room in her heart for the future. A future she wanted more than anything to share with Craig Taggart.

"Welcome home!" Karen called, as Susan and Craig left the helicopter. The turbulence stirred up by the rotating blades buffeted them until they moved out from under their reach. Susan hugged Karen.

"I sure missed you," Karen said. She nodded a greeting to Craig, who was carrying Susan's duffel bag.

"I missed you, but I didn't miss this place," Susan responded with a laugh. Together, the three of them walked toward the hospital.

"Well, it's been nonstop craziness since you left," Karen told her. "But you look well rested. Much better, if my eyes don't deceive me."

Susan felt her cheeks heating up, and realized she was blushing. Craig walked confidently at her side, the duffel bag slung across his left shoulder. "It was like a vacation, Karen," she confided. "Clinic work is great. I helped deliver a baby girl!"

Karen grinned. "Don't tell me you're going to leave surgery for obstetrics?"

"I'm seriously thinking about it," Susan admitted. "Maybe when I get rotated next time, I'll put it on my dream sheet." The dream sheet was a paper that every military person filled out as to where they'd like to be stationed. There were three spaces, and often the last choice was granted, not the first. Dream sheets were exactly that: a dream. Still, Susan wasn't going to be deterred.

"If you're filling out a dream sheet," Craig told her somberly, "then put down Paris, France. I'm going to be an embassy officer for the U.S. ambassador there for two years."

Susan stared at him wide-eyed for a moment. She nearly stopped walking, the blow to her heart felt so real. Her mind whirling, she jerked her gaze from Craig's, reeling from the unexpected news. It was the last thing she had imagined. They'd just found each other.... No, he couldn't go!

Karen raised her eyebrows and grinned delightedly. "Just put it down three times, Susan. I think the boys in BUPERS, the Bureau of Personnel, will get the idea you want to go there."

Susan avoided her teasing, but she didn't miss the unhappy look on Craig's face as he slowed his step to walk at her side. The worry in his eyes broadcast what she wanted to know: he didn't want to leave any more than she wanted him to. The last week had gone by too quickly. Craig had backed off, given her the room to adjust to the new relationship that was forming between them. In small but important ways, he had let her know he wanted back into her life—and Susan had never felt happier...or more scared.

In the parking lot, Karen waved goodbye to them and headed back to the hospital, where she had duty. Susan was aware of Craig at her side.

"Tomorrow we both get back in harness," he told her, slowing his stride as they approached Susan's blue car. He glanced down at her. "Are you looking forward to it?"

Grimacing, she dug into her purse for the car keys. "Not really."

"I'm sorry to drop that bomb on you back there— about being ordered to Paris." He stared down at his polished black boots. "I don't want to go."

Avoiding his gaze, she whispered, "I don't want you to leave, either...."

Heartened, Craig said softly, "Well, maybe I can work something out. I'll have to see, okay?"

She nodded, unable to speak through the emotions that had risen in her at the possibility.

Craig glanced up at the pale sky and the gulls circling overhead. The last few days had been torturous for him. He wanted to hurry everything—hurry Susan toward a more permanent relationship—but his instincts told him he had to bide his time. He watched as the breeze blew several strands of dark hair across her cheek. Fighting the desire to reach out and gently remove them, he forced himself to remain still.

"Finally," Susan muttered, holding up the keys at last. "I hate purses."

He grinned and watched her open the door of her compact. "I wouldn't like to carry one," he agreed.

Susan knew Craig was trying to make her smile—to make her feel better. Giving him a tender look, she tossed her purse into the passenger seat. The last thing she wanted to do was leave his company. Raising her head, she met and held his dark gaze. "You don't have to, but I do," she retorted, managing a small smile.

Craig sobered as he stood there. "I'm going to miss you, Susan. All I have to look forward to is another week of duty at HQ before I can go back into the field."

"I'm going to miss what we shared, too," Susan admitted softly. She would miss Craig. Military duty played havoc with any relationship, but with their very separate duties, time together would be at a real premium.

With a shake of his head, he placed his hands on her shoulders. "Just take the day and relax. Get a good night's sleep." His fingers tightened on her shoulders. Craig wanted Susan to realize how much he cared for her. He *didn't* want to go back to HQ to push more paper around. Maybe he could eke out some kind of field assignment. More than anything, he wanted Susan to realize he wasn't going to lose her a second time.

Susan tried to smile, but didn't succeed. Longing to take that one small step into his arms, she remained where she stood. "That's good advice for you, too."

Glumly, Craig knew he had to leave. He wanted to lean down and kiss her, but he decided against it. He didn't want Dr. David or anyone else to know about their tentative, burgeoning relationship. It was too fragile yet to stand the teasing he knew Susan would take if anyone found out she was dating a recon marine.

"I'll try to drop by and see you tomorrow," he promised. "I don't know what the colonel has planned for me, but as soon as I do, I'll let you know."

Susan felt the power of his hand on her shoulder and ached to move those few additional inches and kiss Craig. She saw the desire burning his eyes. He had made no move to kiss her since that night at the clinic.

"I'll be okay," she told him. "Drop by when you can."

Craig was surprised and pleased by Susan's boldness. He allowed his hand to slip from her shoulder.

Catching her fingers, he squeezed them. "Tomorrow then?"

"Yes, tomorrow...."

Where had all their tomorrows gone? Susan wondered, as she quickly packed her duffel bag. The last two months had passed so swiftly that she felt nearly breathless.

The door to the nursing lounge opened and Susan looked up from her packing. It was Karen.

"Almost ready?" Karen asked.

"Just about."

"If I didn't love surgery so much, I'd be tempted to go with you and Craig and your clinic team," she teased.

"I'm glad to get the opportunity to work with another clinic," Susan agreed. The trauma team had been working nonstop, unfortunately, for two grueling months, and Susan was definitely ready for a change of venue. Besides, the field work would give her and Craig some badly needed time together.

"Craig will be team leader again?"

"Yes."

Karen grinned. "As much as you try to hide how much you like the guy, you can't, you know."

Frowning, Susan finished packing. "I just want to take it slow, Karen."

Sitting down, her friend nodded. "I understand. Not that I blame you after what you went through with Steve."

Attaching the metal snap over the end of the duffel bag, Susan glanced at her watch. In another twenty minutes Craig and his team would drop by to pick her up. She sat down, noticing that Karen looked more tired than usual.

"The pace of the place is getting to you, too," she said ruefully.

With a wave of her hand, Karen leaned back in the plastic chair. "I love it, though. Are you going back to National City?"

"No, it's a different clinic this time. A new one. Craig has been working with officials from Los Angeles to allow us to go into the southern section and work out of a Hispanic clinic there."

"Ohh, that area belongs to two rival gangs, the Bloods and the Crips," Karen warned, frowning.

"I know." The two large gang factions in Los Angeles had made frequent violence and shootings a normal part of life in that area. "I don't think it will be any more dangerous than National City. There were gangs there, too," Susan explained.

Rubbing her brow, Karen muttered, "I don't know. I have a bad feeling about this."

"That's because you would say or do anything to keep me here at your side in surgery," Susan teased.

Karen grinned. "I have been working you like a slave, haven't I?"

"You've been working yourself to death, too."

"I'll survive."

"I won't." Susan gave her friend a fond smile. "Thanks for okaying the orders letting me go to the clinic with Craig."

"Well," she said archly, "I have to do *something* that will put you two together in the same space at the same time. I've seen ninety percent of your dates broken either because of you being on call at the hospital or Craig and his recon team flying all over for international military exercises. You never seem to be together."

"Don't I know it," Susan agreed softly. She shook her head. "It seems like the moment I decided I did want to date Craig, the military decided to ship him all over the map."

"Recons are a breed apart—I warned you about that."

"But I didn't realize the teams would literally go all over the world."

"Welcome to reality. How do you think the wives and kids of these guys feel? Just like you do."

"Except I'm not married to Craig."

Karen eyed her without saying anything for a long moment. "He really likes you, you know."

"I know."

"You're scared."

Looking down at her sensible black leather shoes, Susan nodded. "It's stupid, I know. Why should I be afraid, Karen? Craig has been wonderful."

Reaching over, Karen patted her friend's arm. "Look, you're still healing from your marriage. Give yourself a break."

"That's what Craig says." She glanced worriedly at Karen. "But in four more months, Craig will be gone to France. And I'll be here. I can't follow him. I can't be with him. . . ."

"No easy answers, are there?"

Unhappily, Susan shook her head. "Never have been, in my experience."

"Never will be." Karen smiled slightly and rolled her eyes toward the ceiling. "Choices. Life is always full of choices. Do I love him and leave him? Do I commit to him? Do I not get close, so that when he leaves, it'll be easier on me?" She glanced at Susan. "I know the tightrope you're walking."

"You've been there yourself."

Sadness touched Karen's eyes. "Brother, have I."

Susan knew that at one time, Karen had fallen in love with a navy doctor and it had ended painfully, but her friend had shared none of the details. Susan ached for Karen, who was one of the finest women she knew. She deserved happiness, too. "You want the truth?"

"Nothing but."

"I vacillate about letting Craig know how much I care for him. I keep remembering he's leaving in four months." Biting her lower lip, Susan whispered, "I guess I'm too chicken to get involved with him on a serious level, Karen. I'm afraid of the future—of what it might hold if I tell him how much I care for him."

"It takes courage to live, Susan. It's much easier to run."

Susan cast a glance at her friend. "I won't disagree."

"You're afraid to really reach out and love again. That's what it boils down to."

The words hurt deeply, and Susan hung her head. Swallowing with difficulty, she rasped, "There's something inside of me that keeps telling me I don't deserve him. It's like an old tape or something."

"That's called a conditioned reflex. Joyce, the shrink, would tell you that."

"Where does it come from?"

"Your past." Karen shook her head, her voice low with feeling. "Look what happened to you, Susan: you got locked into caretaking, always giving, from the time you were twelve years old. First your mother, then Steve. When you're in a position of giving everything away all the time, down to your very soul, you don't know how to act when someone like Craig wants to give back to you. It's so foreign to you that you have a tough time knowing how to accept it. You only know how to give." Her mouth quirked. "A lot of women have the same problem. When they're faced with a truly healthy give-and-take relationship, they bolt and run."

Miserably, Susan acknowledged that the shoe fit. "I don't know what to feel about Craig," she admitted. "When I'm around him, my emotions veer from sheer terror to a happiness that I've never known. But you're right—I am uncomfortable when Craig gives to me. It's hard to accept without instantly turning around and giving back to him."

"That's why they call it a conditioned reflex, Susan. The only person who can break that old tape and set you free is you. Craig can't do it for you. I can't do it for you. You have to want to be free."

With a sad little laugh, Susan held her friend's kind gaze. "Wouldn't you think a woman trapped by her past *would* want to be free—to bolt out of her cage the moment the door was opened?"

Karen sat up and clasped her hands on her lap. "I think it's time to tell you about an experiment that a group of scientists did back in the '60s, Susan. I read about it in one of my psychology classes at med school. I've never forgotten it, and maybe it will help you.

"The scientists had this large cage. Half of the floor delivered a mild electric shock, the other half didn't. They put a dog in the cage, and it quickly learned to stay on the side that didn't have the shock. The scientists then switched which side had the shock, and again, the dog learned to avoid that half of the cage. In the third test, they electrified the entire floor. The dog got the shock no matter where it stepped. At first it was confused, then panicked. Finally, the dog gave up, lay down on the floor and no longer tried to figure out how to avoid the shock. In the fourth test the scientists kept the floor electrically activated but opened the cage door so the dog could leap out."

Karen became grim as she stared at her friend. "They were stunned when the dog didn't scramble off the floor that was delivering mild shocks, and make its leap to freedom. They concluded that an animal exposed to unavoidable pain will eventually adapt to it, so that when it's given a chance for freedom, the natural instinct to run has been negated. The dog stayed. Women stay in abusive, violent relationships, too." She sighed and added, "Psychologically, it's called learned helplessness. It's normalizing the abnormal until you accept the condition as normal. So, like the dog, when you're given the chance to flee or make a change from that conditioning, you don't. You can, but you don't unless there's help through friends, family, a therapist or whatever, to help you realize that the situation really was abnormal."

Susan was quiet for a long time, absorbing Karen's words. "It must have been horrible for that poor dog," she whispered.

"I'm sure it was. The shocks were mild, but that doesn't take away from the inhumanity of the test. I felt sick to my stomach when I read about it, but I never forgot its lesson." She held Susan's bleak gaze. "And you shouldn't, either."

"You're saying that I became desensitized by Steve's abusiveness and neediness until I thought it was normal and no longer thought about trying to escape from it?"

"What do you think?"

"I think you're right."

"Maybe that's why you're afraid of what Craig is offering you, Susan. He's offering you freedom from the painful life you've been conditioned to accept as normal."

A warmth stole through Susan, laced with hope. "I am like that dog. At first I tried to avoid the negative, and when I couldn't, I did panic."

"You panicked, but you didn't run, because there was no place for you *to* run," Karen murmured. "You see marriage as a permanent commitment. You took the marriage vow 'for better or worse' to heart, and you stuck it out with Steve. In a way, it was a trap you couldn't escape except through Steve's death."

Rubbing her hands together, Susan nodded, tears in her eyes. "I'm still not sorry I stayed, Karen."

"I'm proud that you did. But it took a terrible toll on you."

Sniffing, Susan wiped her eyes and tried to smile. "Emotionally, I'm warped."

"But not destroyed," Karen whispered, tears in her own eyes. "The good news is, if you've got the courage to reach out to Craig, to walk with your fear, you've got a chance of getting back your normal feelings and emotions. He'll teach you, if you let him, about the positive male and a different kind of life."

Taking a shaky breath, Susan shook her head. "I've been such a fool. . . ."

Getting up, Karen came over and gave her friend a hug. "No, you were caught in a trap. But you see that now, and I know you well enough that you won't let it stop how you feel toward Craig. For once in my life, I'd like to see a happy ending somewhere." She gazed down at Susan. "I'm not saying Craig is perfect. He isn't. A relationship takes two people working all the time to make it successful. Life has no fairy-tale endings, but it can be happy and rewarding. I think you can have that with Craig."

Giving Karen a squeeze of thanks, Susan got up. Any moment now, the official military vehicle would arrive to take them to southern L.A. "Thanks," she whispered, quickly wiping away the last of her tears.

Handing her her duffel bag, Karen smiled. "You're a fighter, Susan. My bet is on you to win."

Chapter Ten

Craig briefly wondered if Susan had been crying as he met her just outside the hospital emergency room. As he took the duffel bag from her hands, he gave her a smile he hoped would let her know just how glad he was to see her. The ragged smile she gave him in return made his heart beat more in fear than anything else. Susan's cheeks were flushed, and her eyes too bright, he thought, as he stowed her bag in the rear of the dark green station wagon with its USMC insignia on the door.

The three other team members selected for this L.A. trip, all of whom knew Susan, waited in the car. Susan followed Craig to the rear of the vehicle, where she'd be sitting, while he sat up front next to the driver. As he shut the door, he turned briefly to her.

"You okay?"

"Yes, fine. I'm fine," she insisted.

Craig stared down into her soft, luminous eyes. When her lower lip trembled, it was nearly his undoing. He opened his mouth, wanting to say so much, but as usual, it wasn't the time or place. He looked up to see Karen standing just inside the ER area at the window. She raised her hand in greeting, but even she looked grim. Craig waved in return, then momentarily touched Susan's elbow as he guided her around the car.

"You've been crying," he said in a low voice.

Susan gave him a wobbly smile. "Yes. But it's okay, Craig. Really." She slowed her step and he released her arm as he opened the door for her. Wanting so badly to speak, but knowing his men were within earshot, she whispered, "Tears of happiness. Don't worry...." And she slid into the car.

The ride to Los Angeles was long—too long, in Craig's opinion. Typical of Susan, she was the introvert in the group and didn't say much, although the other team members laughed and joked, happy to be free of the military base for a while, to be headed for different adventures. Every time Susan did speak, he honed in on the tone of her voice and tried to detect if she was still upset.

Tears of happiness. What was she talking about? For the last week he had been unable to meet with her because of recon duties. Frustrated at being blocked time and again from seeing her because of military priorities, Craig found himself wanting to howl like a wolf too long without his mate. Seven days of not seeing Susan, then realizing she had tears in her eyes, had left him shaken. Everything about their relationship was so tenuous, so fragile.

Worried, Craig clenched his teeth, afraid that he was slowly losing Susan when he'd never really gained her

back. The last two months he'd seen her slowly slipping away from him, had noted the fear in her eyes
again, and he'd been helpless to stop her retreat. What
was she afraid of? Craig sat tensely in his seat, locked
in a private hell. He loved Susan. Desperately. Yet he
would not coerce her, force her or trick her into returning what he yearned for her to share with him. *One kiss.*
With it, she'd melted into his arms, seared his aching
soul with her love, if only for a moment.

Closing his eyes, Craig thought he would never forget her wonderful, soft mouth pressed shyly against his.
Would never forget the softness of her breasts against
him, or her long, slender fingers opening and closing
against his chest as their lips joined and their souls
seemed to become one through the fire of their sharing.

Wrestling with fear that loomed larger than ever before, Craig prayed that the Los Angeles clinic would
give them the time they so desperately needed with each
other. His mind bounced restlessly over a number of
things that could have upset Susan. The trauma unit
was hard on her emotionally, he knew. Why she continued to put herself on the firing line when her feelings were so susceptible to such horror was beyond him.
Was it a leftover fragment from the past, when Susan
had loyally cared for her dying mother? For Steve? He
had so many questions. Perhaps this clinic trip would
provide some answers.

Dr. Miguel Orlando welcomed them to the shabby-
looking clinic that stood surrounded by what Craig
considered some of the most appalling third-world
conditions he'd ever seen. The National City clinic
seemed a palace in comparison. The buildings sur-

rounding this place were dilapidated, the poor without work and hanging out on every corner. The ethnic mix included Asians, Latinos and African Americans, all stirred into the giant cauldron of south Los Angeles.

Introductions were quickly made and Craig had no time to pull Susan aside and speak privately with her. But her eyes no longer held tears, he noted, and her cheeks had lost their fiery flush. She gave him a brave smile, her eyes wide and guileless as she met his searching gaze. Tearing his attention away from her, Craig walked into the clinic with the Hispanic doctor and two of his nursing assistants.

"We are very poor here, Captain Taggart," Orlando said with a sweep of his arm as they stood in the foyer of the clinic.

Craig looked around. Everything was in a state of disrepair, although the white walls were freshly painted, the tile floor, yellowed with years of use, was clean, and the two nurses obviously worked very hard to keep the building as antiseptically sterile as possible under the circumstances.

"Your place looks fine," Craig reassured the short, heavily built doctor.

"We are more than grateful that you have come, *Capitán*. I am always short-handed here. My two nurses work fourteen hours a day, six days a week. I am blessed with their hard work and care, for without them, this clinic would not be open."

Susan approached the nurses. One of them, dressed in a loose cotton muumuu of bright orange, was in her sixties, her round, soft face breaking into a smile that revealed several missing front teeth. But the warmth dancing in her eyes at Susan's presence was genuine and undisguised.

The other woman, Dolores Naldo, was even older, with coal black eyes and dark gray hair pulled into a bun atop her head. She, too, gave Susan a welcoming smile and reached out her spindly hand to grip Susan's.

"Welcome, *señora*, welcome."

"Gracias, Señora Naldo," Susan murmured. She felt like hugging the two older women, taking hope from them. They were wonderful mentors for any young woman because, despite their age, they came from the heart, and their worn faces mirrored their belief in humanity.

"Come, come," Dr. Orlando said with a smile, "I will show you around."

The team was circumspect and silent as Dr. Orlando proudly showed off his facility. The day was drawing to a close, the sunset orange against the heavy pollution that cloaked the city. Craig followed the doctor from one room to another, noting the lack of even such basic equipment as an extra stethoscope. The clinic was obviously impoverished. Tonight he'd make a call to Reed to see if he could get some additional medical items released and driven down to them by tomorrow morning.

Orlando and his nurses were fighters on the front lines of war on poverty, as far as Craig was concerned. The two old nurses had Susan bracketed, he noted, chatting animately to her about their duties and where the various medical items were kept, opening and closing many drawers in each room. He'd seen the look in Susan's eyes—proof that these people's plight touched her as deeply as it did him.

Back in the foyer, Craig ordered his men to bring in their equipment to store in the clinic overnight.

"Captain," Orlando said, "you asked that your team stay with people from our clinic, and this has been arranged. You will accompany me to my humble home three blocks from here. Señora Dolores Naldo will open her home to your nurse. She lives only two blocks from the clinic. The other men of your team will stay with my cousins, who live a mile from here. Is this all right with you?"

Craig nodded. "That's fine. I was hoping that there could be some room here at the clinic, but that's okay." He didn't like the gang problems here. In National City, the gangs respected the clinic. But here in L.A., the clinic's walls had graffiti all over them, as if the building were right in the middle of the war. Craig felt uneasy despite the iron bars over the windows.

Susan moved next to Craig. "Doctor, what about the gangs around here? How active are they?"

He sighed and opened his hands. "They are very active, and that is why your team stays with either my nurses or my family."

"Do you have a pact with them to leave you and the clinic alone?" Craig asked.

The doctor shrugged sadly. "Members of both gangs have promised not to harm us or the people who work here, because we care for them."

"And the clinic?"

"No, Captain, the clinic is not necessarily safe after dark. During the day, yes. At night, things change around here. We sit in the middle of two warring territories, and bullets have hit the walls of our clinic before." He gestured to the broken window to the right of them. "I don't have the money to replace it or I would."

Grimly, Craig looked down at Susan. If he'd have known how dangerous this was going to be, he wouldn't

have allowed her to come along. Unfortunately, he'd
been out on recon assignment, and the setup of work
with this clinic had been handled entirely by an office
pogue from headquarters who didn't always know how
to ask the right questions.

"And Señora Naldo's house is safe from gang attack?" he demanded.

"Sí, sí, yes, yes. She is considered one of the old, wise
women in the Latino quarter. No gang member would
dare to harm her or her home. Your nurse will be safe
there, I assure you."

Still not liking the situation, Craig knew there was
little he could do. At least they all wore civilian clothes,
which was good, since gang members hated uniforms
because they represented authority.

A young Hispanic man came running into the clinic,
speaking rapidly in Spanish to the doctor. Craig
scowled.

"Doctor! You must come quickly! Two gang members have shot my father and my brother! Hurry! The
ambulances won't come into the area." The boy reached
out, gripping Orlando's sleeve. "Please," he sobbed,
"we need your help! Help!"

Gasping, Susan looked over at Dr. Orlando. She saw
Craig move toward the door.

"Susan, you stay here," Craig ordered. "I'll take my
team with the doctor. You stay with Señora Naldo, and
you'll be fine."

Openmouthed, Susan moved aside. The younger
nurse, the doctor and the four marines quickly left the
clinic as the fiery orange of the sky deepened. Shivering, Susan watched from the door as they ran to the
marine vehicle and got in.

"It will be fine," Señora Naldo whispered, patting her shoulder. "The boy lives a mile from here. He must have run all the way." She clucked sympathetically. "We will pray for his father and brother. Come, let us do some last-minute work before I lock the clinic doors. Then you will come home with me."

Torn, Susan hesitated. She realized the folly of walking outside in the gang-infested neighborhood, so she turned and followed Señora Naldo to a room where the medical supplies would be stored. Her heart beating erratically, Susan tried to concentrate on what she was doing, but she worried for Craig. Worried that any member of the team could be randomly shot by some young, unthinking gang member.

Her hands shaking as she put away the bottles of vaccine in the small, dented refrigerator, Susan couldn't shake the ominous overtone of their assignment to this clinic. This was a war zone, she realized belatedly. A genuine war zone.

Wearily, Craig climbed out of the military station wagon that he'd parked in the driveway of Dr. Orlando's small, modest stucco home. It was nearly two hours later, and the sky over Los Angeles gleamed as it reflected millions of lights from the millions of homes. He couldn't see any stars overhead at all. It was depressing.

The front of his shirt was streaked with blood. All he wanted to do was call Señora Naldo's home and make sure that Susan was there and safe. Then he would take a hot shower and wash away the dried blood and sweat.

Dr. Orlando showed him to the small living room filled with bamboo furniture. Sitting on the edge of the couch, Craig dialed the Naldo residence.

"Hello?"

"May I speak to Susan Evans, please?" he asked in Spanish. The woman on the other end wasn't Señora Naldo.

"¿*Que?*"

"The nurse," Craig calmly repeated, "from the marine base, Camp Reed."

"Oh, oh! My mother and the nurse are still at the clinic."

"What?"

"Sí, they are taking inventory and will be home soon. Shall I have her call you?"

His hand tightening on the phone, Craig growled, "No, thanks." He hung up, his heart beating hard. Dr. Orlando had said it was dangerous to be out after dark. What did Señora Naldo and Susan think they were doing? Leaping to his feet, his fatigue evaporating, Craig walked quickly through the house to find the doctor.

Dr. Orlando, who was a widower, was out in the kitchen preparing them an evening meal. Craig halted at the entrance, and he looked up from the stove where he was cooking.

"Is something wrong, Captain?"

"Yes, there is. Señora Naldo and my nurse are apparently still over at your clinic. What's this about inventory?"

"Ahh, I forgot, Captain!" Orlando quickly turned off the stove. "I am sorry. Before you arrived, my nurses were taking inventory. In the rush, I forgot to tell Señora Naldo to stop and finish it tomorrow." He shook his head. "Come, we must go over there now and escort them home. It is not safe at night for women to walk alone."

His heart pounding, Craig moved quickly toward the door of the house and pulled it open. At that moment, there was a huge explosion from the vicinity of the clinic. A fireball, massive, rolling and thunderous, rose above the trees and homes.

"Oh, my God!" Craig rasped. "Susan!"

Craig leapt into the station wagon, sure that the clinic had been bombed. Orlando tore open the other door and jumped in. "Hurry!" he cried. "Oh, *Dios,* hurry!"

As he wrenched the wheel of the vehicle around, the rubber screaming against the pavement, Craig died inside. A second fireball thundered skyward, the sonic impact moving outward from the explosion. He slammed his foot down on the accelerator, the car careening drunkenly down the darkened, empty streets toward the clinic. Had the rival gang retaliated against Dr. Orlando because he'd gone to the aid of the wounded father and brother?

Fighting back tears, Craig raced toward the clinic. As the car screeched around the corner, he saw for the first time what the two explosions had done. One entire end of the clinic looked as if a rocket had hit it. Uncontrolled fire was erupting and leaping skyward. Men, women and children were running everywhere because the clinic was lined on all sides by hovels where they lived.

Susan! Where was she? Oh, God, had she died in the horrendous explosion? Slamming on the brakes a block from the clinic, Craig leapt out. From the opposite direction came at least four fire trucks, their lights flashing furiously through the darkness. Hundreds of people were milling about in the general area. Frantically, Craig sprinted toward the clinic. Susan!

Suddenly, Craig heard gunshots. Automatically, the hundreds of onlookers began scattering like sheaves of wheat before an invisible wind. Shrieks filled the air. Pandemonium set in. Craig slammed down on the biting surface of the asphalt, his hands over his head. More gunshots rang out. But what direction were they coming from? People raced and leapt over him, some stumbling into one another. The wail of police sirens began to fill the air.

Dazed, Craig got to his knees. He couldn't believe the size of the crowd of onlookers—the curious, the horrified. Although his hands and elbows had been torn when he hit the ground, he knew he had to make it to the clinic before the police and fire fighters set up roadblocks. Susan was either in the building or— He couldn't face that possibility. Wiping tears from his eyes, Craig began to zigzag rapidly through the crowd toward the burning building.

For the next hour, he looked frantically for Susan. The clinic was a raging, out-of-control fire and the heat from it drove him back whenever he tried to get close. A policeman grabbed him and hauled him behind a barricade. He hadn't been able to find anyone—not Señora Naldo, not Susan, not even the men of his team. Once he saw Dr. Orlando with the fire captain, his face wet with tears. Bitterly, Craig wiped the tears from his own blackened face with the back of his hand as he stood, exhausted, behind the barricade. Was Susan dead? More tears leaked into his eyes. Was she one of the charred remains to be found after the fire fighters put out the blaze? His throat closed on a sob and he turned away, not wanting anyone to see him cry. Intuitively, he knew Susan had been in the clinic.

Unable to stand the pain, Craig turned, heading toward the neighborhood where Dr. Orlando had told him Señora Naldo lived. By some small chance, Susan might be there with the old nurse. Maybe...

Señora Naldo's house was empty. No one answered the door. Bleakly, Craig looked around the darkened neighborhood. All the people from at least a four-block area had left their homes to go and watch the fire at the clinic. Anguish serrated Craig's heart as he turned and trudged wearily back in that direction. He would check with the ambulances set up at one end of the street. Maybe, by some chance, Susan was there.

Stumbling through the crowd, Craig gripped a burly ambulance attendant, a man in his late twenties. "Have you seen a woman named Susan Evans? She's got brown hair and blue eyes."

"No, sir," he said, "I haven't seen anyone like that." He grimaced. "Hell, in a place like this, you're lucky to know anyone except the people you work with."

His vision blurring, Craig wearily trudged between the ambulances to check for himself. A number of people had been injured by the blast—particularly people who lived close to the clinic. *Susan.* Oh, God, he loved her. He'd lost her. The pain was almost too much for him to bear, and he stopped, swayed, then caught himself. Lifting his head, Craig knew he had to know for sure. He had to see Susan's body before he'd accept that she had died in the fiery explosion. Tears trickled down through the stubble of his beard.

Trying to control his rampant, shattered emotions, Craig made his way back through the groups who worked unerringly at the ambulances. Where to go? He considered the morgue, but it was too soon to do that. Right now, he couldn't bear to see the black plastic body bags. Wiping his mouth, Craig decided to keep searching through the crowds. It took everything he had to look into the faces around him, praying he'd find Susan among them. On the opposite side of the clinic, another first-aid station had been set up. His heart started pumping erratically. Maybe Susan was there... or Señora Naldo.

A huge, tightly packed crowd surrounded the small station. Craig forced himself among frantic, helpless parents of children who had been injured in the blast. A woman paramedic with blond hair was closest to him.

"Excuse me!" He gripped her arm to halt her.

"Yes?"

"I'm looking for Susan Evans. Is she here?"

The paramedic gave him an exasperated look. "I'm busy! We've got people dying in there. I don't know anyone named Evans. Please—" she pulled out of his grasp "—everything's a mess. I don't know who's here. Doctors and nurses from all over the area are assisting. You're just going to have to find her on your own."

Numbly, Craig stepped aside as the paramedic rushed by him. He pushed his way among the gurneys, patients and fire fighters, his heart sinking. Shouts filled the air, doctors barking orders and nurses running in response. Everything was in chaos as he slowly examined the area. The stench of smoke filled his nostrils, as did other, worse odors. His stomach rolled threateningly.

She wasn't in the first-aid area. Disappointment cut through him as he made his way toward the fire truck to see if they were ready to begin searching the heated rubble of the clinic for bodies. Things were less hectic now that the blaze was under control. He halted at one fire truck, searching. A black fireman frowned and moved toward him, scowling.

"Hey, get outa here! You ain't supposed to be here."

"I'm looking for a woman, Susan Evans. She was in that clinic with an older Mexican woman. I—"

The fire fighter halted, some of the anger leaving his sweaty, grimy features. "I'm sorry. We can't get near that clinic yet. It's too hot to search for. . ."

"Well, if I described her—"

"I'm sorry." The man glanced back at his team. "I have a lot to do, buddy, so why don't you go see the police about this problem? I can't help you. . . ."

Craig turned away, tears burning his eyes. Moving between the fire trucks, he heard a woman's voice, high, off-pitch. Exhaustion made him dizzy, and he slowly turned on his heel toward the sound.

"Craig!"

What he saw froze him in his tracks. *Susan!* It was Susan! He blinked uncertainly, time slowing down to single frames as it did during combat. Susan's face was blackened and dirty, her white blouse splattered with blood. Her hair was tangled and her blue eyes were red rimmed. She was running toward him, her arms outstretched, her mouth contorted in a cry, his name on her lips.

Craig had no time to prepare for her throwing her arms around his neck. Staggering backward off balance, he caught himself, his arms moving around her slender form.

"Susan. Susan, are you okay?" He looked down at her dirty features. Her black pupils were huge, telling him she was in shock.

With a hysterical laugh, she said, "Yes! Oh, God, Craig, I thought you were dead!"

"Me?" he croaked, framing her face with unsteady hands. He anxiously studied her. Craig saw the paths of tears through the dirt that marred her velvety skin. Her eyes were huge, filled with fresh tears.

"Oh, Craig," Susan sobbed, and she reached up hesitantly, as if afraid to touch his darkly bearded cheek. "You're okay. You're okay. I thought— Oh, God, I thought you were dead! The blasts, the bombs hit everywhere! They hit the clinic," she babbled hysterically.

"Shh," he ordered thickly, capturing her, holding her tightly against him. Craig buried his face in her smoky hair. "Just let me hold you," he said, his voice cracking.

Susan murmured his name over and over again, burying her head against his chest, surrendering to Craig's superior strength.

"I thought you were dead," she repeated tearfully. "I tried to get away, to find you. I tried to find Dr. Orlando's house but I couldn't. All I could see was the black smoke rising from the clinic. No one knew where you, the team or Dr. Orlando were. After the gang threw bombs at the clinic, I thought you'd been killed." Susan sobbed. "I was so afraid I'd turn around and see you dead on a gurney over in the ambulance area."

Craig tightened his hold on Susan as she sobbed wildly against him. "I'm okay, okay," he quavered. "We're both okay." And he shut his eyes, squeezing her against him for fear that she might disappear. He felt as if he were in a dream—a frantic dream of his own making—and that if he let go of Susan, she would evaporate before his eyes. He kissed her hair, her temple, her damp cheek. Blindly, he sought and found her lips as she lifted her chin to meet his questing mouth.

A groan started deep within Craig as he claimed her parting lips with a hunger that overwhelmed him. Susan's mouth was soft, haunting and sweet-tasting as he moved with desperation against her. She's alive! his mind screamed as he tasted her mouth, molded it to his and gloried in the returning fire she shared with him. Alive! They were both alive! How long he stood there, capturing Susan in his torrid embrace, he had no idea.

Finally, he tore his mouth from hers, breathing hard, his eyes narrowed on her flushed, dirty features. Susan's blue eyes were dazed, and as he tried to control his need to prove that she really was alive, Craig realized the extent of her shock. He rubbed his hands gently up and down her shoulders and back, gradually realizing that Susan had never been in a wartime situation. He had— in Grenada, Panama and Desert Storm. Trying to think, trying to overcome his own selfish need of her, he remembered back to the first time he'd come under attack.

"Where were you going?" he demanded unsteadily.

"What?"

She was looking at him, confused, so Craig slowly repeated his question. When he finally started taking inventory of her, he realized that her shirtsleeve on her upper arm had been torn. Upon closer examination, he realized that she'd been injured—more than likely by a shard of flying glass. He discovered another tear in her shirt on her forearm, which was bloody. The wounds weren't deep, but Craig knew what even small wounds could do to a person who wasn't prepared for such violence. The resulting shock often took at least a day or two to come out of. Susan was in shock.

"I, uh, I'm so tired, Craig...." Susan whispered. She closed her eyes and gripped his arms. "I'm so glad you're alive...."

"Come on," Craig whispered grimly, placing his arm around her waist and making her walk, "you're coming with me."

She gave him a confused look. "With you?"

His mouth turned down into a thin line. "That's right. With me. What you need right now is a little care. You need to be held." And he sure as hell couldn't do it here. Susan didn't try to argue with him or move out of his firm embrace. Instead, she wearily leaned against him, her head resting on his shoulder.

Craig led her through the thinning crowd to where he'd left the marine station wagon. The other members of his team had found it, too, and were waiting there. This was no place for any of them, Craig decided, rapidly devising a plan. After telling Dr. Orlando they were leaving, Craig ordered everyone into the vehicle. Luckily, no one but Susan had been injured.

Opening the front door, Craig placed Susan in the passenger seat. In all the pandemonium, he'd left the keys in the car, but through some miracle, no one had stolen the vehicle. Now he twisted the key in the ignition and the engine roared to life.

Casting a quick glance at her, he saw that she sat tensely, her hands in her lap. Her pupils were large and black, and the slackness on her facial features was typical of someone suffering from shell shock.

"Hang on," he told her encouragingly as he put the car into gear, "we're going someplace safe."

Craig knew Los Angeles well, because he'd visited many times, whenever he wanted to get away from base. He'd spent a number of weekends near the beach, and he knew of many small but well-kept hotels. Craig knew of one nice little French-owned hotel, *La Petite Fleur*— the little flower—south of Los Angeles, only about an hour's drive away.

This particular inn was quaint, out of the way and terribly private, embedded in groves of silver-barked eucalyptus in the hills south of the city—the perfect place, he'd discovered, to forget about the rigors of military life.

After dropping the other three team members at a nearby hotel with orders to rest until he picked them up tomorrow at noon, Craig drove on to *La Petite Fleur*. The two-story structure was completely surrounded by a black wrought-iron fence, with colorful bougainvillea climbing up the historic building's stucco walls, covering them with vivid colors. The rates here were high, and Craig knew most of the patrons were rich businessmen. Few marines could afford to pay a hundred and fifty dollars a night for the pleasure of quaint solitude.

Susan's head was bowed, her hands pressed to her eyes when Craig pulled up in front of the hotel. Worriedly, he got out of the car, and a young man dressed in a starched white shirt and black pants opened the wrought-iron gate for him. Glancing back at Susan, Craig called, "I'll be back in just a minute."

If she heard him, she didn't acknowledge it. Craig was torn between taking her with him to sign in at the desk and leaving her alone in the car. But he wanted to spare Susan the embarrassment of being seen in their present condition. A lovely young girl, her black hair long and shiny, smiled questioningly at him as he approached the desk.

"I need a room with a shower and a lot of privacy," he told her, digging into the back pocket of his filthy jeans to retrieve his billfold.

The girl hesitated, looking him up and down, then went over and opened her book. "Sir, we have a lovely suite, a corner room. That will be very private."

"Fine," Craig muttered, "I'll take it. How much?"

"Two hundred dollars a night."

It was highway robbery, but Craig didn't care. He knew the woman who ran this hotel, a Frenchwoman whose husband had been killed during the war between France and Vietnam. Marie Gerard was in her fifties and every inch the smart, stylish businesswoman. He filled out the proffered registration card and counted out bills in twenties on the highly polished teakwood counter.

"Make sure we're not disturbed," he growled as he picked up the key.

The girl nodded uncertainly, her eyes wide with curiosity. "Of course. Mr. Taggart."

As he hurried down the redbrick sidewalk lined with a profusion of flowers and shaded by tall eucalyptus trees, Craig's gaze fixed on Susan. Her brow rested against her raised knees and her arms were wrapped around her shins. The adrenaline he was sure she had operated on for so many hours was leaving now, and she was not only in shock but physically exhausted as well. Craig helped her out of the car, noticing that the young bellman was waiting to take their bags.

"No luggage," Craig announced shortly. "Just get the valet to park the car."

"Yes, sir!" He hurried off to find the valet.

"Come on," Craig coaxed as he placed his arm around Susan's waist. She stumbled, and he tightened his grip. "It's all right," he soothed, guiding her up the steps and into the lobby. Craig pushed the button to call the brightly polished brass-and-copper elevator. As the doors slowly opened, he led Susan inside.

"Craig? Where are we? What's going on?" Susan lifted her chin and stared up at his grim, taut features.

"I'm taking care of you. You're in shock, Susan. You need a little care, that's all."

Susan felt her knees becoming weak as she walked out of the elevator and down a long, blue-carpeted hall-way. Everything was so quiet. She could smell her own singed hair and the metallic odor of blood on her clothes. Frilly white curtains with ruffles covered a window at the end of the hall. The blue wallpaper was sprinkled with tiny white rosebuds. Susan felt light-headed and gripped Craig's arm as he opened an or-nately carved door.

"Dizzy?" he demanded as he guided her into a plush suite of rooms.

"Very. Just . . . let me sit down. I—I'll be okay."

Craig pulled out a French provincial chair from the Queen Anne desk, carefully helping Susan sit before he left her to close the door quietly behind them, shoving the dead bolt into place. Under no circumstances did he want anyone bothering them. All his focus, his emo-tions, funneled into helping Susan.

Kneeling before her, he quickly removed her dirty white shoes. Straightening, he smiled into her half-closed eyes as he began to unbutton her blouse.

"Wh-what are you doing?"

"Undressing you," he said matter-of-factly. "I'm going to get you into a hot shower, Susan. You're skin's as cold as ice and you're trembling." Quickly, he shed the blouse and threw it to one side on the blue carpet.

"But—"

"Hush, babe. You're in shock. Come on, stand up. Put your hands on my shoulders while I get these slacks off you."

"Everything's like a nightmare," she whispered, standing and gripping Craig's shoulders as he unbuttoned her trousers.

"I know it is. It's always like this when you've been in combat. Your mind shorts out, Susan. You don't think two thoughts without screwing it up. I know. I've been there. Come on, lift your foot. That's my lady...."

Leading Susan, now clothed only in her white cotton bra and underpants, into the bathroom, Craig kept a grip on her upper arm while he leaned into the glass stall and turned on the faucets. The color was rapidly leaching out of her face, and he hurried to stop the toll that shock was taking on her. Making her sit down on a small stool, he quickly appraised the two shrapnel wounds on her left arm. They were fairly deep but not serious. The blood had dried, flaking and cracking off as he ran his fingers over it.

Steam was rising from the stall, and Craig got to his feet and adjusted the temperature. Shutting the bathroom door, he quickly removed his shoes. Grabbing a washcloth hanging near the basin, he brought Susan to her feet.

"Come on, we're going to take a shower, babe."

Craig drew Susan inside the shower and slid the door closed. She was like so much putty in his hands, offering no resistance. He washed her free of the stench of smoke and perspiration and the blackened grime that streaked her face and hands. He cleaned out her injuries with the hotel's fragrant French milled soap, and the scent of lilacs combined with the steam rising around them.

Craig was soaked, his shirt and jeans clinging to him, but he didn't care. As he scrubbed Susan's hair clean, he saw a bit of color returning to her cheeks and life returning to her eyes. The heat of the shower combined with his brisk movements with the washcloth were bringing circulation back to her skin, and she was reviving. When a person went into shock, Craig knew, the blood moved deep within the body to protect the most vital organs. Consequently, the person began to lose precious body heat, becoming cold and often semiconscious, sometimes losing consciousness altogether.

Susan's hair hung in straight sheets around her perfectly shaped head. She tried to help him clean her, but Craig gently placed her hands back at her sides. Her bra and panties were soaked, so he slid them off her, letting the lingerie drop to the shower floor. If Susan was embarrassed, she didn't show it. That told Craig how far removed from reality she really was, because he knew she was shy about herself.

Shutting off the shower, he slid the door open and retrieved a thick white terry-cloth towel. Leading Susan out of the stall, he wrapped her in it. When he opened the bathroom door, the steam rolled out like silent fingers of fog into the rest of the suite.

"Hang on," he warned her, and he picked her up in his arms. Susan was trembling. She gave a little sigh and laid her head against his shoulder, her hands resting against her breast beneath the towel.

Craig was angry. Someone back at the clinic should have realized Susan's condition. He knew all hell had broken loose, and probably, in the panic and chaos, no one had noticed that she was in shock, thinking she was just another onlooker watching the clinic burn.

He gently placed Susan on the bed, pulled the heavy gold bedspread across her and went back to get another towel. When he returned, she was lying on her side, curled up in the fetal position, her eyes closed. Craig began to dry her hair with a towel and saw her lashes barely flutter.

"Where are we?" she asked, her voice a mere whisper.

"At a nice little French hotel way south of Los Angeles," Craig explained. He urged her into a sitting position and quickly dried her off as best he could. She was holding the towel around her shoulders, her fist wrapped tightly in the folds across her breasts. Craig knelt down, vigorously rubbing her thighs and legs to force the blood back to the surface.

"You're wet." Susan reached out and touched his shoulder. "Why are you wet?"

Craig straightened and threw the towel aside. "Because I just took a shower with you." With shaky hands, he unbuttoned his shirt and dropped it to the floor. "Susan, I'm going to get in bed with you. Do you understand me?" He shoved off his Levi's and dark blue socks. Looking at her upturned face, he realized she wasn't really aware of much at all, her eyes huge and dark. Her lips were parted and so vulnerable looking that he groaned to himself.

"You're cold and I'm going to warm you up." He pulled back the bed covers and allowed her to keep the towel around herself as he slipped her under the sheet. Then he crossed to the large picture window and pulled the silken blue curtain across it. The room became very dark when he turned off the light, and Craig carefully made his way back to the bed. His boxer shorts were wet, so, getting quickly out of them, he slid beneath the covers and found Susan, drawing her into his arms.

"Come here," he rasped, closing his eyes, feeling her gradually unwind from the fetal position, her body flowing against his. "Let me get you warm." Turning on his side, Craig was aware of the roughened texture of the damp towel, providing a thin barrier between their naked bodies. He felt Susan sigh, and he released a breath as her arm slowly moved across his chest. She sought his warmth, he realized. Her flesh was covered in goose pimples and cool to his touch.

For the next fifteen minutes Craig gently rubbed huge circles across her shoulders and back. Little by little, she stopped trembling. When he finally stilled his hand against her spine, he realized Susan had fallen asleep.

Uttering a little groan, he relaxed and lay on his back, with Susan snuggled against his length. Her breath was soft and moist across his shoulder, her head tucked beneath his jaw. He brought his arm across her, his other hand gently moving up and down the expanse of her arm that was thrown across his belly. Moments passed, sweet and heated for him as he closed his eyes, the trauma overwhelming him.

Susan was in his arms, where he'd always dreamed of her being. Four years of dreams, and she was here, with him. Craig was too raw from nearly losing her to even think about what would happen when she awoke to find herself here. His mind spun, groggy and disoriented.

Nothing mattered, he told himself as he felt fingers of sleep dragging him down into darkness, except that Susan was safe, and he loved her.

Chapter Eleven

The unexpected attack on the clinic plagued the early morning hours of Susan's sleep. She saw the red-and-orange explosion strike directly at the building. Susan had screamed as she'd been knocked down by the blast. Señora Naldo had been knocked unconscious and Susan had dragged herself, dazed, toward the door, pulling the older woman along as smoke rolled, choking and hot, through the building. A second explosion struck and the earth shook violently.

Flinging the back door open, Susan had tugged and pulled until Señora Naldo was safely outside. Neighbors who had seen them had pulled them even farther away from the heat of the inferno. Moaning, Susan had looked from side to side, seeing the carnage as they were drawn to safety. Somehow, she'd become separated from Señora Naldo and screams shattered her as fire fighters ran around her, trying to tame the flames, their dark shapes outlined by the roaring blaze.

The shrieks of people rose and fell as Susan stood frozen amid the carnage, realizing that gang members were shooting indiscriminately into the crowd of people gathered near the burning clinic. They had come out too soon, concerned for those who might have been injured in the blasts. Flames shot skyward, and Susan frantically threw her hands up to her face against the rolling, searing heat. She was confused and dazed.

She had no time to think, to reason. Panic and chaos surrounded her as gunfire again shattered the night. Out of the darkness, a stranger tackled her from behind, yelling at her to hit the ground as bullets flew into the scattering crowd. Susan crashed into the pavement, the wind knocked out of her.

A third blast erupted, created by oxygen tanks exploding inside the clinic. Susan was pummeled by the aftershock, a scream tearing from her lips. Pain blazed up her arm, then she felt numbness. She lay there, dazed, the breath knocked out of her. Blood dribbled from her nose, and she sat up, looking around. The man who had tried to protect her from the bullets lay on his side, only a few feet away from her, wounded. She started to scream, her fingers digging into her temples....

Craig jerked awake, automatically gripping Susan when she cried out. Momentarily disoriented, sleep torn from him, he felt her shivering.

"Susan?"

Craig's sleep-thickened voice reached her, and she sobbed, clinging to him, gasping for breath. It was so dark, so dark. His body was warm and strong. Where was she?

"Craig? Craig..."

"Shh, I'm here, babe, I'm here." He forced himself awake. Glancing at his wristwatch, he realized it was four in the morning. He pressed Susan back down on the bed, one arm beneath her shoulders, his other hand cradling her tear-stained face. "It's all right," he crooned, leaning down, holding her tightly against him. "It's all right...." But it wasn't and he knew it.

"It's so dark," Susan cried brokenly.

Craig leaned across her, fumbling for the switch on the lamp next to the bed. There. A small amount of light penetrated the darkness, and Craig eased back next to Susan, holding her tightly. His heart nearly broke as he realized just how much damage the attack on the clinic had done to her. Her face was pale, her mouth contorted in a silent scream, her fingers digging into the flesh of his chest, her fact pressed against him like a hurt child who was afraid of the dark.

"Just take deep breaths," he rasped, tunneling his fingers through her hair, trying to soothe her. So many impressions struck Craig at once: the slender length of her body along his, her small breasts against his chest, her gasping sobs wrenching him apart.

Gradually, Susan focused on Craig's deep, strained voice and the nightmare of the attack began to dissolve beneath his ministrations—his hand stroking her hair, his mouth pressing small kisses to her temple and cheek. Where was she? Pieces, fragments of the last twenty-four hours of her life weren't making sense. Was she going crazy?

"Craig? Where are we? What happened?" Susan realized for the first time that they were in bed together, undressed, in each other's arms. Lifting her head, she met and drowned in the tenderness of his gray gaze.

Quietly, he explained the sequence of events, leaving nothing out. "I brought you here, to a hotel. You were in shock. It was my decision," Craig admitted. "I didn't want to stay in the immediate area because of the gang activity." He swallowed hard. "For a long time after they bombed the clinic, I thought you were dead, Susan." His hand stilled against her hair, his eyes filling with tears. "I knew I could take anything but that. Do you understand?" Looking around the gloomy depths of the suite, Craig said, "Maybe I was wrong to bring you here, but—"

Her hand tightened on his shoulder. "No," she whispered, "it was right." So right. She slid her hand along the length of his broad shoulder, feeling the muscles grow taut beneath her touch. Craig's eyes were filled with agony, with indecision...with desire. "I was so scared," she quavered. "I thought I was going to die." And she explained what had happened to her before he found her.

Craig lay tense and quiet, Susan's story tearing him apart. "I didn't know you were in so much danger," he offered quietly when she'd finished. Gently, he touched her arm where the glass had injured her. "Now I know how you got these."

"It was awful, Craig. Awful!"

"I'm sorry, Susan. I should have known better. I should have checked the place out myself instead of letting the office people do it."

"It was a war zone, Craig. A terrible war."

Grimly, his mouth compressed, he nodded. "It reminded me of Grenada and Panama, when we parachuted in with the SEAL teams." He held her tightly. "You're right, south L.A. is a war zone."

Susan lay still, protected by Craig's body, vibrantly aware of him as a man. "It wasn't your fault, Craig. How could you have known? We both could have died," she whispered brokenly. "I ran to Dr. Orlando's house, hoping to find you there, to tell you I was still alive. But there was no one there. No one...I didn't know where you were. I was worried you had been shot like that poor man protecting me at the clinic."

He nodded sadly. "One thing you learn from war and violence: live each minute like it's going to be your last, because it might be...."

Urgency throbbed through Susan as she eased up on her elbow. With her hand, she caressed Craig's stubbled cheeks, his grim features. He was right. Searching his tortured eyes, she felt his body tensing, his hand resting on her hip becoming firm against her skin.

"Love me," she begged hoarsely. "Love me, Craig. I—I need you. I need to feel alive, not like this. I feel so dead inside, so horrible...."

With a groan, he leaned over and hungrily captured her parted, tear-stained lips.

The urgency to drown herself in him screaming through her, Susan closed her eyes, feeling his weight press down upon her. His mouth was plundering, searching and hot against hers, and she lost all sense of time and place, honing in on his touch, his scent, the texture of him as a man. As his hand moved downward, to curve against her breast, Susan gave a little cry that was drowned by his mouth. Mindless, feeling her world pulling loose from the seams of reality, she surrendered to his hands, his hard, pressing body and his mouth, which enkindled the fire of life within her.

His breath was rapid, moist against her face, and Susan responded with just as much need. As his thumb brushed her nipple, she moaned and arched upward. He tore his mouth from her wet, throbbing lips to capture that hardened peak, and she gave a startled cry of surprise and pleasure as he suckled her. Her fingers opening and closing frantically against his shoulders, Susan threw back her head as his hand trailed down across her rounded belly to the juncture of her thighs. Blood pounded furiously through her, and she surrendered utterly to her need of him as a man.

Time...there was no time left. She'd almost died. So had Craig. As Susan lifted her hands, shaking with desire, she could only respond to his questing hand sliding between her slick thighs. She opened to his search, explosive sensations blossoming and thrumming through her under his intimate exploration. Never had she felt more a woman, meeting and matching Craig's hunger for her.

With a sigh, she felt him cover her, his knee guiding her to receive him. His weight, the trembling strength of his body against hers, was all she needed. As his hand slid beneath her hips, she arched, taking him deep within. The power of their coupling shocked her and her eyes flew open to meet and drown in Craig's burning gaze. Beads of sweat covered his face and his fists had knotted into the bed sheets on either side of her head as he filled her, making her one with him. Her lips parted, only to be captured by his strong male mouth. Each twist, each movement of his hips brought her new pleasure—each thrust more exquisite, deeper, more fusing than the last.

Caught in a golden explosion that rippled like a hot torrent of lava from deep within her, Susan felt Craig groan. He gripped her hair, his brow pressed to hers, his mouth contorted as he thrust hard into her. It was then that Susan realized he had shared himself with her. With a little cry, she weakly raised her arms and slid them around his damp body. He lay still, breathing hard, his muscles taut. Then, as the molten moments melded together, Susan gradually felt him begin to relax against her. She searched for and found his mouth, kissing him deeply, silently telling him of her love.

With a groan, Craig realized he must be crushing Susan beneath his weight. He felt her hands, warm and evocative on his back, tighten to prevent him from leaving her.

"No..." she whispered, opening her eyes, looking up into his face, mere inches from her own. "Don't move."

He managed a slight smile and reached down to smooth away the dark strands of hair that clung to her brow, taming them into place. "I'm pretty heavy."

"You're like a wonderful, protective blanket," Susan said softly, so dazed by the joy flowing from her heart that she could barely think, much less talk coherently.

Craig relaxed slightly, shifting his weight a little. "You're so beautiful, do you know that? Your cheeks are fiery red, and your eyes are sparkling like sapphires." He kissed the tip of her nose, then trailed a lingering kiss across her full, slightly pouty lips. Just the feel of her hands moving lightly against him made him growl with satisfaction.

"And I've never seen you look so relaxed," Susan said, amazed to see Craig's face look almost boyish in the dim light. She caressed his features with her fingertips, aware of the sweat, his glistening flesh. "The lines around your mouth aren't so deep," she marveled, her fingers brushing that area. Her gaze shifted. "And your brow—there are no more deep lines there, either."

Craig closed his eyes, enjoying her discovery of him. "I've dreamed of this moment so many times." He opened his eyes and gazed down at her vulnerable features. "I was afraid to dream again."

A soft smile shadowed her mouth. The moments spun together as she assimilated Craig's admission. She saw his mouth lift in a wry smile as he leaned down and kissed her nose.

"I've never been so glad to be alive as now."

She blinked once and stared at him, never more aware that they remained coupled, his strong, vital body covering her. With a choked sound, she whispered, "I had hoped... but I didn't know...."

Craig eased off her and brought her into his arms. Pulling the sheet up to their waists, he settled on his back, with Susan lying across him. "I never stopped dreaming about you, babe. Not ever." He picked up several strands of her hair and tucked it behind her delicately shaped ear. "That very first afternoon, when I met you in the emergency room, I think I fell for you."

Susan nodded and bit her lip. Her emotions felt like a vibrant, living rainbow of color within her body. Did he love her? Susan wasn't sure, and she vividly recalled Karen's talk about the dog in the cage who was afraid to leap to freedom. She was too scared to ask Craig if he loved her. Ashamed of her lack of courage, she whispered, "I was too young, Craig, too easily dazzled by everything that Steve did to get my attention."

"That's because," Craig told her as he caressed her velvet cheek, "he loved you in his own way."

"I've made so many mistakes," Susan rattled.

With a sigh, he framed her face. "You were young and impressionable, babe. No one can blame you for that, especially me. I could've been more aggressive, I could've elbowed my way in and fought for you. Instead, I backed off."

Susan absorbed the tender touch of his fingers spanning her face. "What I felt for Steve was puppy love."

"Don't minimize how you felt about him," Craig counseled. "There are all kinds of love in the world."

"I know he loved me."

Gently, he touched the bump on her nose. "Yes," he agreed, "but it was a love that turned on you and hurt you." *Badly.* Would those scars keep her from trying to love again? To love him, possibly? Everything was so tenuous, even now. Craig knew she held many hidden scars from her marriage to Steve. A smile eased the hard planes of his face. "I know you don't believe this, but love can be good and freeing, too, babe."

Fear began to eat away at Susan's euphoria. She snuggled into his arms and tried to avoid the feeling. "What's going to happen, Craig? I've been scared before, but not like this." Her voice grew raspy. "Either of us could be killed at any time."

His embrace tightened around her. "I know," he said. "There are no guarantees, Susan. I wish I could promise you that everything will always be all right, but we're both old enough, mature enough, to know I can't."

Her arms moved around him and she squeezed him, the words dying in her throat. "No tomorrows."

"No. We'll take this a day at a time." Craig smiled a little and gazed around the room. "We'll plan times like this in the future whenever we can, Susan. With you working twelve hours a day and me being out in the field or away on assignment, it's going to be tough—but we'll do it."

As Susan rested securely in Craig's arms, she realized with a frightening new awareness that life wasn't to be taken for granted ever again.

Craig looked at his watch. "Let's try to get some more sleep—it's the best thing for you right now."

Susan closed her eyes as he switched off the lamp. "When do we have to be back?"

"I have to pick up the team at noon," he said unhappily.

Smiling softly, Susan moved her hand across his chest, her fingertips tangling in the soft hair. "At least we have this time."

"Yes," he murmured gratefully, pressing a kiss to Susan's fragrant hair.

The ride back to Camp Reed the next afternoon was somber. Susan took her place in the rear with the other team members while Craig and the driver shared the front seat. Her body tingled hotly in memory of his hands exploring her as if she were some exquisite, priceless vessel. Lowering her lashes, Susan hoped she wasn't blushing at her wanton thoughts, but her cheeks felt hot.

Their time together had been precious. Running her tongue across her lower lip, she could still taste Craig, the strength of his mouth cajoling, coaxing and matching her passion. Out of the brutality of southern Los Angeles, from the ashes of a clinic desperately needed by the poor, Susan had discovered her love for Craig. But was it love on his part? Last night, despite the fact of almost losing their lives, he hadn't whispered those words to her. What was it she saw in his eyes, then— that gray brilliance touched with diamonds that made her feel as if she were being pulled into his soul?

Susan took in a deep, ragged breath, not at all sure she knew what love was. Wasn't she that dog in the electrified cage? Was Craig opening the door to her own self-imprisonment? She hadn't made love with a man in two years. Going to bed wasn't a lark—to her it was a serious commitment. But how did Craig view it? Torn, Susan closed her eyes, feeling an exhaustion that was soul deep washing across her. She longed to be sitting next to Craig, to have his arm around her shoulders. She felt bereft and confused, and she was no longer sure whether it was due to the shock and violence of last night, or to the beauty of Craig loving her as an equal, as someone who meant the world to him.

If only he did...

At Susan's apartment, later that day, Craig got out and opened the door for her.

"I'll walk with you," he said, holding out his hand to her. He saw the uncertainty in Susan's face. Faint circles of darkness showed beneath those glorious blue eyes, and he remembered the golden highlights in them as they'd culminated their love for each other last night. He gave her a slight smile meant to encourage her to reach out to him. Chafing because, once again, they didn't have the time they so desperately needed, he grasped Susan's cool fingers.

As much as he wanted to continue to hold her hand, he released it once she'd stepped out of the vehicle. Walking slowly at her shoulder, he thought how pretty and fresh she looked in the buttercup yellow blouse and white slacks and sandals. They had stopped at a department store after picking up the rest of the team, and they all bought badly needed clothes. The sidewalk was surrounded by green grass, and he followed her around the corner to a set of stairs. There, out of earshot and view of his men, Craig relaxed and placed his arm around her shoulders, feeling the tension in them.

"How are you doing?" he asked, drawing her to a halt at the base of the stairs. The day was warm without being oppressively hot.

Thrilled by Craig's unexpected intimacy, Susan relaxed beneath his concerned gaze that searched her own. "Tired, exhausted and confused, just to name a few feelings," she admitted.

Craig rested his hands on her small shoulders, aching to kiss her again. "I can understand the tired and exhausted part. What's the confusion about?"

She smiled slightly and absorbed the natural warmth he shared with her. "I guess I'm a lot more conditioned by Steve, by our marriage, than I thought."

Tenderly touching her hair and grazing her cheek with his finger, Craig whispered, "What do you mean?"

Just his featherlike touch sent a tremor through her, and Susan swallowed convulsively. Tears flooded into her eyes, and Craig's serious features blurred. Swallowing, her voice cracking, Susan said, "It's you. You're so different from Steve. I mean, I never expected you to stop me, to touch me like this, to ask me what I was feeling."

Gently, he cupped her cheek and looked deeply into her tear-filled eyes. "A lot of men have a tough time talking to a woman."

Blinking, she lowered her lashes. "I—I know that."

"Your head knows it, but your heart doesn't. At least, not yet." With a sigh, Craig cupped her face and, with his thumbs, dried the tears from her cheeks. Susan's face was flushed and he saw shame in her eyes. "We need time, babe. You need time to adjust to the fact that I'm different from Steve." He gave her a one-cornered smile filled with deprecation. "I need time to learn not to push you too far, too fast. I thought I had patience, but I don't—not with you."

She gave a little laugh and reached up, sliding her arms around his neck. Susan wasn't disappointed, hearing Craig groan as she leaned her body against him. Almost instantly, his strong, steady arms went around her waist and the air rushed from her lungs as he squeezed her close. Shutting her eyes, she surrendered thankfully to his strength, knowing that she had none of her own left on which to draw.

"When will we see each other?" she whispered, nestling her face against his neck.

Kissing her hair, her temple and cheek, he rasped, "In hours, if I have my way." He sought and found her mouth, warm and waiting for him. He drowned in her softness, her long, slow-burning passion that multiplied with every pounding heartbeat in his chest. His head spinning, his senses wildly alive and throbbing with yearning, he slowly, reluctantly, broke the kiss.

"You're like hot sunlight," he whispered against her wet, full lips. "You can melt a man with one of your kisses."

Trembling, she sighed and lifted her lashes. The diamondlike gray of his eyes impressed her that he meant every word he spoke. "I've never thought of myself that way," she said, a tremor in her voice.

With a shaking hand, Craig smoothed her hair. He gave her a very male smile, one meant to convey just how much she touched his heart, the very core of his being. "You are," he rasped. "You always were. I've always felt hope and lightness when you smile. And when you laugh, it sounds like a spring brook to me."

Her heart spilled over with an ache that could only be love. The feeling was as new as it was deep, so profound that Susan had no words to describe it.

"I've got to get going," he muttered, lightly stroking her hair and staring down into her eyes. "It's the last thing I want to do. I want to be here, with you. I wish . . . well, my wishes are pretty wild." He laughed huskily.

Susan laughed with him. Euphoria swept through her, and she reached up and touched his recently shaved cheek. "Are you for real, or are you some figment of my repressed imagination?"

The smile disappeared, replaced with hunger. "I'm real," he growled, claiming her mouth with a fierceness and primal beauty that he wanted her to remember forever—because he would.

"Captain Taggart, your CO wants to see you right now." The sergeant at the motor pool had a grim look on his face.

Signing off the paperwork on the station wagon, Craig nodded. He'd dropped his team off at the enlisted-men's barracks and hadn't been in the motor pool ten minutes when the sergeant had hunted him down.

"Thanks, Sergeant."

"Yes, sir."

Handing over the clipboard, Craig saluted and left the garage. What now? All he wanted to do was go over to headquarters, fill out the reams of paperwork that would be demanded after the unexpected events surrounding the clinic, then go home, call Susan and ask her out to dinner. Right now, she needed his support. She needed to realize he loved her and would be there for her.

Colonel Morton, the recon commander, didn't look very happy, Craig thought, as he walked into the two-story headquarters building. Perhaps he'd heard the news from some local L.A. station about the bombing of the clinic.

"Reporting as ordered, sir." Craig came to attention in front of his superior's gray metal desk.

"At ease, Craig," the colonel muttered, waving his hand toward one of the chairs in front of the desk. "Have a seat."

Something was up. Craig could smell it. He knew better than to speak until spoken to. Morton was one of the old-guard officers who took his rank seriously and didn't fraternize with lowly lieutenants or captains, so he remained patient.

Quickly signing some paperwork, which he handed to an awaiting marine office pogue, Morton focused his attention on Craig. "Captain, I'm sorry, but I've got to pull your team for a clandestine insertion. You will work with the navy SEAL Team Six. We've got terrorists who have taken over a piece of Caribbean real estate. The mission profile specifies that you will do a high-altitude, high-opening parachute onto the island. The political government officials are being held by terrorists. It's your job to go in with the SEALs and get them free."

Swallowing his surprise, Craig remained impassive. Every so often, JSOC, the Special Operations Command, created a make-believe scenario somewhere in the world and coordinated joint operations with another arm of the military. His eyes narrowed.

"Is this real or something JSOC cooked up for us?"

Morton smiled thinly. "Now, Captain, you know I don't have a clue as to whether this is a field exercise or the real thing. You'll treat it as real."

"Of course sir." Further, Morton ordered, he was restricted to base as of right now. Disappointment, strong and deep, serrated Craig. A clandestine operation meant exactly that: no one, especially the press, was to get wind of it until after it had been secured by the military. Craig had been on such field exercises before, and once they parachuted into the situation, he could feel his way through it and find out whether it was just an exercise or not. Either way, it didn't matter. He had exactly twenty-four hours to get his team assembled, work closely with the SEAL Team Six leaders and coordinate a parachute drop at twenty-thousand feet from the back door of a C-130. They would drift under cover of darkness to some small island, land and work their way toward the target. Terrorists, or what was commonly referred to as "tangos,' were the bane of the world, as far as Craig was concerned. And the most-dangerous enemy.

"You're to get over to Operations and begin the coordination effort, Captain."

"Yes, sir." Craig's mind spun with question, with options. He recalled Susan's intuitive feeling that something bad was going to happen. Well, it had.

"SEAL Team Six is working out of the East Coast. You've got a fax, high-priority phones, and a C-130 is already on the ground here at our airport, waiting to take you east. If you need anything, let me know."

"Yes, sir." Craig saw the worry in his CO's eyes and heard it in his voice. Any one of his men could be killed in the high-altitude, high-opening parachute mission they referred to as HAHO. The parachutes could fail to open, and they'd be hurtling to earth with fifty pounds of gear on them. Or they could miss the darkened island, land in the ocean and drown. The dangers inherent to the kind of mission recons and SEALs trained for were always real—whether or not their orders were.

Craig had been through this many times and he knew the steps involved.

The colonel frowned and growled, "You're not going to be back for ten days."

"Yes, sir." Craig came to attention and was dismissed. He hurried out of the building and drove his car to the secure Communications/Operations building. Susan was going to be stunned by the news. She didn't need this on top of what she'd already experienced. That he couldn't be there for her in her time of need struck at him hard. Frustrated and angry because he sensed this was a JSOC exercise with no teeth in it, he knew the first thing he was going to do was call her.

"Hello?" Susan pushed her damp hair away from her face as she answered the phone. Dressed in a cotton robe after taking a long, hot bath, she felt somewhat refreshed.

"Susan? It's Craig."

Automatically, her heart started to beat hard in her chest. Her fingers touched her throat as she heard the harshness in his voice. "Craig? What's wrong?"

"Everything. Listen, I'm being restricted to base. I can't tell you anything more."

Restricted to base. Her mind spun, and she felt dizzy with unexpected fear. Her hand tightening on the phone, she whispered, "Restricted?"

"Yes. Babe, I'm sorry. I just got on board and all hell broke loose. I'm going to be gone for ten days. That's all I can say."

"Oh, no..." She sat down on the edge of the pale pink couch. "This is a mission, isn't it, Craig?"

"I can't say, Susan. You know enough about recons and our top-secret work. I'm sorry...."

She heard the real frustration in his voice. Touching her brow, she felt frightened as never before. "Be careful," she said unsteadily. "Please be careful, Craig."

"Never more careful than now, honey, believe me. I've just found you again. You think I'm going to let you get away? No way. Listen, I've got to go...."

Susan nodded mutely, her hand pressed against her beating heart. It was on the tip of her tongue to say, *I love you,* but she wasn't sure Craig felt as strongly about her as she did toward him. And to say it now on top of some dangerous, clandestine mission could throw him off. She didn't want to risk his focus and concentration being on her instead of his work.

Closing her eyes, she said brokenly, "Come back to me, Craig. I'll be here. I'll be waiting."

"Those are the sweetest words I've ever heard, babe. I'll be careful, I promise. Ten days. Don't worry, okay? Just as soon as I can, I'll be back in touch with you. Goodbye."

The phone line went dead. Already reeling from the clinic fire, Susan gently put the receiver back in its cradle, tears forming in her eyes. She loved Craig so fiercely that it stole her breath. And now he was going out on an operation. Where? Was it genuine or just an exercise?

It wasn't fair! They'd just found each other again. She sat very still, going over the possibilities. Craig, too, was emotionally traumatized by what had happened in Los Angeles. And now he'd been hit with a major operations assignment. He'd had little sleep from the night before. Her hand curling into a fist in her lap, Susan stared unseeing at the pale ivory drapes over the living-room picture window.

Craig wouldn't be as sharp, as focused as he needed to be for this mission. Although he was the most capable marine she'd ever met, he was human, and exhaustion could play havoc with his concentration. His life was in far more jeopardy than normal. Tears leaked down onto her cheeks as helplessness snaked through her. This was how all wives of military men felt when they got these kinds of phone calls. They couldn't be told where their men were going, what dangers they might face or anything that might provide a shred of comfort, because to do so would blow the cover on the entire operation.

Dazed, she got to her feet and wandered toward the kitchen. What if the mission was real? Craig and his team could be in danger far worse than during an exercise. He might die.

The thought made her freeze in the kitchen doorway. Death had stalked her all her life. First her mother, then Steve. With a little cry, Susan sank against the doorjamb, her hand pressed against her heart, the pain almost too much to bear at the thought of losing Craig. She loved him with a fierceness she'd never felt before. He was going somewhere in the world, into a dangerous situation, and he didn't know she loved him.

Wearily, Susan stared across the quiet, neatly kept kitchen. She loved Craig unequivocally. But did he love her? Perhaps she'd never find out. The thought was overwhelmingly painful, and she turned and headed for the bedroom. Sleep was what she needed, but she wasn't sure she would be able to get any now.

Chapter Twelve

"It's been ten days," Karen said as she came and sat with Susan at the hospital cafeteria table.

"Tell me about it." Susan pushed spaghetti around on her plate. Her appetite had disappeared completely when Craig left.

"You need to eat...."

Susan frowned. "I know.... My nerves are raw. I'm raw." She put the fork aside and took a deep, shaky breath. "Ten days. Do you know how many times I've searched every newspaper, listened to CNN for news of some lousy terrorist situation somewhere in the world?"

"I know, I know."

"There's been nothing in the papers or on television, Karen. I've got to think Craig's on some kind of exercise, a stupid war game. Oh, God, I hope it is just an exercise."

Reaching out, Karen patted Susan's hand. "Take it easy. You're tearing yourself up over this. Craig's a professional. He's a recon. They're the best the Marine Corps have, Susan. Whether this top-secret operation he's on is real doesn't matter. He's not going to make mistakes and leave himself or his men as targets. You've got to settle down. You don't eat, you don't sleep. You look like hell. This morning in the operating theater, you were dropping instruments. That isn't like you."

Trying to emotionally gird herself, Susan realized Karen was telling her the truth. "I love him, Karen. And I didn't tell him before he left. It's eating me alive inside. What if he doesn't come back?"

"You can't hurry love," Karen counseled. "Don't feel guilty about not saying anything."

Giving her friend a sad look, Susan whispered, "I've realized over the last few months that I've never really been in love before. Not until now, with Craig." Trying to calm down, she looked up at the tile ceiling in the small cafeteria. They sat in a corner, away from most of the other people. "I've had ten days to really look at myself, my life, my feelings, Karen. Do you know what I've come up with?"

Karen shook her head and picked at her tuna salad. "No. What?"

"That I loved Steve, but it was a romantic kind of love, something that doesn't have a chance of lasting a lifetime. I see that now. I didn't then...."

Karen murmured sympathetically. "A lot of women fall for that kind of love. You were young and naive."

"I'm older now. I—I want a second chance with Craig. I love him."

"Does he love you?"

Sighing, Susan shrugged. "I don't know. I think—I hope he does...." Pushing the tray away, she settled her hands around a cup of black coffee. "I've gone over that, too."

"What?"

"The fact that he may not love me."

Karen gave her a brief smile of understanding. "Age and experience make us a little wiser, don't they?"

"Yes, but it hurts to look at that possibility."

"Still," Karen said gently, "you're taking responsibility for yourself, and that's a step in the right direction. The dog is escaping her cage, so to speak."

"Yes, I'm taking that step," Susan admitted slowly. "This time, I know to ask a lot of other questions. When I was younger, I didn't even know what questions to ask about my relationship with Steve."

"And if Craig doesn't love you?"

Tears stung Susan's eyes. "Then I—I'll have to deal with that, too. Maybe he wants me only as a friend."

"But you went to bed with him. You loved each other." Karen put her tray aside, the lunch half eaten. "Look, I know you very well. I know you'd never have gone to bed with Craig if something really special wasn't in place. This was your first time since Steve passed away. Now, I don't know Craig really well, but from what I've seen of him and know of his past, he's not the type of guy to love you and leave you. He's solid, Susan. Responsible. I've never heard him give you a line."

"I know...." The pain became almost unbearable. "That's why it's so hard to wait...and worry. He could be dead, and I'd never know it...oh, God, it's so hard, the waiting...."

Silently, Karen nodded. "I was convinced a long time ago that to be a wife, mother, sister or girlfriend of a serviceman or woman is one of the toughest ways to live. You're left out of the communications loop, without any information." She grimaced. "Remind me not to fall in love with a military man. I'll take a civilian guy any day. At least I'll know he's not going to be jerked off into some hush-hush operation and be gone for days or weeks on end. What a crummy life you have to lead."

"I love the man, not his work."

With a slight laugh, Karen nodded. "Craig is worth falling in love with. Wish I could find a civilian clone of him around somewhere!"

Buoyed by Karen's teasing, Susan felt a tad better. She'd been working extra duty hours because staying at her apartment only drove her crazy with worry. When she was actively engaged in work that forced her to concentrate, she had a reprieve from her terror and anxiety over Craig.

"I left word at Craig's office that he's to call me when he comes back."

With a wry smile, Karen said, "I'm sure you'll be the first person he calls."

"Susan?" Betty Ross called from the nurse's desk. "There was a phone message for you while you were at chow." She waved a piece of paper in the air and laid it on the desk.

Susan's heart bounded with anticipation as she hurried over. Dread touched her as she reached for the note. Intuitively, she knew it had to do with Craig. Her mouth dry, she stared down at Betty's scrawly handwriting.

Call recon HQ.

The sensation of a knife twisting in her gut followed. It wasn't from Craig.

In ten minutes, she had to go back on duty. Turning, she headed blindly down the passage to the nurse's lounge, where she could make the call in privacy.

A hundred horrible thoughts collided in Susan's head as she forced herself not to run but to walk normally. Clutching the piece of paper in her damp hand, she tried not to imagine the worst: HQ was calling to inform her that Craig was dead. Her rational mind told her that was impossible. If he were dead, his next-of-kin—not her—would be notified.

When the door to the lounge had quietly closed behind her, Susan reached shakily for the phone. Forcing herself to sit down, she gripped the receiver and dialed the number.

"Recons."

"Yes, this is Lieutenant Evans. There was a message for me to call?"

"Oh . . . yes, ma'am. One moment, I'll put Lieutenant Davis on."

Shutting her eyes, Susan groaned softly. Her hand was sweaty, and her heart was beating painfully in her breast.

"This is Lieutenant Davis."

Susan winced internally, the authority of Davis's tone only frightening her more. His voice was crisp, emotionless and deep. "You had a message for me? I'm Lieutenant Evans."

"Yes, I do. I just received a SatCom message from Captain Taggart for you. He will arrive at the base at 2030 and asks that you meet him at the Reed airport."

Relief shattered her tension. "I see—yes, thank you, Lieutenant."

"You're welcome."

The phone clicked. Susan sighed and placed it back in the cradle. Craig was coming home! *Home.* To her. He'd asked her to meet him. Joy, sharp and wild, careened through her, and she sat savoring it like sand absorbing the first drops of rain. She had felt like a desert since Craig had left—parched and empty. He was like life-giving rain, making her realize the beauty of life, the hope that still lived within her.

Waiting at the small Operations desk area of the base airport was torture as far as Susan was concerned. The sun had set, and the sky was a pale gold with some orange-tinted cirrus clouds across the vault. Only a meteorologist and an air traffic controller were on desk duty as Susan stood at the swinging glass doors and looked out toward the revetment area. Her watch read 2100; the plane bearing Craig and his team was half an hour late. Inwardly, Susan chafed.

Soon it would be dusk, and she wanted desperately to see Craig as he deplaned. Sergeant Trudy Wells, the meteorologist on duty, had said a C-130 was slated to land, so at least she knew what kind of plane to look for. Susan had gone home at 1800, taken a shower and changed into civilian clothes. Her hair was freshly washed and hanging in a simple pageboy style, barely touching the collar of her pale pink short-sleeved blouse. White cotton slacks and sandals kept her cool despite the blistering, Southern California heat, which always languished in the hills after sunset.

"Ma'am?" Sergeant Wells called. "The C-130 is on approach right now. If you look east, you'll see it coming in."

Grateful, Susan smiled. "Thank you." She pushed the door aside and moved to the revetment area. Her heart starting to beat with excitement, she hurried away from the building just enough to try to catch a glimpse of the cargo aircraft. There, in the gathering dusk, she could see a black speck with wings. Because she was an officer and on a military reservation, Susan knew she couldn't show any outward emotion toward Craig after he landed. Still, just knowing he was alive was enough for her. She gripped the shoulder strap of her white purse and waited.

The C-130 landed, its four turbo-prop engines whistling shrilly as it slowly approached the debarkation area in front of the small Operations building and control tower. Once the engines were shut down, several marines in dark green utilities hurried out to place chocks beneath the huge wheels of the Hercules and the rear ramp slowly began to open, ready to disgorge its passengers.

Susan saw the first of five marines moving slowly down the ramp. *Craig!* She would recognize his proud carriage anywhere. Her pulse bounded crazily and she practically stood on tiptoe, hungry for the mere sight of him, even though he was a good three hundred feet away. A Humvee vehicle approached the ramp and stopped. The driver saluted, but Susan saw Craig lift his head and look toward the Ops area. Spontaneously, she raised her hand high and waved. If only he saw her!

The moment Craig lifted his hand in return, Susan felt a wave of happiness rush through her. She watched as he saluted the driver, threw in his pack and waited for his four-man team to board the Humvee. It was agony waiting those few minutes, but Susan understood that Craig had to make sure all details of the mission were handled—especially his men. In no time, the vehicle was speeding toward her, and all she could do was wait immobile, filled as much with dread as anticipation.

She was running on raw adrenaline now, she realized as she watched him approach. Her heart beat harder. Recon activity was a shadowy, dangerous world. The first thing Craig would have to do was go over to Intelligence with his team and prepare a long, involved report of the operation.

The dusk was deepening to shadows, as the Humvee slowed to a stop in front of her and Susan searched Craig's grim face. She realized he'd lost weight. His features looked hard, the lines around his mouth and eyes deep. He still wore the yellow, green and black greasepaint that hid his skin in jungle conditions. His face was streaked with sweat, his eyes bloodshot. Susan wanted to cry, but all she could do was stand there, showing no outward emotion.

Craig moved from the Humvee, thanked the driver and told his men he'd see them at Intelligence soon. As the vehicle left, his attention moved to Susan and his eyes narrowed. Each step toward her was purposeful. As he drew to a halt, the bare hint of a weary smile pulled at the corners of his mouth. "Hi, stranger," he greeted her hoarsely.

Susan felt suddenly shaky, her voice low and off-key. "Hi, yourself."

"You look beautiful," he said, aching to reach out and hold her, kiss her.

"You have no idea how good you look to me."

His mouth curved more deeply. "I'm glad you're here."

"I got your message." Susan searched his face, thinking how much a warrior he really was. "You look exhausted."

"A good night's sleep and I'll be fine," he assured her.

Susan felt the hunger of Craig's gaze and heard the emotion in his husky voice as he stood inches from her. She ached to move into his arms, to feel his mouth hungrily claiming her own. "I managed to get tomorrow off—the first break I've had since you left."

Craig nodded. "We'll probably be up half the night filling out reports," he said miserably. "It's the last place I want to be."

She felt heat touch her cheeks but drowned in his darkening gaze. "I know...."

Craig couldn't stand it any longer. He knew there were eyes watching, but he didn't care. Reaching out, he gently slipped his hand into hers. "I'm sorry I had to leave you like that. I got back to HQ after dropping you off at your apartment and they threw this mission at me." His fingers tightened around hers and he saw the gold flecks of joy in her blue eyes. "I wanted to call you, to tell you, but I couldn't say very much."

Thrilled by his touch, the firmness of his strong fingers around her own, Susan felt another cloak of worry dissolve from around her. "It's all right. I understand," she whispered. "You're home and you're safe. That's all that matters."

Worriedly, Craig searched Susan's upturned face, aware of the happiness dancing in her eyes and the aching beauty of her mouth, which he so badly wanted to kiss. "It was a lousy, top-level JSOC test for us, that was all." He grimaced. "Listen, I've got to get going. I have to make sure my men are cared for, and then I'll be in a report office filling out paper until I'm ready to scream."

"Will you get any sleep?"

Releasing her fingers, Craig stepped as close as he dared. Reaching out, he barely grazed her flushed cheek with his fingertips. Her skin was so soft, so inviting, that he trembled from a hunger he'd never experienced with any other woman. "Yeah." He laughed wryly. "I'll probably fall asleep in the middle of typing up the damn report on the computer terminal." When he saw her eyes darken with worry, he quickly added, "I was just teasing. I'll get some sleep, don't worry." Craig sighed. He would much rather be sleeping with Susan than keeping a computer terminal company half the night.

"I'll get tomorrow off," he told her in a low voice. Forcing himself to keep his hands at his sides, he saw the hope spring to her eyes.

"But you need to sleep. You look so tired, Craig."

He shook his head and his smile deepened. "Tomorrow is ours, babe. Unless the world comes to an end tonight, I'm going to be on your doorstep tomorrow morning at 0900 to pick you up and take you to breakfast. Deal?"

There was such warmth in Craig's eyes despite the camouflage makeup. "Better yet," she whispered, "why don't you come over and I'll make you breakfast? I make a mean stack of seven-grain pancakes with apricots that you'll never forget."

A tired smile worked its way across Craig's thinned mouth. "Wild horses won't stop me."

The morning was surprisingly hot, but Craig was oblivious to the baking temperatures that plagued Southern California at this time of year. He climbed out of his car, shut the door and quickly made his way toward the stairs that led to Susan's second-floor apartment. Freshly showered and shaved, he whistled happily as he took the stairs two at a time. In his hand was a bouquet of a dozen pink roses. The day was young, the sky a light blue and Craig had never felt happier—or more apprehensive.

"Come in." Susan stood at the screen door and drank in Craig's tall, proud form. The red polo shirt showed off his chest to advantage, while the Levi's emphasized his trim hips and heavily muscled thighs and calves. She saw the roses and smiled even more. "Flowers at this time of the morning. You're going to spoil me rotten, Captain Taggart." She pushed the screen open and Craig caught it and opened it all the way.

"A beautiful lady deserves flowers that mirror her beauty." He handed her the roses as he stepped inside the coolness of her white-painted apartment, decorated in Southwestern pastels and earth tones. The screen closed behind him and he stood just inside the door, watching her inhale the fragrance of the blossoms. Today, Susan wore a pair of yellow shorts and a short-sleeved tank top that lovingly outlined her slender form. She was barefoot, her hair tousled, and the urge to run his fingers through those strands was nearly his undoing.

"They're wonderful," she said, laying the roses on the lamp table next to the sofa. "But they pale in comparison to you," she said, and moved forward as Craig opened his arms in invitation.

Craig took Susan's full weight, his arms going around her, holding her tightly. Holding her forever.

"Mmm," he growled, "I've missed the hell out of you," and he slanted his mouth hotly against her lips, drinking her into him in great, selfish drafts. In eleven days, Craig hadn't forgotten anything about Susan, from her sweet taste to the fragrance of her skin to the wanton heat of her body pressed fully against him. Moments spun together as he gave as much as he took from her.

Breathless, they parted. Susan laughed giddily. "You're here. You're safe. I can't believe it! This is like a wonderful dream come true."

Craig sobered and touched her silken hair. "You're my dream," he told her, meaning it. "You always have been, babe. Maybe you didn't know that at first, but you do now. At least, I hope you do." He allowed himself the luxury of drowning in her eyes, which were filling with tears. This time he knew they were tears of welcome, tears of happiness.

"I'm just so glad you're home," Susan quavered.

He touched the prominent shadows beneath her eyes. "I heard you were working yourself to the bone while I was gone."

She nodded and absorbed his brief touch. "There are a lot more injuries lately at Reed."

"I happened to meet Karen over at the Exchange a little earlier, and she told me you worked to keep from worrying. Is that true?"

Content to remain in his arms forever, Susan nodded. "I'm a worrywart."

"It's been a long time since someone worried about me," Craig murmured, lowering his mouth to her lips, grazing them, tasting her, absorbing her. The soft moan that came from Susan only made him ache even more fiercely for her. Gently easing back, he stared down into her eyes. The words *I love you* were nearly torn from him. Was it too soon? Was he pushing Susan too quickly? Craig wasn't sure anymore.

Not wanting to leave her, he knew he must. With a smile, he said, "Are those fabulous-sounding pancakes ready to be eaten?"

Her mouth curved into a smile. "All ready. I've got the batter made and the coffee's on." She pulled reluctantly out of Craig's strong, steadying embrace. This morning he looked better rested, but there were still shadows beneath his eyes. Touching his shirt over his ribs, she said, "You've lost weight."

Placing his arm around her shoulders, Craig moved with Susan to the kitchen. "Who doesn't on MREs?" MREs had replaced the old C-rations, and Craig wasn't convinced they were better. In some cases, he knew they were worse. He stopped in the small but cozy kitchen and gave it an appreciative look. The windows over the sink were framed with white curtains tied back with blue sashes. The round table was covered with a blue cloth and a white, crocheted coverlet. A small white vase contained deep yellow black-eyed Susans, their sunny color complementing the blue-and-white color scheme.

"This reminds me of home," he said simply, giving her a warm look. "Ma has a kitchen with blue checkered curtains and a blue tablecloth over the maple table that's been in our family for four generations." He motioned to the flowers, a catch in his voice. "And she always has fresh flowers on the table from spring through fall."

Touched, Susan pointed to the straight, Shaker-style, high-backed oak chair. "I like your mother's taste in decorating. Have a seat, and I'll pour you some *good* coffee."

The soft FM music from the living room intruded gently. Craig nodded his thanks as she handed him a flowery china cup filled with steaming black coffee. He watched hungrily as she tied on a pink apron and began to cook him up a batch of pancakes. Everything was perfect. Perfect.

"Did you want to know about our mission at all?" he asked dryly as he sipped the Brazilian coffee.

Susan twisted to look across her shoulder, the spatula in hand. "Sure, if you can talk about it. I thought it was top secret or something."

With a snort, Craig eased back in the chair, the coffee cup resting on his stomach. "If you stick around me for very long, you'll find we're pulled on all kinds of crazy missions. Most of them are tests, that's all."

"Tests?"

Craig nodded and absorbed the sight of her at the stove. The fragrance of the cooking pancakes filled the air. A pitcher of warm apricot syrup already sat on the table in front of his plate. "To test our readiness."

"Where did you go this time?"

He scowled. "To some jungle-infested little island in the Caribbean. We did a joint HAHO with the SEALs."

"HAHO?" Susan slid the first three pancakes onto his plate. Two more went onto hers.

Craig was starving, but it wasn't for food. It was for Susan. He tried to concentrate on the food and the conversation. "We do high-altitude, high-opening parachute jumps," he explained between bites of the savory pancakes. "This time we got to jump from twenty thousand feet in the middle of the night to hit this damn island. One of my men missed the island and almost drowned."

"Oh, no!" Susan felt terror in her heart that it might have been Craig.

"He's okay," he soothed, taking another sip of coffee. He smiled. "These are great pancakes! You cook like this all the time?"

She smiled a little. "When I get a chance. A HAHO sounds so dangerous, Craig."

"It is," he murmured between bites. Noticing Susan hadn't touched her food, he gestured to her to start eating. "Come on, eat. Stop sitting there with those big, frightened blue eyes of yours, huh?"

He was right, Susan realized. Belatedly, she picked at her pancakes, not really tasting them. All that mattered, all she wanted, was Craig, sitting across from her at the table. There was so much to discuss, to talk about. Did she have the courage to speak of what lay in her heart? After breakfast, she promised herself, she would talk to Craig. Her appetite completely deserted her.

"Come with me," she pleaded to Craig when they'd finished eating. She held out her hand.

Craig smiled and gripped her cool fingers. Rising, he followed Susan into the large, airy living room. A black, gray and maroon Navajo rug graced the hearth in front of a small, redbrick fireplace. Sitting down on the overstuffed couch, he maintained a hold on her hand. The fact that Susan appeared nervous concerned him, and he reached out and touched her cheek.

"Whatever it is," he told her thickly, "let's talk about it. You're nervous and you're going pale on me, Susan. What's wrong?"

She tried to smile and failed. "You read me like a book, Craig. I don't know if I'll ever get used to that. Steve never did...." Her voice failed. Forcing herself to look up and meet his warm gray eyes, she whispered,

"Ten days has given me a lot of time to think about you... about us. After the clinic was attacked in southern Los Angeles, all I could think about was surviving it to get to you, Craig. In the smoke, in the darkness, I found out I really wanted to live.

"When Steve died, I was in a state of numbness." She gave him a sad little smile. "I was totally empty. And then, like a miracle, you stepped back into my life." Touching the back of his hand, she added, "You made me feel again, Craig.... The numbness is gone."

With a nod, because there was a lump in his throat, he caught her hands and brought them together in his own. "You were in a desert the last year of your marriage to Steve. It was understandable under the circumstances." When he saw the surprise in her eyes, he went on, "I've had ten days to think, too. The mission was tough because all I wanted to think about was you—and us. I hated leaving you alone again and running off to this damn JSOC mission. You were in shock from the clinic attack. I wanted to be there with you. I wanted to hold you, to help you through it. Hell," he muttered, looking away, "I needed you to help me."

"What?" The word was spoken softly, in awe.

Craig gently ran his thumb across the back of her hand. His heart beat so strongly he thought Susan might hear it pounding away like a drum in his chest. Swallowing hard, he decided that now was the time. Lifting his head, he met and held her misty gaze. "I need you, Susan. Ever since I met you at Annapolis, I knew that." He felt heat rising in his cheeks and realized he was blushing, but he didn't care. Raising her hand, he kissed it gently and then looked into her eyes again.

"When we loved each other, it was heaven for me. It was a dream come true. At first, I thought you might have made love with me that night out of shock and fear. I know when things get dangerous you can do crazy things to prove that you're alive, not dead."

Tears swam in Susan's eyes as she studied Craig's grim features. She felt his hands tighten around hers. "Well," she said huskily, "we were both in shock, but I don't think that's why we loved each other, Craig." She tilted her head and drank in his shadowed gaze, which was rife with feelings. "When you and I met back at Annapolis, we became friends. Such wonderful friends. With maturity, I now realize that what I felt for you back then was, in many ways, a more genuine love than the romantic 'first love' I felt for Steve. But I was too immature to appreciate all that—then. I love you, Craig. I always have. I just didn't realize it until recently." She lifted her hands from his and touched his face lightly, aware of the anguish in his eyes. Susan felt a terrible dread lifting from her as she admitted, "I don't know if you love me. But I love you. I always will."

Craig cradled her face in his hands. He smiled at her sadly and saw the tears drifting down her cheeks. "Love isn't something that can be killed, Susan. It's like energy—it changes, but it can't be destroyed. Look at me, Susan. Please...."

It took every ounce of her failing courage to lift her head and look directly into Craig's eyes. She saw tears glittering in them.

"I love you, too," he said hoarsely. "I always have. I never stopped loving you through all those years."

With a little cry, Susan leaned forward and felt his arms come around her with such startling sureness, such strength and warmth, that she surrendered completely to Craig's haunting embrace. Burying her face against his shoulder, she sobbed a little, clinging to him, never wanting anything else out of life. She felt him tremble, and she laughed with a joy that transcended all the pain that both of them had carried so long by themselves.

Craig sat with Susan pressed against him, in another kind of shock. He closed his eyes and absorbed her soft, giving form, his breathing synchronizing with hers. The moments passed and the soothing instrumental music flowed gently through the room. Running his hand tenderly across her hair, marveling at its beauty and life, Craig sighed.

"When our helicopter crashed, I thought I was going to die. And then, when I saw you in the trauma unit, I couldn't believe my eyes." He smiled and pressed a kiss to her hair. "I was in shock from the crash, from knowing that two men might not make it. And you were there, Susan."

She lifted her head so that she could see Craig's face. His features were drawn, but his eyes shone with the love he felt for her.

Touching her warm, soft cheek, he tried to smile and failed. "All my life I dreamed about meeting a woman who would make me feel whole. When I met you in Annapolis, I knew you were the one. When Steve married you, I hardened my heart. I had a couple of relationships with women, but they were empty—I couldn't find the intimacy and communion I'd had with you. I can't say I was stellar with them, at all. I was angry and hurting. I took it out on them, and they didn't deserve it. I screwed up with them, Susan. I hurt them out of my own place of hurt. After the last breakup, I sat down and figured out what I was doing. Then, six months later, you suddenly dropped into my life. After I found out you'd been widowed, I prayed for a second chance with you."

Raising his head, Craig stared up at the plaster ceiling, his voice choked. "I know I didn't deserve the chance, either—not after how I handled those two other relationships. But I wanted to try and make things right again—for both of us."

Closing her eyes, she sighed brokenly. "Love isn't easy, is it?"

"No, it's more like a mine field," Craig said wryly, and squeezed her hard, absorbing her against him. "We all get wounded because of our own shortcomings, our training and the brainwashing we receive from this culture of ours."

Easing away from Craig, Susan smiled gently. "I think we've earned our time together, don't you?"

"Yes."

Susan had never seen Craig so happy, so spontaneous. He released her and dug into the pocket of his Levi's, hunting for something. His face was flushed, and she loved him fiercely for his ability to share his love and excitement with her.

"What are you pawing around for?" she asked with a laugh.

"Something," Craig told her conspiratorially, "that I've been holding on to for over four years, lady. Ah, here it is." He grinned broadly and brought out a small, well-worn jewelry case. Craig held it reverently in the palm of his hand as he extended it to Susan.

"What you don't know," he said, losing his smile, "is that I had a lot of plans for us. Remember when I asked you to meet me for dinner?"

Susan clasped her hands and stared down at the red velvet box. "Yes..."

He touched the box lightly. "I had finally gotten up the guts to ask you to become engaged to me."

Susan gasped, her hands flying to her mouth.

"Now, wait a minute," Craig counseled, seeing tears come to her eyes. "I never let you know that I loved you, Susan. You saw me as a friend only, but I was hiding a lot more from you. I had bought this ring probably six months earlier, that's how badly I wanted to marry you. But I was chicken. Finally, I built up enough confidence to ask you, because you had told me you were going to break up with Steve. I was hoping against hope that you would agree our friendship was a perfect base to build a lifetime together on.

"So," he went on huskily, "I got my courage together and made that decision. I wasn't exactly up-front about my feelings for you, but that was four years ago." He gave her a little grin. "I'm older now—a little bolder, maybe. At least—" he laughed wryly, placing the box in her hands "—I'm not making the same mistake twice. I'm going to move on how I feel, and I'm going to be up-front about it."

The box was light on her damp palm. Susan gently touched the jewelry case as if it were Craig she was touching. "If I'd only known..."

"It's no one's fault," he said.

"No," Susan said softly, "it's not."

"Well," he soothed, anxious to know if she liked the ring or not, "that's behind us. Let's use our experience and move forward—together."

Susan gave him a tender look as she fingered the latch.

"Now," Craig cautioned quickly, holding her hand down on the lid before she could lift it up, "you have to remember, I was pretty poor at the time. It's a real plain ring, Susan. If you want something fancier, bigger, I can afford to get it for you."

Touched beyond words, she lifted the lid, to find, instead of the usual engagement ring, a simple gold wedding band. She knew how economically strapped Craig had been at that time. Loosening the band, she picked it up and tried it on her left hand. The ring moved easily into place. Susan whispered, "No, it's beautiful. I love it." And she blindly reached out, throwing her arms around Craig's shoulders. "And I love you so much it hurts...."

As Craig held her, crushing her to him, he knew there was only one more hurdle to scale. Kissing her tear-bathed lips with reverence, he refused to even mention it to Susan. Not now. No, they deserved the time they were going to share with each other. As he held her, his eyes tightly shut, he dreamed future dreams. That was dangerous, because Craig knew that recon training was fickle and had no favorites—not even two people who were madly in love with one another.

"I want us to have the time to get to know each other again," Craig rasped as he framed her face with his hand. The joy in Susan's eyes made him feel larger than life, invincible.

"But you're going to France in just four months," Susan whispered.

It was the very subject he'd been avoiding. His smile was very male and very proud. "Not anymore. What you don't know is that I've been working like hell behind the scenes to get my orders changed. This morning, before I left HQ, Lieutenant Davis, who was wanting to make the trade with me, came in and told me BUPERS had agreed to the switch in personnel. I've got Davis's three more years here at Reed, and he's jumping up and down for joy to be going to Paris."

"That's wonderful!" Susan cried, throwing her arms around Craig. She wasn't disappointed as his arms swept around her and held her tightly against him.

"I couldn't leave you. Even when I didn't know if you loved me the way I loved you, I couldn't leave," Craig murmured against her hair, then kissed her cheek. Moving her hair aside with his hand, he tilted her chin, leaned forward and placed his mouth gently against her lips. "My world," he whispered, "is here, with you."

With a small cry, Susan met and molded with his giving mouth. There was such strength in Craig, such powerful convictions and principles, and they all revolved around his love for her. As she drowned within his heated offering, the world and its harshness melted away. Their lives would never be easy. She would always have to worry for his safety, because he was a proud warrior, a recon. Despite all that, Susan never wanted anyone more than Craig. Forever.

* * * * *

It's our 1000th Silhouette Romance, and we're celebrating!

Join us for a special collection of love stories by authors you've loved for years, and new favorites you've just discovered. Join the celebration...

April
REGAN'S PRIDE by **Diana Palmer**
MARRY ME AGAIN by **Suzanne Carey**

May
THE BEST IS YET TO BE by **Tracy Sinclair**
CAUTION: BABY AHEAD by **Marie Ferrarella**

June
THE BACHELOR PRINCE by **Debbie Macomber**
A ROGUE'S HEART by **Laurie Paige**

July
IMPROMPTU BRIDE by **Annette Broadrick**
THE FORGOTTEN HUSBAND by **Elizabeth August**

Silhouette Romance...vibrant, fun and emotionally rich! Take another look at us! And as part of the celebration, readers can receive a FREE gift!

You'll fall in love all over again with Silhouette Romance!

CEL1000

MILLION DOLLAR SWEEPSTAKES (III)
AND
EXTRA BONUS PRIZE DRAWING

DANGEROUS ALLIANCE
Lindsay McKenna
(SE #884, May)

Vulnerable Libby Tyler intrigued Captain Dan Ramsey.
He was willing to take a chance at love, but Libby had
promised she'd never fall for a marine again. Drawn
together in the face of a perilous situation, could they
deny their dangerous attraction?

MEN OF COURAGE

It's a special breed of men who defy death and fight
for right! Salute their bravery while sharing their lives
and loves!

MENC2